AF483593

The Point Man and the Peacenik

America in 1968

Also by RW Holmen

NOVELS

A Wretched Man: A Novel of Paul the Apostle

*Wormwood and Gall: The Destruction of Jerusalem and
the First Gospel*

Lost in the Land of Milk and Honey: An Immigrant Saga

NOVELLA

*Gonna Stick My Sword in the Golden Sand: A Vietnam
Soldier's Story*

NONFICTION

*Queer Clergy: A History of Gay and Lesbian Ministry in
American Protestantism*

The Point Man and the Peacenik
America in 1968

A Novel

RW Holmen

Wretched Man Publications

Paperback published by IngramSpark

It don't mean nuthin'.

Anonymous

Chapter One

How the hell was he supposed to know who was friendly and who was the enemy? He figured he wouldn't know until someone blew his head off with an AK-47 or slid a satchel charge between the tracks of his tank. Should he shoot first and ask questions later?

As gray dawn filtered in, Beans heard the first stirrings of life, and ghostly shapes floated in the mist rising from the Ia Xoi River. He nervously fidgeted with the innocent-looking butterfly-shaped thumb trigger of a fifty-caliber machine gun aimed ominously across a bridge. Finally, in the innocence of morning when the sun peeked over the mountains, the shapes materialized, and he realized that Pleiku villagers had merely assembled to await the opening of the bridge.

Beans survived his first night as a combat soldier on duty in Vietnam, and he didn't kill anybody. After pulling bridge guard duty as a solitary sentry perched atop an M-48 Patton Tank, a jeep pulled up to take him back to base camp, and he breathed again.

****

Beans and the Perfesser both loved Angie, but it was Beans she cuddled with in his father's Ford pickup on their last night together before he shipped off to Vietnam.

Beans' hands slid under her sweater, and his fingertips nervously traced the taut muscles on her back, climbing until they reached her bra strap; he had never been so bold, but he was about to ship out to Vietnam, and he figured now or never as he fumbled with the slide hook.

"Beans, don't," Angie said, drawing back against the pickup seat. With her hands on his shoulders at arm's length, she hesitated while searching his eyes, and then said, "I'll do it myself." She twisted her arms behind her back to undo the clasp, but she set the ground rules. "This is as far as we'll go. We don't need a baby to come while you're over there, and what if …?"

"Should old acquaintance be forgot?"

An hour earlier, Big Jimmie Overskei warbled off-key and slurred the words, as he wagged his finger in the air as if to direct the dozen friends who gathered on New Year's Eve 1967 for a going-away party for Beans, but the others paid little attention. Dave Karlstad, aka the Perfesser, hosted the party in the basement of his parents' home in the small farming community of Kalmar, Minnesota, while on holiday break as a sophomore at the University of Minnesota. Dave, Big Jimmie, and Beans played basketball together and graduated high school in the class of '66. Angie Olson was two years younger, and she was now a high school senior.

As the hands on the bold-faced clock on the wall twitched inexorably toward the New Year, a low conversational buzz wafted over the clink of beer bottles and the clatter of pool balls bouncing against each other. Beans took his turn challenging the Perfesser's home court winning streak of eight-ball on the velvet-covered billiard table.

"I see General Waste More Land keeps asking for more troops," Dave said.

Beans responded defensively.

"Shit man, we all know you're smart, but it seems like college is turning you into a smart-ass. When Uncle Sam calls, you go," Beans said. "What's so hard to understand about that?"

Beans repeated well-worn cliches as if the truth was self-evident.

"Wiser men than you have said we need to stop the commies before these little countries fall one by one like dominos. Better to fight the bastards over there than on our own shores."

"What's the point?" Dave replied, raising his own obvious truth. "Do you really think the peasant farmers of Vietnam will attack America unless we bomb their rice paddies?"

Beans bristled but didn't have a good comeback. After a few seconds, he merely said, "Nice hair," which both men understood as a dig at the shoulder-length locks of the privileged university student who didn't face the same danger of being drafted due to his college deferment.

"Hell, youse guys," Big Jimmie piped in. "Stop yer bitching and have another beer. This night's fer Beans, and he ain't got no say so. Who knows when we'll be together again …" His voice trailed off as he left the thing unsaid.

Big Jimmie was right, and Dave shut up. Arguing with Beans over war policy served no purpose. As a draftee, it wasn't Beans' decision to risk his ass in Vietnam, and it wasn't right to put him on the spot for the military debacle in which he was also a victim. Best not to fracture his friendship with Beans. Best to send him off as his supporter; after all, the odds are pretty good that he won't come home in one piece.

As Big Jimmie started to sing another refrain, Dave interrupted, "Shut your yap and countdown to midnight with us."

"3, 2, 1."

Grain Belt Beer bottles clinked together.

"Welcome to the year of our Lord, 19 and 68," Dave said, and the bottles clinked again.

Dave melted into the plush, well-worn sofa in his parents' basement, nursing a bottle of Grain Belt. A transistor radio tuned to clear channel WLS in Chicago faded in and out with the Beatles number one hit, *Hello, Goodbye*. Yes or no? Stop or go?

His gaze kept returning to Angie. He hadn't seen her in months. Pretty, if not quite beautiful, with milky-white skin and understated makeup, cherry lipstick, and blonde hair, she leaned with her butt against the pool table while talking with a girlfriend. It seemed her hair was longer with a wave that Dave hadn't seen.

Since their parents were best friends, Dave and Angie grew up together: waterskiing, skating on frozen ponds, hiding together in a dark closet playing hide and seek where they shared their first kiss of puppy love. Didn't seem that long ago.

So, when Beans invited freshman Angie to the Junior Prom that began their current romance, Dave was shocked to realize that his childhood companion had matured into a young woman and the object of attraction by others, including his friend Beans. The longing look she gave Dave when they next met remained fixed in his memory, as if she asked, *why wasn't it you, Dave; you should have been the one to notice that I had grown up and wasn't a teeny bopper anymore; you should have been the one to ask me to the prom.*

After well-wishes all around, Beans departed with Angie clutching his arm. She hesitated at the door and caught Dave's eye; she lingered an instant too long before turning and leaving.

Chapter Two

Dave looked up from the spread of newspapers on the library table to see a petite woman in red pigtails homing in on him from across the reading room.

"I'm Wendy, and I hear you will join us in New Hampshire."

"Thinking 'bout it."

"Late for class. Gotta go, but I hope you can make it," she said with an impish smile.

When Alex, the trip organizer, first approached him, Dave didn't know much about the Senator Eugene McCarthy insurgency, so he visited the University library to scour news articles. Not much there since the national press didn't pay much attention, but the popular wisdom said that the undistinguished back bencher in the Senate had no chance against incumbent President Lyndon Johnson. A gadfly, some said. Many press pundits speculated that McCarthy was a secret proxy for Senator Robert Kennedy who had been the first choice of anti-war activists within the party.

Dave's eyes followed Wendy as she ascended a flight of stairs. As he gathered up the newspapers, he decided; he was in.

Dave cranked up the radio of the '60 Chevy Belair as Aretha Franklin, the Queen of Soul, belted out her hit, *Chain of Fools*.

"What the hell, man?" The three male passengers in the rear seat stiffly came alive, stretching and yawning.

"Wake up you chain of fools," Dave said. "It's time for breakfast."

Wendy Cragun rode shotgun in the passenger seat of the cherry-red Chevy with a white top and wing-like fins. She clapped rhythmically, danced with her shoulders, and mouthed the words along with Aretha.

"Can you dig it?" She said.

The five college students from the University of Minnesota traveled east to New Hampshire to join the "Clean Gene" brigade. Their cause was Eugene McCarthy, the senator from their own state of Minnesota who had the temerity to challenge a sitting president of his own party.

For these five Midwestern kids, and thousands of other college students across the country, Gene was their voice of opposition to the illegal, unjust, and cruel war in Vietnam. So, Dave clipped his hair that had gone uncut for over a year, shaved the stubble on his chin, packed a few ties to go with dress shirts, and joined Wendy and three men enroute to New Hampshire and the kickoff primary for the race to be the Democratic nominee for president in the 1968 election.

"My folks are divorced," Wendy said to Dave earlier as the Chevy rumbled along the New York Thruway during the early morning hours while the others slept in the back seat.

Wendy Cragun's ancestors were Irish, and she looked the part with long red pigtails bound by green ribbons, a freckle face, and a fresh, exuberant air about her. In a paradoxical way, she was innocent but not naïve, savvy but not jaded. She wore no bra under her t-shirt, and she spoke with brash honesty, not to shock but simply matter-of-factly.

"Mom is into a whiskey bottle and Dad is into his work. I don't mean to shit on either of them, but it is what it is. Dad's paying my way at the U, and he buys me lunch or coffee once or twice a month. We're past arguing, even though he thinks I'm just a lame-brained hippie. Dad demonizes McCarthy as a godless communist even though he and the Senator attended Catholic prep school together in central Minnesota. He pours himself into making money at his investment firm, but I wish he'd find a girlfriend. What he needs more than anything is a good fuck."

Dave tried hard not to show a reaction, and he kept his eyes on the road.

"What about you, Dave?" Wendy asked. "Who are you?

"I'm pretty vanilla. Small town. Middle class. Republican family."

Wendy screwed up her face.

"Yeah, but they're moderate. You know, Rockefeller Republicans," Dave said.

"What brings you to the cause?" Wendy asked.

"I was ambivalent, but here's how I saw the light," Dave said. "It happened at the University of Wisconsin. A dorm friend invited me to tag along to Madison for a sit in with his cousin, and I thought it sounded like a good time, but when the police kicked the shit out of me, I got religion."

Wendy's eyes narrowed, and she leaned in to hear the story of Dave's conversion.

"Tell me about the police," Wendy said. "Did they really knock you around?"

Dave nodded.

"We sat in the hallway to block recruiters from Dow Chemical, the manufacturers of Napalm, from reaching the interview room. Not for an hour, not for a day, but for however long it would take to cause Dow to give up and leave. We remained peaceful and non-violent with guitars and singing. Maybe a hundred of us sat in. It wasn't that many, but the word spread around campus, and a huge throng of kids gathered to watch. Some were with us, and others weren't. Some sang along and others just watched with curiosity."

Dave hesitated and drew a deep breath through his nose then exhaled a slight whistle through his mouth.

"That's when the city police arrived. Not the campus police, mind you, but the regular Madison city cops who already had an attitude about the campus community. They arrived in riot gear and riot they did. Without provocation, they began swinging their clubs and throwing us around. I heard that over sixty of us ended up in the hospital that day. More than half."

Dave rolled up the sleeve on his right arm.

"See that lump there? I hope it never goes away. It's my badge of honor. Before that cop belted me with his Billy club, the clear shield on his helmet couldn't mask the hatred in his eyes. He called me a 'long-haired, greasy pig.' He wasn't just doing his job or following orders, he was fighting a war, and I was the enemy. They may have won the battle, but they lost the war as they turned me and many others into true believers."

"What about the draft?" Wendy asked. "Aren't you guys jeopardizing your college deferments by being here?"

Dave didn't know how to answer because he wasn't sure himself. Not only was he missing class, but the Director of the Selective Service warned about pulling deferments for anti-war activities. Where was the line between free speech and resistance to the draft? What did it say about military service if it was punishment for exercising the right of free speech?

"No, I mean it. What will you do if your draft board comes after you? Will you burn your draft card? Will you go to jail? Will you join the National Guard, the Navy, or the Air Force so you don't get sent to Vietnam? Will you flee to Canada or Sweden?"

Wendy tried to look him in the eye, but Dave froze his gaze on the freeway.

"Don't tell me you'll submit to induction and go to Vietnam!" she said, more as an indignant statement than a question.

Finally, Dave sighed and shrugged his shoulders. "Haven't thought that far ahead."

Chapter Three

On a clear January day, the snow-capped eminence of Mount Rainier slowly passed by Bean's window as his Northwest Airlines flight from Minnesota descended into SeaTac Airport between Seattle and Tacoma. After a couple days of processing at Fort Lewis, an olive drab military bus transported Beans and a load of men toting duffle bags to nearby Fort McChord Air Force base where they boarded a Boeing jet. Beans was surprised that it was a commercial airliner on contract with the military. He wondered if they would pass out weapons before landing in Cam Ranh Bay, imagining that Charlies--the enemy--might be waiting in ambush for fresh arrivals. The flight attendants didn't seem too concerned, but they weren't friendly either. They remained standoffish, and they didn't serve drinks.

Beans slept an uneasy sleep on the overseas flight and dreamed of his recent sojourn in the swamps and sand hills of Fort Polk Louisiana for training as an M-16-toting infantryman bound for Vietnam.

"If'n one of them coral snakes bites you, here's the proper military procedure," droned the drill sergeant.

Smokey hat tilted forward over dark glasses, uniform tight and full of starch, the tall and lean instructor stalked the stage of the outdoor amphitheater with a manner that said this was his domain.

Who knew the army had a sense of humor? The joke was on Beans and the sorry asses assigned to infantry training at Fort Puke, the armpit of America. The irony kicked them in the balls on that day near the end of basic training when they posted the lists for advanced training assignments. The screw-ups in basic training--the swinging dicks who couldn't hang on to the monkey bars outside the mess hall, who puked during forced marches, and who shot holes in the sky during rifle training--found themselves on various training lists, but not on the list for 11B. The reward for running fast and shooting straight was to be placed on the shit list: Eleven fucking Bravo--the infantry, the basic foot soldiers of armies ancient and modern. Grunts. Straight legs. Ground pounders.

"... You can also use this procedure for the cobras of Vietnam, if'n one of them crawls into yer bunker when yer sleeping," the sergeant continued.

The pine slab benches sagged with fools like Beans, baking in the sun. While men on the other lists learned their specialty training here and there in comfortable camps around the country, the Eleven Bravos sweltered in the Louisiana humidity and learned how to treat snake bite.

"Spread yer legs to a comfortable military stance ..."

Normally, the sleep-deprived trainees had difficulty keeping their eyes open during training sessions, and the drill sergeants jokingly warned them not to be caught checking their eyelids for pinholes, or the sergeants would poke them in the ribs. Not today. Today, they had no trouble staying awake when the drill instructor told tales of the rattlers, water moccasins, black-widow spiders, and small but deadly red-yellow-black banded coral snakes that crawled the hill country of northwest Louisiana ... and the cobras of Vietnam.

"... Put yer hands on yer knees ..."

Wouldn't it be the shits to get snake bit before shipping out for the Nam? Course, if you're gonna catch a bullet anyway.

".... Bend down at the waist as far as you can ..."

The drill instructor removed his Smokey hat and wiped the sweat from his shaved head, glancing up at the merciless sun. Next, he removed his wire-rimmed dark glasses and wiped them clean as he scanned the peach-fuzz faces of the innocents. Then, he offered his wisdom, his enlightenment, his sage advice, like he did every day to countless Eleven Bravos who passed through his outdoor classroom on their way to on-the-job training in the Nam.

"... and kiss yer sweet ass goodbye."

Beans awoke with a start as the jet bounced on the tarmac runway of a remote military base for refueling and a crew change. Beans checked his watch, but how many time zones had been crossed? The runway lighting barely muted the starry sky as the jet taxied on some God-forsaken spit of land somewhere in the Aleutian Islands of Alaska, and Beans couldn't see much from the inside of the plane. He wondered if Siberia would be visible during the midnight sun of summer. The Soviets were the smart ones. They sent their AK-47s and their anti-aircraft batteries, but they let Charlie do their fighting.

Finally, the Boeing touched down at the Cam Ranh Bay Air Base. There were no Charlies in Cam Ranh Bay after all, but plenty of fucking new guys (FNGs) like Beans, spending the first days of three hundred sixty-five, their scheduled one-year tour of duty. Mounds of white sand dunes surrounded low-lying gray buildings with tin roofs held down with sandbags. Water tanks on wheels marked as potable water or non-potable water squatted here and there outside the buildings, but Beans could never remember which one was for drinking.

Even his underwear was olive green. Freshly attired in loose-fitting combat fatigues and jungle boots, Beans affixed a three-cornered pin on his collar indicating he was a PFC, Private First Class, just like all who had completed infantry training at Fort Polk, Louisiana.

After Cam Ranh Bay finished its processing, the Army decided to send Beans to the 4th Infantry Division up in the rugged mountains and jungle of the Central Highlands. Following a short hop aboard a C-130 transport plane, Beans arrived at Camp Enari near the small city of Pleiku. More processing. Between rain squalls, two-and-a-half ton trucks called deuce-and-a-halfs transported new arrivals outside the perimeter for M-16 rifle training. Fort Polk had already trained Beans and other infantrymen on M-16s, but the in-country welcoming festivities included an introduction to the M-16 for all FNGs, even the non-combat rear-echelon warriors.

Beans imagined a horde of Charlies lurking in the tall grass, and he worried that the clerk/typists needed protection. He kept a close eye out for Charlie, but the only real danger was if one of the desk jockeys shot himself in the foot, or worse.

Chapter Four

The sign at the exit from the New York State Thruway said "Albany," and Dave swung the over-sized sedan onto the off ramp toward the capital city of New York state. Snowbanks lined the side of the roadway, typical for mid-January, but the winter weather had cooperated, and the travelers enjoyed clear and dry highways in their cross-country pilgrimage.

For twenty straight hours the five students from the University of Minnesota traveled east, but now it was time to leave the system of freeways and toll roads across the northern tier of the U.S. and follow a winding mountain road across Vermont, headed toward the Granite State of New Hampshire.

"Two eggs, sunny side up with a side of bacon, toast, and coffee—boatloads of coffee!" Dave ordered without looking at the menu.

"You got it, Hon," the middle-aged waitress in a faded orange uniform said, smacking her chewing gum.

Two of the back-seat sleepers, Jonathan and Hank, had already been to the men's room.

Tall and nerdy with a slumped over posture, Jonathan always wore the same brown corduroy sport jacket with patches on the elbows. He walked with a stooped gait, his arms dangling low, too long for the jacket's sleeves. He owned the tank of a car that carried the fivesome on their idealistic journey.

The other guy, Hank, seemed aloof, and he didn't say much unless it was a sarcastic remark, always gazing off as if not heeding the others but then weighing in with a cutting comment when the moment seemed right.

After Dave ordered, he replaced Alex, the trip organizer and third sleeper, in the head and passed Wendy returning from the ladies' room. She winked at him. He didn't know her well until this trip, but they enjoyed a great discussion as they took the latest shift in the wee morning hours as driver and navigator.

After breakfast, Jonathan, the Belair owner, took over behind the wheel of his one-time family vehicle handed down from his folks. Hank served as navigator. The four-door sedan lumbered along the twisting mountain roads across Vermont as the radio blared hit tunes, and the political neophytes sang along with Aretha. *Chain of Fools.*

Hanover, New Hampshire, and Dartmouth College on the east bank of the Connecticut River would be their first night's stop where they would meet up with local organizers and receive their marching orders. A fraternity house was their rendezvous point, and the Belair pulled into the small fraternity parking lot by noon, but the meetup wasn't scheduled until that evening, so the Minnesota invaders tromped around campus in gently falling snow. They toured Baker Library (very traditional) and the sprawling Hopkins Center (very modern) and returned to the fraternity house by nightfall.

That evening over pizza and beer, the conspirators laid out their plans. A tall, slender woman with long brown hair draping over a cardigan sweater and off-white blouse led the discussion. Her maxi skirt swirled as she moved energetically around the room welcoming the Minnesotans and other volunteers.

"I'm Amanda Crosby, and I'll be your moderator tonight. There are nearly one hundred thousand registered Democratic households in New Hampshire. With your help and hundreds of others like you fanning out across the state, our goal is to ring the doorbells on most of them by primary election day."

Turns out Amanda Crosby was a political science honors student from Smith College just down the road and across the border in Massachusetts. Dartmouth College undergrads remained strictly male even as coeducation loomed on the horizon. Progress for the Woman's Movement.

She continued to explain.

"Ask voters questions, and listen politely to their answers," she instructed. "Never argue with them or berate them. Be deferential to the housewives and factory workers. Offer them a McCarthy button."

"What should we say about the war?" Alex asked.

"Speak in terms of its endless nature. Tell them we need common sense to bring it to an end, but don't sound like a radical or a pacifist."

When the meeting broke up, fraternity brothers invited the men to bunk in the frat house, but females had to exit the premises by 11:00 pm according to Dartmouth College parietals.

"The Hanover Inn sits on the corner of the main intersection across from the college Green," Amanda said to Wendy. "I'll be staying there. Why don't you join me?"

"It looked bourgeois to me," Wendy said. "I've got my sleeping bag, and I'll camp out in the back seat of the Chevy."

Amanda shrugged.

Dave walked outside with Wendy.

"Not sure I'm up for what she had in mind," Wendy said.

Dave canted his head and furrowed his brow, not understanding.

"The way she looked at me, I'm pretty sure she's a dyke. Not that I care, but it's not my bag."

Dave raised his eyebrows and followed Amanda's newer model Buick Riviera as it exited the parking lot.

"You gonna be ok in there?" Dave asked Wendy as he turned up his collar against the chill wind whipping around the frat house.

"Come inside and smoke a joint with me." she replied.

She was one step ahead of the small-town boy, but he did not resist following her on a path that led him far, far away from Kalmar. He shared the joint, coughing, but didn't see what the big deal was. When they finished, she slid into her sleeping bag, tossing her articles of clothing one by one onto the floor.

"Come and snuggle with me," she said. "Help me stay warm."

Far, far from Kalmar. That was his first time, and it happened quickly.

Dave awoke with a start the next morning when Wendy opened the car door and cold air rushed in.

"Gonna find a shower," she said.

Dave sheepishly entered the frat house where Hank greeted him.

"How's the room service at the Belair Hotel?"

Jonathan looked peeved at what had taken place in the back seat of his car, but he said nothing.

Dave showered and pulled on a dress shirt and tied a tie.

"Hey, it's the middle of January already." Alex said. "Time to get a move on. The primary is only about eight weeks away. We've got doors to knock and voters to persuade."

Chapter Five

After returning from his overnight guard duty atop the tank overlooking the bridge, Beans was allowed to nap. After catching some Zs, Beans stepped outside the tent that served as a barracks, and he watched as an E-7 First Sergeant paced in front of a formation of sorry-assed new arrivals. The sergeant belted out instructions that laid out the process the FNGs would follow for the next couple of days. Beans recognized a black man from Fort Polk slouching in the back row. When the sergeant bellowed "DISMISSED," Beans approached the familiar face.

"Hey, it's Harris, ain't it?"

After a quick glance, the tall and heavy-set black man kept his eyes forward and spoke out of the side of his mouth.

"Yah, that's me. I recognize you from Fort Polk, but I don't 'member your name."

"Name's Jeff Pfeffer but folks call me Beans."

"Let's grab a beer," Beans said.

Nate Harris looked sideways at the whitey that he barely knew. The look on Harris' face suggested he had never carried on a personal conversation with a white man, to say nothing of sharing a beer, and the reverse was also true for Beans.

Harris shrugged. "What the hell. Where do we get a beer?"

Misery loves company, and if there are no atheists in foxholes, the same may be said of racists, and the two men with little in common except orders for front-line duty in

Vietnam found their way to a crowded and smoke-filled NCO (non-commissioned officers) club where they shared beers and conversation over a blaring juke box.

"Funny name. Beans. Where the hell did you get that?"

"I played high school basketball back in Minnesota. Small town, and I was pretty tall. They first called me 'String bean' or 'Beanpole' before "Beans" stuck. I'm ok with it. How 'bout you? You're tall as me. You play some ball?"

"Nah. I woulda liked to, but I quit school to help Mama. I been working since I was fourteen. That's the way it is in my Detroit neighborhood."

Nate took a long swig of his beer.

"Mama didn't want me in the army," Nate said. "'I didn't raise my boy to go off and fight in a white man's war,' she said. 'You're the man of the house, and your sisters need you,' but what could I do after I got my draft notice? Anyways, I'll send my combat pay to help Mama with the bills."

Nate chugged down the remainder of his beer and slammed the bottle down so hard it nearly broke.

"I guess the next one's on me," he said.

Nate inserted a coin in the juke box, choosing Sam and Dave's *Soul Man*, and his shoulders danced as he weaved his way to the bar.

Finally, the replacement depot placed Beans and Nate Harris with Alpha Company, a regular infantry line unit consisting of around eighty men led by a captain and three lieutenants in charge of the three rifle platoons, which were each subdivided into three squads that included a squad leader, an M-60 machine gunner, an M-79 grenade thumper, and the rest of the men carried M-16s. Each squad carried a pair of PRC-25 radios, and they assigned one to Beans that he stuffed into his rucksack with the antenna sticking up and the handset clipped to the shoulder strap of his ruck. He figured it would be cool to listen to the radio chatter.

Beans was twenty years old, and that was typical for the troops. Some were younger. The first or second lieutenants who served as platoon leaders were slightly older products of college ROTC programs or Officer Candidate School (OCS) training. Beans was assigned to the 1st platoon led by butter-bar 2nd Lieutenant Wolsey fresh from college ROTC and new in-country himself. Captain Connally, the Texan who served as commanding officer (CO), was older still, and he had seen twenty-five but not yet thirty. Then there was the grizzled First Sergeant, an E-7 lifer on his second tour of duty in Vietnam, who was well past his thirtieth birthday. The troops called him Top, and Beans wasn't sure of his real name. Finally, Beans' squad leader, who would soon become Beans' best friend, was Specialist 4th Class Francisco Rodriguez, a Puerto Rican by way of the Bronx.

The buzz cuts from basic training had disappeared as hair returned atop the heads of the men of Alpha Company, but Top was the sole exception. The gray hair on his head remained bristly stubble. When Beans stood in line before plopping into a barber chair at the start of boot camp, it surprised him that the inductees themselves paid for their military-mandated haircuts from private barbers imported onto the army base. Sweetheart deal for the barbers. *Zip,*

zip, zip. Up one side, then the back, and then the other side with the clipper set at the lowest setting. *Next.*

The whole company flew in a helicopter airlift escorted by Cobra gunships. Six men per Bell UH-1 Iroquois helicopter, aka Huey, aka chopper, aka slick, aka bird. When the door gunners tilted their M-60 machine guns to the ready, the grunts slid their asses to the edge of the helicopter floor, feet dangling and groping for the steel runners. Gaining firm contact, they shifted their weight, including eighty-pound rucksacks, onto their feet. With his left hand grasping the edge of the chopper's door and the pistol grip of his locked and loaded M-16 clenched tightly in his right, Beans glanced at the door gunner for reassurance, but the dark visor of the gunner's helmet merely reflected Beans' own bug-eyes under a steel pot helmet, set in a worried face. Though the pilot and crew wanted to get in and out fast, the landing zone (LZ) slipped under the belly of the bird in slow motion. Beans scanned the tree line for any telltale muzzle flashes of a hot LZ; nothing could be worse than for a couple of Charlies to empty their AK-47 magazines or to fire a rocket propelled grenade (RPG) into a hovering helicopter. For all the goddammed firepower on the army's side, the endless moment when troops slowly descended into Charlie's jungle was when Charlie had them, if he was there; the best the troops could hope for was that he wasn't. *Ready or not, Charlie, here we come.*

They jumped the last few feet and scrambled for the cover of the tree line. As the rapid *wump-wump* beat of rotors gradually receded, the solitude of the jungle swallowed the men. The awful silence screamed of absence, aloneness, and detachment from former life. The warriors sat back-to-back, rucksack to rucksack, to let their senses and their souls transition from helter-skelter to stealth. But how stealthy could eighty men tromping through the jungle be?

The records would show that Alpha Company went humping--officially a search and destroy mission-- for eighteen days, but Beans felt it was a goddammed lifetime. He began as a fucking new guy (FNG), but eighteen days later he was a savvy vet promoted to Specialist 4th class; he had loaded dead comrades onto a helicopter; he had crawled over a dead enemy body to retrieve that friggin' Prick-25 radio; and he had seen buddies collapse from heat exhaustion and dehydration.

Whether the terrain was triple-canopy jungle or grassland, it was thick, and the company humped single-file. From the head to the tail, eighty guys strung together in a snaking line, one after the other, stretched over two hundred meters. There were times in the elephant grass that all the point man could do was push into it, lean against it, and when it squashed down, he stood up, took a step forward and pushed into it again, hoping the snakes slithered away from the ruckus. Of course, that was just the guy on point, and once he tamped the grass down, the rest of the company passed through easy enough, but it was a slow slog. The three rifle platoons within the company took turns leading the way. Within the platoons, the squads similarly rotated the hazardous duty, especially for the point man.

When the company came to the edge of a ridge overlooking a ravine, Captain Connally could see no way around, so down they went into the gully. Going down was no problem, but climbing to the other side was more than the captain counted on. The men grabbed onto scrub brush to pull themselves forward, one bush at a time, but they held a weapon in one hand with an eighty-pound rucksack on their backs. If the bush uprooted, the soldier tumbled back into those following him. The guys in front pulled, and the guys in back pushed.

They never made it up that day, and finally darkness poured over the valley like somebody spilled a bottle of ink over the cliff. They remained in place through the night, clinging to the side of the slope, wedged against a bush or rock so they could snatch a little sleep. The fool killer didn't visit that night, which was a good thing because there sure were plenty of fools. With first light, they started up the slope again, and the last swinging dick clambered over the edge by noon. Captain Connally allowed the exhausted men to set up right there for the day.

Normally, the daily hump ended around 3:00 p.m. so there would be time to create a defensive perimeter, a night location (NL) or November Lima. Army slang was often based on the letters of the phonetic alphabet: night location=NL=November Lima, and from there creativity took over. "Loud and clear" radio transmissions became lima charlie and then lima chuck. "White phosphorous" became whiskey papa and then willie pete and then Wilson Pickett. They called the enemy combatants "Charlies," derived from Viet Cong=VC=Victor Charlie, or simply dehumanized as dinks or gooks.

First, the men swung machetes to clear the small trees and brush to create a line of fire, and then they filled the empty sandbags lashed to the bottom of their rucksacks with dirt from the holes dug with entrenching tools. They piled the full sandbags in front of the holes with gaps for shooting, creating bunkers. Next, they arranged hand-activated, directional Claymore mines around the perimeter at the brush line with the thin electrical wires trailing back to the bunkers. The three rifle platoons encircled the headquarters platoon. Each rifle platoon delegated four men to set up a nighttime listening post just outside the perimeter in the brush line, and the troops took turns with that extra hazardous duty. There would be time before nightfall to crack open C ration tins and scribble a letter home.

And that's exactly what Beans was doing one evening early in the hump when he thought he heard popcorn popping. *Pop. Pop. Pop-pop. Pop-pop-pop.* When he realized it was rifle fire, he thought some asshole, probably one of the FNGs, was dicking around, but when the whole perimeter exploded with the frantic chatter of M-16 fire, he knew different.

Exhilaration washed over him. He joined with warriors from time immemorial in mortal combat. A bond stretched through the eons, and he was at one with every soldier, in every army, in every war. That was Beans' first reaction, but such silly notions evaporated quickly.

Beans dropped his writing pad and dove into the bunker. He located the clackers connected by wire to the Claymores, and he detonated them all.

"Here comes a dink!" someone yelled, but Beans never saw him as his comrades mowed down the man who came charging toward them.

Everybody loaded and reloaded and poured thousands of rounds into the brush encircling the perimeter until the order came from Captain Connally to slow down and preserve ammo. They probably expended half their ammunition just like that. Some tossed frag grenades into the brush. Charlie was too close for an artillery strike, but Captain Connally called for illumination rounds fired by distant artillery as the evening darkened. Beans heard a puff above in the dark sky, and then white phosphorous burned as it slowly descended with a mini parachute, lighting up the night. As the parachute drifted on the night breeze, shadows danced in the bushes, and Beans imagined Charlie was everywhere. Choppers circled overhead, but they never fired their rockets or miniguns.

The firing stopped. Had it been five minutes? An hour? More? Had time stood still?

Captain Connally called around to obtain a situation report.

"Are all the men accounted for?"

Yes, but there were four KIA and half a dozen wounded. The company medic, a conscientious objector who carried no weapon, would check them out. A medic accompanied every line unit, and they would invariably be called "Doc."

"Are all the PRC-25s accounted for?"

Frankie, the squad leader, looked at Beans. Francisco Rodriguez had been in-country for a few months, and he now served as the experienced squad leader.

"Where's your radio?" Frankie asked.

"In my rucksack in the listening post."

Beans was supposed to be one of the four in the listening post that evening, and he prepared by carrying his poncho and rucksack into position, and then he returned inside the perimeter to write letters and wait until dark when Beans and three others would creep out. Be prepared, they say, but Beans had been too goddammed prepared.

Frankie reported to Captain Connally that one of the radios was unaccounted for, that it was in a listening post outside the perimeter. Beans huddled close to Frankie while he waited for Captain Connally to respond, but it didn't take long before the slow Texas drawl crackled over the radio.

"Ah need to know if Charlie has that raaydio. If Charlie has it, our security has been compromised. Ah need to know one waay or the other."

Frankie looked Beans in the eye, but he was just an FNG, and Frankie quickly looked to the others.

"I need a volunteer," he said.

Before anyone could speak, Beans did.

"I'll go," Beans said.

Beans was no hero, but it seemed the thing to do. He brought it out there, and he knew where it was. No one argued with him.

"Stay low, slide on your belly," Frankie cautioned.

Those endless alligator crawls back at Fort Polk paid off. Bean's left hand was empty, and his right hand grasped the pistol grip of his M-16, thumb on the safety to click to rock and roll in an instant. He barely crawled eight or ten meters when he came face to face with the wide-eyed stare of the Charlie who came charging in just moments earlier. Bullet holes riddled the man's blood-soaked fatigue shirt, but his eyes followed Beans. His lips moved as he attempted to speak, but he uttered no sound.

"Here's the dink," Beans hollered back to the others. "He's still alive."

"Be careful he doesn't have an unexploded grenade in his hand. Put a round in his head."

It happened naturally without any second thoughts. Beans grasped his M-16 like a pistol, and his thumb flipped the safety to single-shot. He lifted the muzzle to within inches of the black-haired head and squeezed off a round, hastening the man's inevitable death before he bled out. The head twitched slightly at the force of the bullet slamming into the temple and penetrating the skull.

"He sure as hell is dead now," Beans called back to his squad.

Beans wriggled his way past the dead man, keeping his gaze fixed on his blank, black eyes, as if Beans could see a reflection of what the dead man could see, as if Beans could know what he knew. What had his moving lips attempted to say? Beans never figured out what he was thinking to come charging in like that. Doped up, some said. A willing martyr, according to others. Was he just as scared as the rest of them, and when he tried to hightail it out of there, he ran the wrong way? Was he a fool or a brave hero? Only God knows, and maybe God doesn't know either.

So far so good, and Beans soon crawled to the brush line, but then he tripped a booby trap. *Christ almighty.* The squad had stretched a thin wire between trees about six inches off the ground, and they affixed a white phosphorous grenade at one end that exploded about ten feet from Beans. This was a smaller version of the illumination flares fired by the artillery. Willy Pete burns hot and bright; Beans was not close enough to be burned, but the illumination lit up the night. There he was, lying in a spotlight with butt muscles clenched tight. If his nose had been pressed any tighter against mother earth, he would've been breathing worms. There wasn't a goddammed thing he could do except lay still and wait for the AK-47 round that he would never hear or for the white phosphorous to burn out, whichever came first.

Darkness was now his friend, and when it finally settled over him again, he crabbed his way forward. He didn't have far to go, and his instincts were sound. He crawled straight to the spot, and there was the rucksack with the PRC-25 antenna jutting up from the back. He lugged it with his left hand as he crawled with his elbows and knees back to the bunker. He didn't know it then, but he would get a promotion to Specialist Fourth Class (E-4) and a bronze star for his actions.

The mood that night was somber, but that doesn't really say the truth of it. Beans' exhilaration had long since dissipated and depression set in as they waited for the next onslaught. No one slept, and they remained at the ready through the dark night. They had all seen too many cowboy movies and expected the Indians to attack at dawn, but they didn't; Charlie had hit and run and hauled ass.

Who knows how many attacked that evening? A search the next morning didn't find any bodies except for the sorry soul who had come charging in—Beans' intimate. Had there been other bodies dragged away? That's what the official report said, but that's bullshit. That's the way you snatch victory away from defeat.

Under tall trees and surrounded by thick brush, their location prevented helicopters from landing. Word came down for volunteers to carry the dead while the company humped to a clear patch that could serve as an LZ about a click away (1,000 meters) where choppers would pick up the wounded and the dead while resupplying with ammo and delivering FNGs as replacements.

No fucking way did Beans want to carry a body, but he got picked anyway to help with a dead man wrapped in his poncho. Two in front grabbed his arms and two in back lifted his legs. He was a big son-of-a-bitch, and Beans grabbed onto his left boot. Beans didn't see his face, but he knew. Nate Harris, the black kid from Detroit, would soon be on his way home to mama in a body bag.

That was the longest walk of Beans' life. He feared the next night, the next week, and the next month. As he walked that click with Nate's foot in his hand, he wanted to die. He was mere weeks into a twelve-month tour of duty. If this was the way it was going to be, he didn't think he could take it. This stiff, heavy body in his hands was the lucky one. Nate got it early. He was finished being scared. Maybe that's why the dead dink charged in like that. He didn't want to be scared any more.

That firefight happened early in the eighteen-day hump, so there's more to tell. The real story of the remainder of that hump was the rain—that is, the lack of it. Every swinging dick had canteens and water bladders hanging all over their rucksacks, but when the temperature reached a humid 90 to 100 degrees, the thirsty soldiers soon

drained their water supply. Streams appeared on their maps
as blue lines, and the troops planned to refill their canteens
in the blue lines, but they were unexpectedly dry except for
pools of stagnant, foul-smelling water. A couple of times
headquarters attempted to resupply by dropping empty
artillery shell canisters filled with water from helicopters,
but many split open, and the water rations were barely a
drip. Cans of fruit in C rations disappeared quickly.
Dehydration became dangerous, and it was a good question
whether the men would slog out of that jungle in time
before ... well, they weren't sure what could happen, but
they were about to find out.

The last evening, Beans saw Frankie licking
something.

"Whatcha doing?" Beans asked.

"Eatin' jelly," he replied. "Got any?"

They went through their rucks and licked every tin of
jelly they could find because there was a little moisture in
there.

On the last day, they needed to go up a steep slope and
down the other side where they would reach a highway and
friendlies waiting to transport them back to the base camp.
In fact, one squad of the friendlies would come up the
backside of the mountain to hook up with Alpha Company
and deliver water. It fell on Beans to be on point that day,
to go up the mountain first to meet up with the guides.

Goddamn Beans was thirsty, but he was strong and fit,
and he was able to get to the mountaintop with four or five
of his buddies, but the rest of the company languished
behind. Normally, the snaking string of grunts spread over
a couple hundred meters moved together, but that day the

troops got separated. Maybe the promise that the friendlies were bringing water pulled Beans up that slope, lifting one heavy boot after another up the steep incline, but he made it, and he met up with four or five grunts, but they had no idea. They had enough water for three or four but not for eighty.

Beans called Captain Connally.

"Alpha six, this is two-two. Over." Beans had learned how to talk on the PRC-25 and how to use the appropriate code words.

"Go ahead two-two."

"Confirm rendezvous with the Delta element," he said, "but negative on the H two O."

There was silence for a moment, and then the radio crackled. "Roger. Copy. Carry on two-two. Alpha six out." Even over the radio waves, the worry in the captain's voice came through loud and clear.

Beans looked at the others. Should they stay, or should they wait? The escorts settled it.

"Head straight down," their leader said, pointing with his M-16. "We've been up and down plenty, and you can see our trail. There's a wide river in the valley and tanks are waiting on the far bank to carry you to the highway. We'll wait here until the rest of your unit makes it up the mountain."

Down they went, and it was easy like he said, especially since they all had several glugs of water from the escorts' canteens. Damn, the canteen water tasted good, but Beans felt a tinge of guilt at chugging it down, knowing the others behind him wouldn't be so lucky. Beans' squad soon reached the valley and the river. He waded into the knee-deep flow. He pulled out his canteen cup and filled it to the brim and chugged it down. He splashed the second cup over his head. Then he drank down another, more slowly than the first. He filled his canteens and waded to the shore, plopping down in the sand. The C rations included plenty to mix with the water. First, Beans mixed a canteen cup with Kool-Aid. Then, he heated a cup and mixed it with chocolate. Then ... hell, he didn't remember all the ways he drank water, but drink he did, and he didn't care if it was potable or non-potable. He drank a couple of gallons over the next few hours, and he didn't piss once.

Back on the mountain, the sorry bastards experienced heat stroke or dehydration. Beans heard it all on the radio. There were seven heat casualty Medivacs by helicopter that day, "dust offs" they called them, and those were only the ones who passed out. Others threw away their heavy rucksacks. Some muckety-muck colonel who was the battalion commander tried to take charge from his light observation helicopter circling over the troops. He got on the company radio push and heard all the disjointed, angry talk.

He broke in. "Keep the radios clear for official business. Use proper military decorum."

Someone keyed their mic. "Fuck you." And then a moment later. "I mean, fuck you, sir."

After the hours passed and the last stragglers made it down the mountain, with Captain Connally bringing up the rear--Beans gave him credit for that--they all climbed atop tanks that were waiting for them, and they carried the men of Alpha Company a few clicks to the highway. A line of deuce-and-a-halfs awaited them, and they climbed down from the tanks and into the open backs of those trucks. Somebody in the rear had their shit together that day. In the back of every truck was a corrugated steel cattle trough-- where they found six cattle troughs, Beans didn't know-- and each trough was filled to the brim with ice and cans of beer. It took a while to drive back to Camp Enari, and they were some drunk sons of bitches by the time they got there: chugging, shaking cans and squirting beer on each other, and pouring it over their heads, like they just won the world series.

"Hell, we can celebrate New Year's all over again," someone hooted. "It's the fucking new year in Vietnam, and I hear there's parties every damn place. It's the biggest Vietnamese celebration of the year."

"They call it Tet."

Crack the sky, Shake the earth. You are about to inaugurate the greatest battle in the history of our country. Thousands of North Vietnamese soldiers (NVA) secretly filtered through the valleys and jungle of the Ho Chi Minh trail to coordinate with the South Vietnamese villagers who toiled in the rice paddies by day but took up arms by night as Viet Cong (VC). Across South Vietnam, the enemy attacked in a massive, coordinated effort to convince the colonialist invaders that they would pay a dear price to prop up their corrupt puppets in the south.

Shit-canned after the first night of their stand down at Camp Enari, Beans had no idea why the sirens blared or where the ear-splitting explosions came from, but he sobered up in a hurry.

"Where's my fucking rifle?" he said, stumbling around in the dark tent protected by a low level of sandbags stacked around the exterior.

Along with the others, Beans scarfed up what he needed: his ruck sack filled with poncho, poncho liner, C-rations, the Prick 25 radio with a spare battery, boxes of ammo, and hand grenades. Bandoliers of M-16 magazines slung over his shoulders. His steel pot helmet. Canteens and water bladders filled with water. When ready, they hastily moved out to bunkers and trenches near the perimeter. Rockets and mortars exploded around them and set buildings and tents on fire. The radios blared with confused shouts of alarm. Tracers fired from machine guns in perimeter guard posts lit up the brush and grassland that surrounded the Camp Enari plateau. Helicopters lifted off and provided rocket and mini gun support for defenders at key points along the sprawling perimeter of barbed concertina wire.

"Why the hell are they attacking a well-defended base camp?" Beans asked. "This ain't some remote firebase."

Frankie merely shrugged his shoulders. Only later would they learn that coordinated attacks hit US forces all over South Vietnam that night, nearly overrunning the US Embassy in Saigon.

For days and nights, the shelling continued, off and on. Beans never saw the enemy, but with the others, he set his M-16 to rock and roll and emptied a full magazine in a second or two whenever something outside the concertina wire seemed threatening. They slept in shifts--if you could call it sleep--they ate cold C-rations, and they prayed. They seemed alone in their bunker, as if the world forgot them, unknowingly sharing their plight with thousands of fellow GIs under siege across Vietnam. With few exceptions, such as the ancient, historic city of Hue, the U.S. forces repelled the offensive, killing thousands of VC and NVA in the process. By traditional military standards, Tet was a great American victory, but this wasn't an ordinary war. The very notion of American military invincibility was under attack, and if the battle was won, perhaps the war was lost.

When the shelling finally stopped, the rain started. Squawking radios quieted. Except for raindrops drumming the corrugated metal roofs of bunkers and hooches, silence descended upon the base camp.

Around 3:00 am, Beans wrestled with sleep in the mud as the rainwater pooled around his ass, and his poncho became useless. He was cold, wet, and discouraged, so he exited the bunker and wandered in the darkness and pelting rain before he plopped down on an upended pail with his poncho draped over his head, and he chain-smoked Kools, as if the glowing ember would give off heat, and he warmed his insides with swigs from the bottle of Jim Beam bourbon leftover from the first night of the stand down. He figured a little whiskey in the rain was called for, even if it was a bit early in the day.

When the raindrops softened to gray mist, first light revealed an unexploded enemy 122 mm rocket stuck in the mud next to him. For no good reason other than serendipity, the troop-killing, anti-personnel warhead, filled with explosives and shrapnel, had not detonated. For the NVA soldiers who humped the slender rockets south along the Ho Chi Minh trail, the 122s long-range capability allowed distant and untraceable launch sites. The portable rockets merely required a tripod of bamboo to aim at targets miles away. Guided by small stabilizer fins at the rear, the rockets flew far but without precision, and most of the hundreds of rockets launched against the base camp failed to hit buildings, aircraft on the ground, or bunkers; only fate decided where the random rockets might land and who they might strike: a crapshoot; a roll of the dice; snake eyes.

Beans removed his steel pot and hung it atop the fins at the butt end of the rocket jutting from the ground.

Fucking A, man, maybe the warhead will explode, maybe it won't. It don't mean nuthin'.

Chapter Six

"Ashes to ashes, dust to dust."

On an unusually balmy winter day, Pastor Olafson made the sign of the cross over the coffin waiting to be lowered into the frozen ground of the Kalmar Lutheran Church cemetery. A warm, gentle breeze wafted from the south and created slushy, muddy ground for the graveside service.

Dave's dad paid for Dave's airfare to fly home from New Hampshire for the funeral. Jonathan and his Chevy Belair delivered Dave to Logan Airport in Boston, and Dave's older sister, Hannah, picked him up at the Twin Cities Airport to deliver him to Kalmar. Hannah attended Gustavus Adolphus College in St. Peter, Minnesota.

Dave's eyes remained fixed on Angie Olson standing with the family across the open grave. Dressed in a demure dark dress, she dabbed at her eyes but stood tall and remained stoic. Dave saw another side to her. She was composed and classy. Elegant.

Back in the fellowship hall of the church after the graveside service, the church ladies served a variety of sandwiches and homemade pastries washed down with coffee or grape Kool Aid spiked with frozen lemonade.

"Thanks for coming home," Angie said as she clutched Dave's hands in her own. Dave didn't settle for that and hugged her, but other well-wishers waited in line, and Dave moved on.

"Later," was all he said.

Ben Olson, Angie's father, died suddenly in his office at a boat factory in nearby Little Falls where he worked for many years as the comptroller. Heart attack they said. Ben was the best friend of Harvey Karlstad, Dave's father, and the two families had always been close. So, when Dave got the call from his dad, he readily agreed to fly home for the funeral. Of course, he came back for Angie more so than his dad.

It wasn't until the next afternoon that Dave and Angie got together.

"Hello, Joyce," Dave greeted Angie's mother at the door. "I'm so sorry. Ben was like my favorite uncle."

Joyce teared up, nodding, but said nothing.

Angie appeared and pulled on her winter coat.

"We're going to drive around a bit," Angie said.

"Come back for supper," Joyce said.

Dave and Angie weaved their way slowly through the back streets of Kalmar: trees barren of leaves, snow-covered lawns, and familiar houses that seemed smaller and meaner than Dave remembered. Kids puffed up in their winter clothing looked like the Pillsbury Doughboy as they skated on the Lion's Club rink on a corner of the town ballpark.

The metal roof of the high school gymnasium glistened in the late-afternoon sunlight. The gym was part of the 1956 addition to the original schoolhouse built in 1920. Dave spent all twelve years of school here; he could almost hear the creaking hallway floors and radiators rattling as hot water throbbed through the pipes. Many of his classmates started in one-room schoolhouses spread around the area before joining Kalmar High in seventh grade or as freshmen.

He remembered the school assemblies in the old auditorium watching Ma and Pa Kettle movies on the last day of school before holiday vacations, the Mercury rocket launch propelling astronaut John Glenn on his way to orbiting the earth, and the Minnesota Twins in the '65 World Series. His 10th grade geometry class had just begun working silently on a daily assignment when the ashen-faced teacher ducked back in to announce that President Kennedy had been shot. Snow days and class plays. Leopard frogs that unwittingly hopped into the basement window wells, awaiting rescue by kids in town. Kittenball on the playground when the pitcher would ask the batter, "where do you want it?" The playground slide and merry-go-round where their parents played when they passed this way a generation earlier; only the jungle gym and monkey bars were new since their parents' student days. Dave always won the elementary school foot races on the last day of the school year.

Locals packed the gym for the high-spirited home games that rendered the Kalmar winters tolerable. Beans was the raw-boned center on the basketball team and the leading scorer, but Dave captained the team as the coach on the floor, and along with Beans, he received all-conference honors, less for talent than cussed grit.

Dave didn't remember who first called him the "Perfesser." He knew it was envy, but he took it as respect, and he didn't mind. He was the classroom whiz, whether by intellect or competitiveness, and it surprised no one that he offered the valedictory at the commencement ceremony for the class of '66.

Angie was a leading student in her own class, two years behind Dave and Beans. She epitomized the all-American small-town girl: bright enough to be on the honor roll but not nerdy; captain of the cheerleading squad; a soprano in the high school chorus and Lutheran Church choir; a clarinet and piano player; and she had been invited into the National Honor Society as a sophomore. She wasn't flighty or shallow but an old soul with both feet planted firmly on the ground. She spent lots of time with her grandma in a nursing home until she passed the previous summer, but she recently returned to the facility over Christmas to play piano and sing carols for the old folks. Much appreciated, but that was Angie.

Pleasant memories, all, of a simple but charmed childhood.

Dave was a townie; his dad ran a small business providing petroleum products to the community: gasoline delivered to the farmers to run their machinery and fuel oil to everyone to heat their homes in the frigid Minnesota winters. The Karlstads enjoyed a middle-class existence, which seemed rather well-to-do in the Kalmar community, all things considered.

The parents of Dave and Angie, the Karlstads and the Olsons, belonged to the same social circle emanating from the Kalmar Lutheran Church. The church perched atop a small hillock at the south end of Main Street. Angie's eyes fixed on the fresh dirt set against the white snow that marked her father's grave. Other relatives of Dave and Angie rested in the cemetery surrounding three sides of the brick building in a semi-circle. Around the turn of the century, Dave's great-grandmother on his mother's side and others in the Ladies Aid Society bought the church bell shipped all the way from Philadelphia. Cost more than the pastor's annual salary, it was said. Town boys rang the bell for hours in 1919 and twice in 1945 as world wars ended.

The Roman Catholic Church, a newer addition to the once solidly Scandinavian community, nestled into a grove of spruce trees on the edge of town. With the buzz following Vatican II, the Lutheran pastor and the Catholic priest often enjoyed morning coffee together at Margie's Café. Just a decade earlier, high drama followed a high school romance between a Catholic boy and a Lutheran girl, but that was no longer an issue with Beans and Angie.

The state highway that sliced through town doubled as Main Street. Sidewalks fronted the businesses on either side, including Margie's Café, the Gambles hardware store in the building that had always been "The General Store," the post office, the Lofgren Grocery, Halverson's Dry Goods, the Farmer's and Merchant's State Bank, the Anderson Insurance Agency where folks could also receive tax return assistance, an old two-story building that had been converted to apartments, the Williams Funeral home, and a couple of empty buildings. Dave's dad owned the gas station on the corner. Off a backstreet, the Farmer's Coop Creamery and Feed Mill overlooked the creek that flowed past town winding its way to the Mississippi. The silver-painted water tower with KALMAR scribed in large black letters on two sides cast a shadow over the Feed Mill. Dave once climbed up the ladder to the top of the tower on a dare, a seeming rite of passage for local boys. At the north end of Main Street, a blacksmith shop looked across the roadway at the Municipal Liquor Store & Bar. The smithy would often be found perched on a barstool, sipping on a glass of beer, and joking that he closed his shop because of "a bomb scare." A half mile outside of town, the garages and livestock pens of Kalmar Trucking occupied several acres. Beans' dad worked there as a truck driver. In addition to shipping livestock from central Minnesota farmers to the slaughterhouses of South St. Paul, the trucks transported other heavy goods, such as fifty-five-gallon barrels of oil for Harv Karlstad's business.

Dave and Angie eventually made their way out of town and parked at a beach alongside a frozen lake. Fish houses clustered across the bay over a traditional panfish hotspot.

Conversation flowed easily and naturally.

"Have you heard from Beans?"

"Yes," Angie replied, "but only a few letters. I'm surprised. I send him two or three letters a week."

"I've only received one letter," Dave said. "It didn't sound like Beans. He didn't say much, almost like he's hiding the truth of how miserable it really is."

"Yes, that's my impression, too. I worry so much."

A pickup pulled past them and drove onto to the lake, following wheel tracks in the snow to the fish houses across the bay. The sun would set soon, and the crappies always bit best at dusk.

"I worry about you, too. Folks around here don't know about you and New Hampshire. Your dad sure hasn't told anyone. What has he said to you?"

"Nothing yet, but I'm sure that's coming. How about you? What do you think?"

Dave hadn't shared his story of the Wisconsin police riot with Angie or his folks, much less the welt on his arm that left a lump.

Angie shrugged her shoulders.

"I know you believe in what you're doing, but I don't know what to think. I just worry about Beans over there. I want to get through this year and finish high school. When he's home and I'm off to college, then I'll think about it. You know, high school is not the same without you guys. I'm paying the price for hanging out with the classes ahead of me. It seems like most of my friends are gone."

He understood her ambivalence. He didn't know much about the war when he was in high school, either.

"I'm so sorry about your dad. How's your mom doing?"

Angie stared straight ahead and bit her lip. Her shoulders began to quiver.

"Your dad was like an uncle to me, a favorite uncle, and you were like my kid sister."

Angie lost it. Sobs poured out, with greater intensity than at any time since her dad's sudden death. Dave hugged her close, and the sobs only increased, and her whole body convulsed in his arms. After a bit, she cried herself out and regained her composure. She pulled a Kleenex from her purse and blew her nose and dabbed at her eyes with a second tissue. She drew a deep breath and turned to face him. Her eyes scanned his face and bore deeply into his. Suddenly, she lurched forward and kissed him, hard, on the lips.

"I'm not your sister, Dave."

The aroma of fried chicken greeted them at the door, and Joyce already set the table. A small TV flickered on the kitchen counter with the sound turned down. The NBC evening news with Huntley and Brinkley was just starting.

"Mind if we turn up the volume?" Dave asked. "All this news about the Tet Offensive is crazy. Can you believe it? The Viet Cong attacked and nearly overran the US Embassy right in the heart of Saigon. They're still fighting in the streets and every damn place in South Vietnam."

"Mom normally turns the news off when they talk about Vietnam."

"Oh, it's ok," Joyce said, and she turned up the volume just as they heard a warning about the graphic nature of the film to follow, but she didn't look away in time as the announcer described the chilling scene blasted over American airwaves.

On a street of Saigon filled with debris from the recent skirmishing, South Vietnamese allies of the Americans delivered a raggedly dressed and harried looking VC captive to the National Chief of Police. The officer nonchalantly put his pistol to the temple of the captive and blew his brains out.

Dave's mouth dropped.

Angie shrieked.

"Oh my God," Joyce stammered and staggered to the kitchen sink, holding her stomach. She retched in the greasy pots and pans.

Harv Karlstad rose early, like always, and sipped his standard single cup of coffee with a dash of cream but no sugar followed by a large bowl of Wheaties—also, no sugar. Twenty pushups and a like number of sit-ups kept his slight belly paunch at bay. By the time he showered and shaved, the winter sunrise appeared through the steamed-over translucence of the bathroom window. He dabbed gel in his palm to rub into his hair to keep his crew cut spiked up in front like a tufted blue jay. He plucked a gray strand.

He sucked in large gulps of the brisk morning air as he swept the sidewalk and driveway clean of an overnight dusting of snow. For heavier snowfalls, he plowed his own driveway, and his neighbors' as well, using a blade affixed to the front end of a three-quarter ton, four-wheel drive Chevy pickup. During the summer, no lawn in Kalmar was better groomed than the Karlstads', but now a thick blanket of snow covered the dormant grass and the flower bed sleeping along the front of the house. Snow clumps clung to the branches of the lilac hedge defining the western edge of the Karlstad property, and leafless burr oaks filtered the sun falling on the pair of bedroom dormers peering out from the second floor of the Cape Cod style house built under Harv's direction a decade earlier.

In the years prior to construction, the family rented a house on the cheap from Meg's mother Doris, the matriarch of one of Kalmar's leading families. Grandma Doris never cared much for the house owned by her second husband, and when he died in 1950 after only three years of marriage, she moved back to the ancestral home she had shared with Grandpa Dick and rented the empty house to Harv and Meg and their two young kids.

Dick and Doris Alekson raised five kids, including Meg Karlstad, nee Margaret Ann Alekson, the baby of the family. Grandpa Dick had passed in 1944 soon after

Richard Jr. was killed during the battle of Anzio in Italy. When Grandma Doris died in 1956, both houses were sold, and Meg's inheritance helped pay for the Cape Cod that dominated Bergstrom Avenue on the city's edge, an area that had been a cow pasture during Meg's youth.

Harv came from lesser circumstances: a small, rocky farmstead north of town where he grew up during the depression in a tiny house with no running water shared with six siblings. He remembered well the poverty of his youth epitomized by the code "FHB" (family hold back) if guests visited around mealtime. Harv and Meg had been high school sweethearts in the Kalmar class of 1943, but he shipped off to Navy boot camp shortly after graduating high school, and Meg enrolled in nurses training. After Harv's discharge following service aboard a destroyer in the Pacific theater, Harv and Meg rekindled their romance, and they were married in 1946 only months before Dave's sister Hannah was born.

Meg interrupted her nursing career to serve as a stay-at-home mom to rear her pair of kids, but she rejoined the work force as the Kalmar school nurse when Dave entered first grade. Harv had attempted college at the University of Minnesota, but standing in line to register was more than he could handle after the "hurry up and wait" experience in the Navy, and he worked out a deal with his father to take over the farm. Farming the meager acreage didn't last, and in 1950, he sold the farm at auction and bought out the Kalmar oil business where he had been working as a truck-driving delivery man. His timing was excellent as his boss was anxious to retire, and the price was right for the aspiring small businessman. Ambitious and hard-working,

Harv expanded the business in the next few years by purchasing both gas stations in town and buying out his principal competitor in Kalmar.

He was a joiner and community leader: the American Legion, the Lions Club, the town council, the church board, and the local Republican party caucus. Harv's own father had favored FDR and the New Deal, but to a man like Harv who saw himself as a businessman who pulled himself up by the bootstraps and didn't need the government meddling in his affairs, Ike's Republican party seemed the place to be, and Harv often represented the local party caucus at county conventions and occasionally state conventions.

Later that morning, Harv drove Dave back to the airport for a return flight to Boston. Icy silence prevailed for the first half hour while Dave waited for an opening, a question about New Hampshire, even a critical comment. Dave wanted to evangelize his father, to persuade him that the war was a hopeless cause. Perhaps more than anything, he desired his father's blessing for the honorable path he had chosen.

Oedipus got in the way.

"Sounds like Romney's support is drying up," Dave said, trying to start a conversation. "Too bad. He's preferable to Dick Nixon. I've crossed paths with a couple of Romney supporters on the campaign trail in New Hampshire."

Harv growled incomprehensibly. George Romney, the moderate Republican governor from Michigan, had been his choice, but it was clear that Nixon would be the one, and Harv's bond to his Republican tribe would prevail.

"I'm disappointed in you, son," Harv's first words came out as a hiss.

Harv could not have uttered more poisonous words. Approval is the greatest gift a father can give a son, and disapproval the deepest sting.

Harv, like other fathers, expected his son to follow a certain path, to mature into an image of himself. Harv's eyes grew misty when Dave delivered the class valedictory, and he shook Dave's hand with extra gusto just before Dave turned to climb the steps to his dorm at the U. Dave would go far and make his father proud, but Dave's departure from college for a fling with Democrat McCarthy seemed an irresponsible departure from the plan.

Dave misjudged the psychology of the moment. He didn't appreciate that his anti-war flirtation with the Democrats challenged his father's authority. A father's pride can be tricky in the face of a son asserting independence, especially when assumptions are questioned. It was all a mulligan stew of ego, identity, authority, and coming of age, and Harv vomited out his bile:

"There were no yellow bellies in my generation, and when Uncle Sam called, we stepped up. We did our duty, and we saved America. We stood up to the Nazis and the Japs. Seems like this pampered generation doesn't have the backbone to stand up to the communists."

Dave was briefly taken aback, but then he responded with a youthful lack of discretion.

"Don't be ignorant and get your head out of your ass; pay attention to what's going on over there."

So much for gentle persuasion. Rational discourse didn't fit the moment, but Dave tried.

"After the Vietnamese kicked out the French colonialists in 1954, the Geneva Accords called for democratic elections to unify the country. But who blocked the elections? Who doesn't have faith in democracy and self-determination? Who moved in after the French moved out? Who are the colonialists now? There was a time that Ho Chi Minh admired American democracy and principled support for self-determination, but we certainly proved to be a disappointment."

Harv's fingers squeezed the steering wheel, and his clean-shaven jaw jutted out. The creases in his ruddy face tightened. His breathing picked up like a race car revving its engine, and then he released the brake.

"Goddammit, Boy. Show some respect for your father and for your country. Fine. If you ever grow up and go back to college, I'm not gonna pamper you anymore. Don't expect me to pay your way."

Dave was silent but not surprised, and he stifled a smug response. The amount his dad paid was peanuts compared to the scholarship and loans that Dave relied on. Many miles passed under the wheels of Harv's Oldsmobile Cutlass before either spoke again. As the car turned into the airport drive, Dave had the last word.

"Did you see that Vietnamese general, our ally, murder a prisoner on the street in Saigon? There it was; that said it all. Any pretense of standing on the moral high ground died along with that poor man."

Dave hesitated momentarily to gain control of his emotions, and he spoke calmly.

"I admire what your generation did, and I'm especially proud of your service in the Navy. I agree with the existential necessity to fight the Nazis and the Japanese imperialists, but not all wars or threats of war are the same. Not all wars are just. America isn't right just because we're America. Jingoism isn't patriotism. We were the good guys in your war, but I don't believe the same is true of my generation's war. It's not that I don't respect America; no, I have the greatest respect for the idea of America, the ideal of America, the promise of America, and my generation merely asks that she live up to her own high standards. I hope you still respect my intelligence and my character. You don't need to agree with me, but I wish you would trust me to act according to my best judgment and conscience. Give me that much, Dad."

Harv merely grunted.

The Oldsmobile pulled up to the curb, and Dave hopped out and grabbed his suitcase from the back seat.

"I'll see you when I see you," he said and disappeared into the Departures concourse.

"Man, it's happening," Jonathan said to Dave as he steered the Chevy out of Logan Airport in Boston and headed north toward New Hampshire. "Since you been gone, our momentum has shifted. When I knock on doors, people start to listen and ask questions. I swear to God I've been invited inside for milk and cookies! More than once!"

"No shit."

"That Tet offensive in Vietnam has really got people thinking. The administration and the military had been blowin' it out their ass that the war effort was going so well that the enemy's military was about to crumble. Well God damn if Tet didn't put the lie to that, and it ain't over yet.

Bloody reports from places with strange names like Hue and Khe Sanh continue to dominate the nightly news. The brass touts thousands of enemy body count, but the hundreds of dead GIs, though fewer in number, count for more to the American public."

Dave had no idea where these places were on a map or how close Beans was to the action.

"Have you seen McCarthy?" Dave asked. "I heard he finally came to New Hampshire himself to do some in-person campaigning."

"True enough. The crew went to listen to him one night, and he ain't a great speaker. Recited poetry. Spoke over people's heads. He just droned on and abruptly quit when it seemed he had talked long enough. It sure as hell ain't his charisma that's got folks talking. People are just so pissed about the war and the lame excuses and lies coming out of Washington. Some say he's a lazy campaigner, but I think he's just laid back. It's his style to appear calm and rational."

Jonathan shook his head and laughed.

"Hell, even some conservatives are pissed enough at Johnson that they said they'll vote for Gene because Johnson ain't doin' enough! More'n one old geezer told me he'll vote for McCarthy to send LBJ packing because he has totally bungled this war. They say American bombers should blow the commies to kingdom come."

"But here's the thing," Jonathan leaned toward Dave and continued in a low voice, like he was sharing a secret. "Here's why we know we got the momentum. Johnson ain't taking Gene for granted anymore. His proxies are trying to sow fear. New Hampshire's governor said Hanoi will see a McCarthy victory 'as a sign the American people are ready to quit.'"

Dave nodded. "They may be right."

Suddenly, Jonathan started spinning the radio dial. "Let me find a New Hampshire radio station. Johnson is up with ads. Lemme see if we can find one."

They drove in silence for ten minutes as Jonathan twisted the dial.

"Here's one. Listen to this:"

The Communists in Vietnam are watching the New Hampshire primaries. They are watching to see if we here at home have the same determination as our soldiers.

"Told ya. They're running scared. Since Tet demolished the old lies about the war, they bluster and demonize us. When they goad us as draft dodgers and quitters, the people we meet know different. The politics of sowing division and name calling doesn't work when the voters can see for themselves that we're serious minded, cordial, and reasonable."

Jonathan looked at his watch and sped up. "I wanna make it back in time for the CBS special on Vietnam. Walter Cronkite is s'posed to report on his trip to Vietnam in prime time."

"Uncle Walter" was the patriarch of American news. Everyone knew him and everyone trusted him. He was not partisan although he had been hawkish on the war. He recently left his news desk to travel to the front lines to see for himself, especially in the aftermath of the Tet offensive. He was a straight-forward newsman, not prone to personal opinions, and that's why people trusted him. Now, he was back, and America was curious to hear what he had to say.

Jonathan pulled up in front of the Manchester campaign headquarters too late. It was already half an hour into the broadcast, and the volunteers who had assembled around a TV chatted nervously.

"He hasn't said much yet," Alex said. "Just lots of scenes from Vietnam. He's dressed in combat fatigues with an unstrapped helmet canted on his head and a microphone in his hand."

Cronkite waited until the last three minutes of his hour-long newscast. Back at his New York desk, he spoke solemnly but matter-of-factly:

It seems now more certain than ever that the bloody experience of Vietnam is to end in a stalemate . . . It is increasingly clear to this reporter that the only rational way out then will be to negotiate, not as victors, but as an honorable people who lived up to their pledge to defend democracy and did the best they could. This is Walter Cronkite. Good night.

When he signed off, stunned silence filled the McCarthy campaign headquarters. Someone started to slow clap, and others joined in. Then cheers broke out. And hugs. Wendy Cragun wiped away tears.

Dave wondered if his father had watched the special newscast. Harv Karlstad revered Cronkite and seldom missed his daily broadcast. Dave's dad was middle America, and that's who Cronkite spoke to. Dave considered calling home, but he thought better of it. His folks must find their own way.

Wendy sidled up to him and poked him in the ribs. "Welcome back stranger. Seems you brought good luck. Can you dig it?"

They hugged, and he was happy to see her, but it was different. After they first slept together in her sleeping bag in the back of the Belair, they made love a few more times, but now Dave was confused. Just as his relationship with Wendy Cragun was developing in New Hampshire--it was more than just sex, wasn't it?--one kiss in Minnesota turned his world upside down, especially since the girl back home was supposedly going with Beans, his friend in Vietnam. Uncertainty and uneasiness gnawed at him.

"Hungry?" Wendy asked. "Can I buy you something more edible than airline food?"

"Yeah, I guess."

Just down the street and around the corner, they ducked into the Pewter Pot Muffin House, a popular New England restaurant chain that presented an old Boston ambiance. Dark wooden beams graced the ceiling, and a cozy fire flickered in a brick oven. After a quick scan of *ye olde* menu, Dave ordered a bowl of New England clam chowder *from a cherished olde recipe.* The waitress' outfit was meant to mimic Revolutionary War era attire, but who knew what a scullery maid from two centuries earlier would have worn. The vest, skirt, and bowtie sported by the waitresses were clearly inauthentic upgrades.

Wendy passed on a plain bran muffin and ordered something called Strawberry Gem from the exotic muffin menu. Neither spoke, and minutes passed as Dave slurped down the chowder and Wendy picked at the crumbles that spilled onto the wooden plank table.

"Anything more I can get for you?" the waitress asked upon returning.

"Please refill my coffee," Wendy said.

"Do you want a cup?" she asked Dave, lifting her gaze from her half-eaten muffin.

"Sure. And maybe some dessert." Dave said, shrugging his shoulders since Wendy didn't seem ready to leave.

After the waitress filled Wendy's cup and brought a fresh one for Dave, Wendy mumbled without looking up.

"What's she like?"

"Who?"

"The girl you went home to see."

"Oh, you mean Angie. I don't know, She's kinda a regular Midwest girl. She sings. She's bright. She's a cheerleader. Comes from your basic middle-class, small-town family, like me. Our families are close, and we grew up together. I didn't go home to see her but to attend her dad's funeral. He was my dad's best friend."

"Were you dating her?"

"Me? No, she was going steady with a friend of mine from the basketball team."

"She *was*? Past tense?"

"Yeah, well, I mean, he's in Vietnam, so they're not dating now."

Wendy pursed her lips and tapped them lightly with her forefinger. She tried to look into Dave's eyes, but he was scouring the menu and attempting to appear nonchalant. She knew he lied, and he knew that she knew.

"Hmm." Dave said, thinking out loud. "Maybe some pie. Apple or Sour Cream Raisin?"

Chapter Seven

Hatless with tangled hair growing back and dog tags dangling over a bare chest, Beans leaned against his ruck in the shade of a gigantic Bodhi tree, sipping on a Minnesota brewed Hamm's Beer. The ancient tree invited reflection. For more than an hour he studied the sinews of vines from root to branch, but they were too many to count and too intertwined to follow. The tree could be thousands of years old. It could have been a sapling when Jesus of Nazareth walked the earth. Beans understood why local villagers considered the Bodhi to be spiritual. Roots and vines twisted into one trunk. Sprawling branches offered sanctuary for birds and shade for pilgrims.

Beans often thought of the enemy soldier whose imminent death came suddenly at the muzzle of his M-16. What had been a spontaneous decision now gnawed at him. What unspoken words were on the lips of the dying man? Was he pleading for medical aid or for a quick death? The morning after the firefight, he was still there, still staring. Maybe he's there still, and Beans would like to have a visit with him one day, to ask some questions, and they never really said goodbye. Somehow, Beans felt a kinship with him because he was there at that holy time when life became death, and he had looked deeply into his eyes, but all he saw was an eternal stare. Maybe the dead man would like to make confession, if he was Catholic, and Beans could offer last rites, even if he wasn't a priest. Or maybe the dead man was Buddhist, and Beans wouldn't know the words to say or the right prayers, but somehow, he expected Buddha would listen anyway. Beans could say he was sorry and that would be the truth, but he couldn't tell him that the men of Alpha Company didn't mean him any harm, shooting him like they did, because they did mean him harm just like he meant them harm, but Beans could talk about that with him, and they could wonder about that and talk about their families and such. At least it would be nice to know his name, this man who visited Beans in that murky place between sleep and wake.

After a crash combat course stretching over the first weeks of his tour of duty, Beans and the rest of Alpha Company experienced weeks of calm. Following the shelling during the Tet offensive, the company hung around Camp Enari to help rebuild with low-lying buildings replacing tents.

More recently, they settled into their current location on the outskirts of a village near the small city of Pleiku, a few miles outside Camp Enari. They first established a circular perimeter around the sprawling Bodhi tree consisting of claymore mines and white phosphorous grenades attached to trip wires, and they dug bunkers and filled sandbags with the soil to create walls at the edge of the bunkers. The men stretched their ponchos from wall to wall over the bunkers to create a tent-like structure. A crapper was set up at the edge of the perimeter. The headquarters platoon encamped in the middle at the base of the tree with radio antennas strung along the climbing vines of the Bodhi.

Beans borrowed a buddy's camera and photographed camp scenes. All the guys flashed the two-fingered V for peace sign when he pointed the camera at them. When the roll of film was full, he included it in a letter home to his Ma.

"When you get this film, please develop it, and you can see what my life is like and who my buddies are. Please share the pictures with Angie."

"Poncho is the short guy with black hair and a big grin. He's an Irishman from Boston. We call him Poncho because he's always wheeling and dealing, and you can get almost anything from him, like a poncho, for the right price. Frankie, our squad leader, is my best bud, real name Francisco. He's the one standing in the hole in the ground with a shovel, digging a bunker. He's Puerto Rican by way of the Bronx in New York City, and he's already been in-country for a few months. He calls his squad, *mis hermanos.* Sam is our machine gunner. He's the black man with the pet monkey on his shoulder. That damn monkey goes everywhere with us, even when we head out on a mission into the jungle. Don is the guy clowning around with the gas mask. He totes an M-79 grenade launcher when we're on a mission. We call him Bulldozer, or Dozer for short, because he dived into a bunker once and that ugly face pushed up a mound of mud. Will, with the tight curly hair, is another guy from New York, but I think he's from upstate and not the city. He's a married dude and kind of quiet. Larry Jones, Jonesy, is a black man from the deep south. I can barely understand his drawl."

He didn't mention Nate Harris, the man missing from the picture.

Compared to his first field experience of humping through the jungle, this duty was downright luxurious. On alternate days, the platoons took turns swimming and bathing in a nearby river. Once a day, a deuce-and-a-half arrived from nearby Camp Enari with a hot meal served from insulated metal canisters, cases of beer, and other supplies, but the best part was letters from home sent to an APO address (army post office) in San Francisco where scores of stateside soldiers sorted the correspondence and forwarded letters and packages to the troops in Vietnam.

His mother, Mary Ann, sent chocolate chip cookies in a care package. Cooking and baking were her strengths, but she didn't send many letters, partly from embarrassment that she couldn't spell, and her eighth-grade education in a small one-room schoolhouse hadn't prepared her well for such refinements, but then she didn't talk much either. A shy woman, she had always been oversized and teased plenty as a youngster. Jeffrey was her only child, followed by a series of miscarriages, surprising because she was a large, sturdy woman; bigboned, she said. She visited the confessional regularly, especially after each miscarriage, convinced that God was punishing her for reasons unknown, and her priest's admonition to pray twenty "hail Marys" as penance only heightened her free-floating shame. Praying the rosary daily while fingering a crucifix and prayer beads helped her anxiety, but only a little.

Beans was a farm boy, but there wasn't much future in it for him, and he had been working a factory job in nearby St. Cloud assembling refrigerators before he was drafted. The farms of the Kalmar community tended to be small and diversified which meant they raised both animals and crops without being particularly successful at either. Nearly a century earlier, Swedish Lutherans immigrated here choosing the same rocky hills and swampy lowlands they left behind in the old country. In subsequent generations, German and Polish Catholics moved in, and Beans' parents reflected the change. His father, Clarence, was German, and his mother, Mary Ann, was Polish. The meager Pfeffer farm consisted of a few chickens, hogs, and rented-out fields, and Beans' father earned his primary income as a truck driver for Kalmar Trucking delivering livestock to the South St. Paul stockyards.

The package included a note from his father written on a piece of birch bark. His anti-social dad was happiest traipsing about in the woods and hunting; Beans was surprised by his father's gesture, but he appreciated it. If his mother was quiet and non-talkative, his father was even more so, which made for an odd but stable relationship; since they didn't talk much, they seldom argued. She cooked, cleaned, tended her egg-laying hens, and attended mass, and he brought home a regular paycheck as a truck driver, picking up livestock from farms around central Minnesota and delivering the beef and hogs to the slaughterhouses of the South St. Paul stockyards.

The first batch of letters included nearly a dozen from Angie. Rather than tearing through them immediately, he treasured each one and imposed self-discipline to pore over one while leaving the others for later. Then another. And another. The letters were his lifeline to reality. Not that soldiering in a shooting war wasn't real. It was too real, damned surreal.

Doc, the company medic, a conscientious objector who carried no weapon, treated local villagers who gathered just outside the perimeter. He dabbed at sores and smeared various ointments. Applied bandages or splints. The villagers loved it. Doc also attempted to treat the boils that appeared on the skin of the sorry bastards who drank the river water at the end of the earlier hump. That included Beans who had boils on the back of one hand and on one knee. Beans finally figured out the problem with non-potable water. Damn, the boils were painful, and Doc did his best, but Beans and a few others returned to Camp Enari for a day trip to have an army surgeon lance the boils and carve out the roots to the core; the pain subsided but scars would remain.

Captain Connally didn't like the idea proposed by Top, but he didn't stop the plan. Somebody dubbed it Operation Cherry Boy.

Without his M-16, Beans felt damn-near naked riding in the back of a deuce-and-a-half for the short ride into the city of Pleiku. After dodging bike riders and Lambrettas in the busy streets, the trucks dumped the troops in front of a backstreet pool hall. Military police strolled by. Beans and Frankie each ordered a beer at the bar.

"*Ba Moui Ba*," the Vietnamese bar tender said. "Vietnam beer. Very good."

With their bottles of beer in hand, they slid into a wooden booth opposite each other. Two young Vietnamese women soon joined them.

"My name Becky." Barely sixteen and likely half-French, a legacy of the French occupation that ended in 1954, the young girl offered an obviously made-up name.

Perhaps the next generation of prostitutes would be half American.

"Becky" sidled up close to him, and her hand groped his crotch.

"We boom-boom," she whispered in his ear. "Five dollah American, and we luv long time."

Beans followed her out the back door and up an exterior staircase. An old man with a pointy white beard squatted in the second-floor hallway. Without looking up or speaking, he simply extended his hand, palm up. Beans placed a five-dollar military payment certificate (MPC) in his hand, wondering how much would go to the girl and her family and how much might end up in the coffers of the Viet Cong. Beans followed Becky into a dimly lit room with a mattress on the floor.

It didn't take long for Operation Cherry Boy to be a success.

Beans cracked open another can of Hamm's and continued to study the ancient Bodhi tree. Local villagers hung around the camp, and they told the story of the Buddhist temple that once stood near there, pointing at the hollowed-out ruins a hundred meters away. An old man from the village with fine strands of a gray beard touching his chest spoke of a similar Bodhi tree far away which offered enlightenment to the Buddha centuries earlier. The old man said when he was a boy in the village, Buddhist priests placed little spirit houses around the trunk and in the low-hanging branches.

Unknown to Beans and the rest of the world, one hundred fifty miles across the mountains in a hamlet near the South China Sea, other villagers died that day. Army troops under the command of Lieutenant William Calley massacred hundreds of occupants of My Lai village. *Papa sans*, too old to put up a fight, *mama sans* shielding children, pregnant women, and dozens of infants fell under a fusillade of automatic weapons and machine gun fire. American soldiers raped young girls and mutilated their bodies. Beans and the world knew nothing about My Lai that day as the military covered up the atrocity. Officially, the first report called the American assault, "well planned, well executed, and successful."

Despite the aura of the spirit tree, Beans failed to attain inner peace that day.

Chapter Eight

Wendy Cragun introduced Dave to pot, sex, and fresh lobster drenched in melted butter, but at least the latter didn't sit well with him, and he hadn't slept with her since his return from Minnesota. Her cheery demeanor masked her disappointment that their growing relationship, sexual and otherwise, had taken a step back following Dave's return to Minnesota, but Dave noticed, and he felt conflicted.

Dave awoke with an uncomfortable rumbling in his belly. Perhaps it was his first taste of fresh New England lobster the night before. Early that day, the team bought live lobsters out of the back of a pickup with a topper. The side of the topper claimed *the fish you buy today slept last night in Casco Bay*. They selected live lobsters from an ice-filled wooden chest layered with seaweed and semi-dormant crustaceans. A dollar seventy-nine a pound. The lobsters idled the day away stuffed in brown paper bags and crammed into a refrigerator at McCarthy headquarters in Manchester before Wendy plopped them into a steaming pot of boiling water.

Or perhaps his unsettled belly betrayed his apprehension. The first in the nation primary day had arrived. The last poll he saw showed LBJ ahead 62% to 11%. He knew too well the utter disdain his father felt for the anti-war movement embodied in Eugene McCarthy, and Dave didn't believe flinty New Hampshire voters, much like his father, were ready to reject the status quo in Vietnam ... or Washington.

He was wrong.

As the first numbers from around the state began to roll in, the enthusiasm at headquarters swelled. Of course, outright defeat of a sitting president was unthinkable, but the numbers said the race was close, closer than the most wild-eyed optimists had hoped. In the end, LBJ barely eked by with a margin of 49% to 42%. Technically, a loss for the insurgent McCarthy, but practically and psychologically a political earthquake.

"Look at him, he's jubilant," Wendy said as McCarthy appeared. "He's not restrained or laid back tonight."

McCarthy grabbed a hand-held microphone and addressed the rambunctious crowd, mostly consisting of the "Get Clean for Gene" brigade.

"People have remarked that this campaign has brought young people back into the system, but it's the other way around," a beaming McCarthy said, "The young people have brought the country back into the system."

Nobody paid much attention to the Republican primary returns, but Dave noted the ominous results. The "New" Richard Nixon garnered more votes than all Republican and Democratic candidates combined. The old, grumpy, vindictive Nixon seemed relatable with staged town halls with softball questions fed to him by a compliant panel of voters.

A domino effect of a different sort was in effect. The first domino to fall was the Tet offensive that rattled America's confidence about the war. McCarthy's showing in New Hampshire was the second. As the Minnesota team drove back to Minnesota four days later, somewhere along the short stretch of Interstate 90 between Gary, Indiana, and south Chicago, the next domino fell.

The Chevy blew a tire, and Jonathan supervised the placement of the jack and the removal of the flat. Just as Dave rolled the spare into place, Wendy shrieked, "Listen to this!"

As cars whistled past on the four-lane freeway, the five Minnesota students clustered on the shoulder next to the disabled car and listened to the news flash on the radio. Senator Robert F. Kennedy, the brother of the slain president, threw his hat into the ring to also challenge the sitting president for the Democratic nomination.

"He's a fucking usurper," Jonathan spit out the words.

Wendy agreed. "He a Johnny-come-lately riding on the coattails of Gene. Gene was the only one with the balls to challenge Johnson, and now that he has knocked the crown off Johnson's head, Kennedy wants to be the knight in shining armor to ride in for the kill."

Dave said nothing, but his mind was spinning. Kennedy's announcement, shocking but not surprising, was expected by many, not the least of which was the national press. For months, the first question directed at Senator Kennedy was always "are you going to run?' Dave heard whispers within the McCarthy campaign that the movers and shakers behind the McCarthy candidacy had first approached Senator Kennedy.

With the spare tire in place, the Belair ambled along I-90 through Chicago traffic before pulling into the Belvidere Oasis for Standard Oil Company gasoline and lunch at the Fred Harvey Restaurant. Kind of cool sitting in the bridge restaurant suspended over the cars buzzing along the freeway underneath.

"Goose liver? Fucking A, man!" Hank said, eyeing the menu item with disgust.

After sandwich orders were in, Dave methodically began to make his case.

"How many think McCarthy can actually win the nomination and then the presidency?" Wendy the spitfire optimist was the only one to raise her hand. Alex shrugged, Hank looked out the windows at the cars speeding by below, and Jonathan sucked on ice cubes.

"Shit has changed," Dave continued. "It's no longer merely about making a statement, about registering opposition to the war that may spur policy change. I appreciate what McCarthy has accomplished, but I doubt whether he can close the deal. Does he even want to be president? He runs to give voice to a movement, to call the war into question. He has done that in spades. After New Hampshire, LBJ is wounded, maybe mortally, and thanks to McCarthy for that, but I don't think he is the one to finish the job. Kennedy might. Bobby Kennedy might win the whole damn ballgame."

"I never liked Kennedy," Wendy protested. "He's too smooth, and he's part of the establishment."

Talk stopped while the waitress set the sandwich orders on the table.

"Could I get a refill on the Pepsi?" Jonathan asked. When he cleared his throat about to speak, all eyes turned to him.

"He's not his brother," Jonathan said. "He's not JFK, and he won't bring Camelot back. Wipe the stars out of your eyes."

Hank joined in. "Rusk and McNamara, LBJ's architects of war policy, are holdovers from the Kennedy administration."

Dave faced a hard sell, and these McCarthy acolytes weren't about to abandon their man.

"Let me tell you about my personal introduction to politics," Dave said, trying another tack. "Any of you watch or remember the Democratic Convention four years ago?"

He didn't wait for an answer.

"It was only months after JFK's assassination. When Bobby was introduced, he stood at the podium for *twenty-two minutes* as the crowd clapped and screamed and cried. Shit, even my *Republican* mother cried as we watched. Bobby didn't stop the outpouring; he knew that they needed to grieve his brother's recent death. He sensed the moment. His political intuition was right on. Charisma matters."

Dave was getting wound up.

"I appreciate that McCarthy relates to our rational intellect, but Kennedy can speak to the head *and the heart*. He can inspire and not merely debate. He's still only 42 years old with the most celebrated name in politics, wearing the mantle of his brother's martyrdom. He's youthful, with striking good looks, and experienced, having served as his brother's campaign manager and attorney general before his own election as a United States Senator. Like his brother, he is capable of soaring rhetoric that can arouse the passion of a movement. Bobby has support across a broad spectrum of the Democratic party: Hispanic farm workers, union members, and African Americans, to say nothing of all levels of party officials."

Dave finished his breathless monologue. Alex, the most seasoned among the group and the organizer of this trip, was thinking hard while rolling his fingers on the table. A senior poly-sci major with designs on a political career, Alex had been active in various causes since Edina High School, an upper-middle-class suburb of Minneapolis.

"Winning," Alex said, nodding. "It's all about winning, and Kennedy's recent statements are just as anti-war as McCarthy or anyone."

Dave pounded his fist on the table, hard enough to emphasize his point.

"Right on! It's about winning! That's what I'm saying. McCarthy has the policy right, but he's no politician. I agree with the message, but I doubt the messenger. Call Kennedy a knight in shining armor, but he's no Don Quixote. There's a long road ahead with many battles to come, and it will take a fighter, someone with heft, someone with clout. McCarthy's poetry won't get it done. Optimism has carried us this far, but now we need pragmatism."

After a brief silence, Hank said, "If you're not going to eat your fries, at least pass them around."

Dave smiled and nodded and took a big bite of his club sandwich. Wendy dabbed at the mayo on his cheek, but he was oblivious as he wound into his summation.

"I repeat what Alex said … 'it's all about winning.' Much as we all appreciate what Gene McCarthy has done, he's not the one to take us across the finish line. Bobby Kennedy is no less anti-war, and he may actually end it."

He could see on their faces that he hadn't convinced them, except maybe for Alex.

"Let's hit the road," Jonathan said, pushing himself away from the table.

"You're kinda cold blooded and ruthless, aren't you? Just like a pol." Wendy said, grabbing his arm as they walked across the parking lot to return to the Chevy and the last leg home to Minnesota. "I like that."

It was already the middle of March, too late to return to class that spring. Dave had the time. He had convinced himself, if not the others. History called. He would figure out a way to join the Kennedy team.

But first, sorting out his relationship with Angie was his number one priority, and he needed to accomplish that before joining Kennedy's campaign. Her relationship with Beans only made the question messy. What did Angie's kiss mean? In the short weeks after the kiss, Dave knocked on New Hampshire doors during the day and pondered the kiss at night. Wendy Cragun found him to be friendly but aloof.

After they unloaded the Belair on the U campus, Wendy pecked Dave on the cheek.

"Will I see you again?" Wendy asked.

"Of course," Dave said, but a wave of sadness washed over him as he realized this could be a final goodbye.

He arrived at his parent's house on Friday evening. Of course, Meg, his mother fawned over him and prepared his favorite supper: meatloaf and mashed potatoes with candied carrots.

Harv, his father, was more restrained, but he did shake his son's hand, an improvement over the harsh words they had exchanged when Harv drove him to the airport weeks earlier.

"That was quite the upset you college kids achieved," he said with grudging respect. Of course, anything that tarnished LBJ was ok with him. "Did you actually meet Senator McCarthy?"

"Sure did," Dave answered.

"Come and sit," Meg said.

Dave slid two thick slices of meat loaf onto his plate and lathered the meat and the potatoes in brown gravy.

"What is New Hampshire like?" Meg asked.

"Climate wise, much like Minnesota. We saw plenty of snow. The terrain is different. Mountains and lots of granite. Not much for farming. The people are different. Flinty. Stand offish. Don't care much for city folks, especially New Yorkers."

Dave smiled, remembering some of the jokes about the locals.

"The locals are called *Emmets*. Not sure why and not sure they like it, but here's a joke that gets at their dry humor."

"A New Yorker in a flashy convertible came to a fork in the road, and there were no road signs, but he saw a local standing behind a rock fence. *Hey Emmet, does it matter which fork I take?* The local looked up the road one way and then the other. The New Yorker asked again only louder. *I say again, Emmet, does it matter which fork I take?* The local slowly shook his head as he mouthed the word, *nope*. As the convertible sped off, the local mumbled to himself. *Not to me, it don't.*"

His dad smiled, but it wouldn't last.

"Is there still time to get back in school this term?" Harv Karlstad asked.

"Don't think so," Dave answered. "Anyway, I'm going to switch horses and see about joining the Kennedy campaign."

Harv's mouth opened, but no words came out. He looked at his wife as if she could make sense of their wayward son.

"Gotta run," Dave said after he cleaned his plate in the sink. "Heading over to see Angie."

Dave had been in Joyce Olson's kitchen often, but it seemed like the first time as Joyce opened the door. Ben Olson's funeral had been a few weeks earlier, and Joyce looked tired.

"Ang, Dave is here," Joyce called out over her shoulder. "Coffee? Cookies?" Joyce said as she gestured for Dave to come in and take a seat at the table.

After coffee and small talk. Joyce excused herself and headed upstairs toward her bedroom.

"TV?" Angie asked, and they moved to the living room. Angie checked the channels, finally settling on Saturday Night at the Movies and *Three Coins in the Fountain*. When she joined Dave on the couch, she sat close, and their shoulders touched. In an instant, conversation didn't matter, the movie didn't matter, and their lips came together passionately and repeatedly.

Dave had his answer, but he couldn't forget Wendy Cragun.

How could Dave join the Kennedy team? And where? And when? Although the papers were full of Kennedy stories, there was no mention of campaign details. Dave called friends from the New Hampshire campaign, but nobody knew much. It was all happening so quickly. So fluid. So uncertain. Then, a breakthrough.

"I haven't heard a thing," a Chicago friend said. "Wait a sec, I think I heard Patrick Kelly--you remember Pat, he was short with a shock of black hair that kept falling in his face—say something about Irish Catholic students going somewhere to do something for Kennedy. What's your number? I'll have Patrick give you a call."

Patrick called, and Dave had the info he needed.

Dave didn't have much money, and he decided against bus fare. Angie would drive him as far as Minneapolis to a freeway entrance heading east. Dave would hitchhike and retrace the route back to Gary, Indiana.

"I don't understand your compulsion to play around with politics," Angie said as she piloted her mom's Buick down the four-lane highway toward the Twin Cities. "What difference will you make? Why not return to school and get on with your life?"

As much as they were alike and a perfect match, in this they differed. She was apolitical and innocent, perhaps even naïve, as he had been back in the day, before graduation, before college, before the police riot in Madison. Angie was still all about apple pie after church on Sunday morning. Nothing wrong with apple pie, but he had changed since leaving Kalmar and small-town Americana. *Once you've seen Paree,* or something like that.

But then, she was right, he thought. What difference could he make? Was it just ego? It was cool to be close to the action, but he and his cohorts had made a difference in New Hampshire, hadn't they? Maybe he was naïve, but isn't citizen involvement a good thing? More than that, he was hopeful. During the Belvidere Oasis discussion, Jonathan had warned that he was captured by the Kennedy mystique with stars in his eyes. Guilty as charged. He was a true believer in Bobby Kennedy, and he would see this through.

"I'll return to the U, soon enough," Dave said. "The Indiana primary will be over in early May, and I'll have plenty of time to enroll for summer classes."

Too quickly, they reached their destination, and Angie swung the car over to the curb alongside a freeway entrance.

"Call me when you get there and call me often," Angie said with a parting kiss. "I love you."

Whoa! Dave was taken aback. Those words had not been spoken.

"I, I love you, too," he said. The words felt strange tumbling out of his mouth for the first time.

His first ride took him as far as Eau Claire, Wisconsin, then another to Madison, then on to Chicago suburbs near O'Hare airport. He waited quite a while before he caught a ride for the last leg through downtown Chicago to Gary, where he met up with Pat Kelly.

"Here's the deal," Pat said. "Bobby decided the Indiana primary would be where he would stake his claim, but there's only a few days left to get on the ballot, and he needs thousands of signatures. We're assigned to canvass Gary."

So, it was back to knocking on doors but not randomly. The congregants of Catholic parishes were strategically targeted. Dave had never been a member of a minority, but the Scandinavian Lutheran from Minnesota was decidedly out of place with the Irish Catholic team knocking on doors in a city that was 80% black. But it worked; in less than a week, teams across the state gathered the necessary signatures. Bobby Kennedy would be on the ballot for the Indiana primary scheduled for May 4. There would be other primaries in the meantime in which Kennedy was not on the ballot, but Indiana would be a critical test of the mood of the Democratic electorate.

Chapter Nine

After lolling about under the Bodhi tree and enjoying the calm, Alpha Company returned to the bush. While the men slashed brush and dug bunkers to create a November Lima, word came to Beans that Captain Connally, the Texan CO, wanted to speak with him.

"Beans, I need y'all to lead a team and head up the mountain ridge. Our radio contact with baayse is spotty. There will be good commo with baayse from the top, and y'all can relay messages back and forth as necessary. Tomorrow, the rest of the company will hump up the mountain and join y'all, but I want good raaydio contact as we're fixin' to move out. Pick three or four guys to be a raaydio relay team."

Within half an hour, Beans, Dozer, Poncho, and Jonesy headed up the mountain so they would have plenty of daylight to get up there and pick a safe spot, a thick brush patch to crawl into. Beans walked point, picking their way through the bush. As a youngster growing up in central Minnesota, Beans spent many hours tramping around piney woods and tamarack swamps, and the others relied upon his woodsy know-how to lead them.

They snaked forward a step at a time in a loose string with five to ten-yard gaps between them--eyes darting, and ears pricked, stopping, listening, searching, sniffing--choosing each step carefully to avoid snapping a branch or kicking against a punji stick, a sharp slice of bamboo used by the NVA to booby trap pathways. Not much chance of that here, they weren't on a path, and there was no evidence of human activity on this primeval mountain.

After moving a couple of hundred meters up the slope, the triple canopy jungle gave way to scattered trees, scraggly bushes, and savannah grass. Within an hour, they reached the spine of the ridge, but the cover was sparse, and they didn't immediately find a suitable brush patch. Nightfall would arrive soon enough, and they needed to settle in well before then. Best to move to the side, to hang on the edge just as the mountain fell away into the valley; they would have scant cover but only one direction to worry about and a handy escape route down the steep slope if they needed to bust ass outa there. They nestled into a thin patch of leafy brush and head-high stalks of grass, placing their rucksacks in a row, backs to the valley. Here would be their November Lima, leaning against their rucks, facing up the slope, the only direction of danger; later, they would sleep side-by-side with one person awake for rotating two-hour shifts.

"Base, this is Alpha team relay, how do you read? Over."

"I've got you 5 by 5. How me? Over."

"We hear you lima chuck. Thanks much. Alpha team relay out."

After confirming contact with the base camp, Beans next checked with Captain Connally down in the valley.

"Alpha six. This is Alpha team relay, do you copy? Over."

"Alpha team relay, this is Alpha six. We heard y'all contact baayse, but we didn't hear baayse's response.

That's why y'all are there. Good job. Keep your heads down. Alpha six out."

With radio contact confirmed, it was time to settle in.

They knew the drill; two kept lookout while the other two set out an array of Claymore mines: C-4 explosive encased in olive-drab plastic with a layer of shrapnel on the outer curve that would inflict mayhem in a controlled direction. They arranged the Claymores in a semi-circle, aimed up the slope, at the outer edge of their brush patch, 15-20 feet in front of them, hidden in the leaves and grass. They also covered up the electrical wires leading back to hand-activated detonators that would lie at the ready near their feet.

With the business of war out of the way, they attended to personal comforts. They spread their poncho liners on the carpet of grass and leaves and opened cans of C-rations with the handy P-38 can opener that came with the rations. Not much bigger than the end of a thumb, the P-38 boasted a sharp blade that flipped out and sliced through the metal can tops like a hot knife in butter. Beans finished with his favorite: a tin of pound cake paired with a tin of peaches in sweet sauce.

Bellies full, they leaned back on the rucks. As dusk settled in, Poncho slipped out the backside and disappeared over the edge with a packet of toilet paper and an entrenching tool to bury the evidence that he was a living, breathing, shitting human being.

Crack.

A branch snapped. Goddamn it, Beans thought, be quiet for chrissake, but when he heard muted voices and realized the snapping branches were up the ridge, dread walloped him in the chest, taking his breath away.

"Poncho, get your ass back here," Beans whispered as loud as he dared. "Here comes Charlie."

Poncho scrambled back, and all four men flopped forward, bellies on the ground, peering through the leaves and grass up the slope, butt muscles clenched tight, sure that their pounding hearts echoed over the mountainside. Without speaking, they instinctively assumed different roles: Beans grabbed Claymore detonators in each hand; Dozer unfastened frag grenades from his belt and lined them up in front of his nose, ready to pitch; Poncho and Jonesy aimed their M-16s up the slope, safeties flipped to rock and roll.

The voices grew louder as Charlie drew near. At that moment, the four Americans were Greeks in the belly of a wooden horse listening to the hoots of Trojans, doughboys waiting to go over the top, GIs on a landing craft chugging toward a Normandy beach.

Vague shapes and shadowy faces filtered through the leaves and grass. In seconds, they would pass in front of the Claymores, unaware Beans' hands cradled their lives along with the detonators. How many? Six. Eight. Maybe ten. Kill or be killed. The politicians in Washington, the generals in their air-conditioned flats, the officer corps, and the lifer sergeants back at the base camp had delegated moral authority to four frightened young men, boys really, lying in the weeds. Alive or dead, their lives could forever change in the next few seconds.

The troops called them gooks or dinks to dehumanize them, these short, yellow-skinned men with hair black as sin whose lands the Americans trespassed. Did their mothers feel a cold shiver pass over them at that moment? Would they leave wives and girlfriends to mourn? Fatherless babies? As the NVA regulars filled up M-16 rifle sights, the four Americans couldn't understand their words, only their laughter.

Grasping their AK-47s by the muzzles, stocks draped loosely upon their shoulders, Charlie didn't suspect anything amiss, completely unaware that four men lay in ambush just a few feet away. Had one of them tripped, or stooped to tie a boot lace, they might have noticed disturbed grass and leaves at the instant Beans detonated the Claymores. At the slightest alarm, Beans would squeeze the detonators, the signal for the M-16s in Poncho and Jonesy's hands to spit out a full clip in a second, and Dozer would lob unpinned grenades into the melee. Some of the NVA, maybe all, would laugh no more; maybe Beans and his buddies would be silenced too. They would all be dead or wounded, in body or soul.

Beans waited for the signal that never came--a cry of alarm or sudden movement. Charlie never sensed danger, and Beans didn't squeeze the detonators. Serendipity, perhaps, because Beans couldn't claim that he consciously decided to live and let live. Before Beans knew it, the young men from the north had passed by and continued down the ridge, smokin' and ajokin'. Perhaps they headed toward thatched hooches and a snout full of rice wine; little did they know they had much to celebrate.

There was a coda yet to be heard. The rhythms of the squad that passed by had barely faded when the drumbeat up the ridge swelled again, only louder. For all the racket, it sounded like a major troop movement through the bush. The squad had merely been the point, Beans was sure, followed by the whole fucking North Vietnamese Army. The Americans buried their faces in the grass again, hardly daring to raise their mud-caked noses. The cacophony moved toward them, but something didn't fit. The high-pitched jabbering threw the men off.

What the hell? The Americans' heads popped up like gophers.

Monkeys. Fucking monkeys. A troop of monkeys, dozens of them, swarmed through the treetops.

"Mornin' Beans," Captain Connally said when the rest of Alpha Company arrived the next day. He slapped Beans on the back. "Good job, men. I trust y'all enjoyed a quiet night."

Chapter Ten

After the Gary, Indiana team finished gathering signatures on the petition to add Kennedy to the primary ballot, the Irish Catholics from Chicago returned home, but Dave hitchhiked his way to Indianapolis to volunteer at campaign headquarters.

The door to the Marriott suite was open, and the only person there was a middle-aged, bespectacled man in a crewcut.

"Sir, I'm here to help."

"Can you drive a cah?" the man replied without looking up from the paper in his hand.

"Yes, sir, I have a Minnesota driver's license."

The man looked up with a smile.

"We could use some diversity on the team. We cahn't all be Irish Catholics from Boston."

Dave barely understood the thick Boston accent.

"Young man, I need you to drive to the airport to pick up volunteers flying in from Beantown." He dug in his pocket to find the car keys. "My name's Gerard Doherty," he said, extending his hand for a handshake. "I'm a friend of Teddy. I guess I'm in chawge heah until somebody tells me I'm not."

In the beginning, there really wasn't much of an organization or staff apart from Mr. Doherty and Dave, but lots of people passed through for instructions and campaign materials. Mr. Doherty directed around seventy Massachusetts volunteers who fanned out to campaign across the state.

After delivering the volunteers, first to the Marriott and then to the Greyhound terminal after they received their marching orders, Dave picked up boxes of materials from a printer, and then he picked up two orders of McDonald's Big Macs and fries for Mr. Doherty and himself.

"You seem like a smaht fellah, and I need a gophah. If you care to stick around for a while, you can sleep on the couch theah, and you'll get $10 a day meal money, same as the volunteers in the field."

"That's ok with me," Dave replied. He felt pretty-damn smug to be so close to the action, and then it got better.

"I've got one more run for you before we call it a day. Head back to the airport to pick up the Senator. He'll be staying heah most nights while he flies around the state to campaign."

Senator Robert Kennedy's entourage included three others, and they barely noticed Dave, their chauffeur, and they chatted away with campaign conversation as if he wasn't there.

"This is John. John Lewis," Mr. Doherty said, sweeping his arm to introduce Dave's new roommate. "John, meet Dave, whatevah his last name is."

After a few days sleeping on a couch, Dave would now share a hotel room with John Lewis who had joined the campaign to organize events within Indiana's black community. John was a black man with close cropped curly hair, well dressed, confident, and earnest. He spoke with a southern drawl and a rural Alabama dialect that clipped the end of words.

"Small town Minnesota," Dave said as he and his new roommate settled in with small talk. "On leave from the University of Minnesota."

"You a farm boy?" John asked.

"Not really. Farm community but Dad had a small business in town. How about you?"

"Oh, I'm a farm boy alright. My folks were sharecroppers in rural Alabama, workin' on half. After paying half the crop as rent for most of their lives, they bought 110 acres of cotton, peanut, and corn fields with an old three-room house. No running water or plumbing. No door to the kitchen except from the outside. We were poor, barefoot, and black, but we didn't know otherwise."

John wrestled with a stuck drawer after transferring the contents of his suitcase into the dresser next to his twin bed.

"Any black folks in your town?" John asked as the drawer slammed shut.

"Nope. I guess this conversation we're having right now is the longest I've ever carried on with a black man."

John chuckled and turned to face Dave.

"Up until I was six-year-old, I had only seen two white men in my whole life. When I went to town for the first time, I met Jim Crow face to face. You know Jim Crow?"

Dave shrugged his shoulders unsure what John was getting at.

"Jim Crow was the way of life in the south, a caste system relegating black folks like my family to second-class citizens, a legitimization of racism. Segregation was the key. When I went into Troy, the county seat of Pike County, I couldn't drink from a water fountain meant for white only. The one for 'coloreds' was merely a rusty spigot. I love to read, but when I tried to get a library card, I was told that the library was for white folk only, not coloreds. I could buy a mixed Coca Cola at the drugstore, but I had to take it outside to drink. Sitting down at the Formica counter or one of the wrought iron tables was unthinkable. Except for the janitors, the local courthouse personnel were all white, including the entire criminal justice system: police, prosecutors, judges, and the juries who would be called to render judgment, but white justice wasn't always meted out by the authorities. Vigilante violence haunted our black community. I knew a man, a distant relative, who visited our community regularly to see his kin, who was shot dead--probably by the Klan because he was active in the NAACP."

Dave sat on his twin bed, wide-eyed and speechless. If John Lewis' intention was to prick the innocence of the naïve, white college student from small town Minnesota, he succeeded.

"I mention all this 'cause I don't want to make any assumptions," John said. "We gonna be ok rooming together?"

That was the start of a fast friendship and Dave's civil rights education. The day after their first discussion, John presented Dave with a present: the hot-off-the-press best-selling Kerner Commission Report. Dave placed the thick tome, over four hundred pages, on his nightstand, but he didn't have time to crack it open, and he would get to it when he could get to it.

John Lewis was a few years older than Dave with many miles of civil rights marches under his feet. He was experienced and savvy, far more than Dave could have imagined, but hours of late-night conversations educated Dave on Jim Crow and civil rights history, and news stories that Dave vaguely remembered came alive with first-person retelling: lunch counter sit-ins, freedom riders, Bloody Sunday in Selma.

As Dave listened to John's stories, he kept his own mouth shut. Years earlier when Dave hired on for a few days to make hay with a Kalmar farmer, he thought pitching hay bales was the most miserable work possible, but it didn't compare to picking cotton for endless hours under the blistering Alabama sun, bent over with a back still aching from the day before and with fingertips chewed raw from the sharp edges of cotton pods. Dave knew about outhouses, but he wasn't familiar with the bucket of lye used to staunch the stench in the Alabama heat or the Sears, Roebuck catalogues and dried corn cobs that took the place of toilet paper. When John talked of the beatings he endured at the hands of white mobs and state troopers, Dave subconsciously rubbed the lump on his arm from a Madison city cop's baton. In a small way, he understood. If racial bigots had brutalized John Lewis, cultural bigots had battered Dave, but the lump on his arm didn't compare to the fractured skull John sustained on Bloody Sunday, and Dave never mentioned his minor scrape with bigoted law enforcement.

When confronted with the reality of poverty and racism, Dave's white, middle-America, middle-class privilege reared up and spit in his face. Did he feel a prick of conscience? Not exactly, but he did sense a gnawing obligation to do something, but what? John's stories certainly piqued Dave's curiosity to know more.

The thing about John was that he was still *out there*, still organizing, still advocating, still preaching the non-violent resistance he had learned from many mentors, not the least of whom was Dr. Martin Luther King, Jr. John *believed.* As a trained preacher, John believed in the social gospel and the beloved community which he understood as God's kingdom on earth: peace, justice, equality.

And, despite all reasons to the contrary, John believed in America.

Late in March, Dave joined others huddled around a TV set in Kennedy campaign headquarters in Indianapolis. President Johnson was about to address the nation with an update on the war. LBJ spent forty minutes droning on, and several volunteers left the room, and others started their own jibber jabber. Johnson made news by announcing a pause in the bombing campaign that was devastating North Vietnam. That was something, if it was true, but few in the room trusted his word.

Then, the next domino fell.

With America's sons in the fields far away, with America's future under challenge right here at home, with our hopes and the world's hopes for peace in the balance every day, I do not believe that I should devote an hour or a day of my time to any personal partisan causes or to any duties other than the awesome duties of this office — the presidency of this country, Johnson intoned, looking earnestly into the TV camera.

"Get in heah," Mr. Doherty shouted at campaign headquarters. Everyone in the room and tens of millions of viewers around the nation suddenly came to full attention. "What the hell is he saying?"

Accordingly, I shall not seek, and I will not accept, the nomination of my party for another term as your president.

Johnson's shocking announcement sucked all the air out of the room, but then it came rushing back in. Euphoria mixed with confusion. Until then, defeating LBJ for the nomination had consumed the campaign energy, but what did it mean now that he had dropped out? Had Senator Kennedy become the *de facto* front runner? Who would fill the void left by LBJ?

In caucus states and earlier primaries where Kennedy couldn't get on the ballot, McCarthy racked up delegates, but the biggest competition in Indiana would be the Democratic governor, Roger Branigin, who was on the ballot as a "Favorite Son." Typically, preconvention primaries and caucuses only anticipated but wouldn't control the national convention. The convention would decide the nominee and not before, and there would be plenty of wheeling and dealing. Governors, state chairmen, and state parties carried great weight by controlling their state delegates, and that was the point of running as a favorite son. If Branigin won the primary (and initial polls said he was well ahead of Kennedy), he would control the delegates and exert influence at the convention. It was raw party politics pure and simple, and for the late-comer Kennedy campaign, the primaries were less about racking up delegates than signaling the mood of the electorate heading into the late-summer convention. If Kennedy could pull off an upset, that would create momentum going forward and bestow legitimacy on the campaign during the convention, even if he didn't have most of the delegates.

"If we can win in Indiana, we can win in every other state and win when we go to the convention in August." Words right out of Senator Kennedy's own mouth.

Dave was learning the game from seasoned pols, especially the Kennedy machine from Massachusetts that had launched all three Kennedy brothers into the Senate and JFK into the White House, and he was learning about the civil rights movement from his roommate, John Lewis.

"Two questions," Dave said to John when they returned to their hotel room after a long day. "Why is the black community so loyal to Bobby Kennedy, and why are you?"

"Big questions. We could be talking for days on end."

John spit out his toothpaste and stepped out of the bathroom.

"The civil rights movement didn't focus on elections at first. Instead, we used non-violent direct action to reveal the horrors of segregation. We trained in non-violence. We expected to be taunted and beaten, but we would not fight back. We learned how to take a blow without hitting back. We meant to raise the rug and expose the dirt underneath and force the public to see the hidden filth. When we were ready, we sat at segregated lunch counters knowing that we would be refused service. Then we would come back, and crowds would gather with insults and taunts, but we kept coming back, and they beat the crap out of us, and then *we* were arrested for disturbing the peace. We refused bail. Others took our place. Eventually, the press caught on, and the taunts, beatings, and arrests made the news. While I was a college student in Nashville, we were successful, and we broke lunch counter segregation in that city. There were mixed results here and there across the south."

Dave had been lying on his bed with his head on his pillow, but he sat up and listened intently as John paced back and forth telling the story.

"Next came the freedom riders challenging the segregation in bus terminals because they were subject to federal law through the Interstate Commerce Commission. The first bus got bombed. I was on a second bus, and white folks beat us while the police looked on and then they arrested *us* after the mob had its way. We spent time in jail and a notorious Alabama penitentiary. As the news spread around the country, dozens of others, hundreds of others, took our place, and freedom bus rides appeared all over the south."

Dave was amazed at the matter-of-fact way John recounted the beatings and the jailings.

"As the violence upon the freedom riders escalated, the Kennedy administration, JFK the president and RFK the attorney general, had no choice but to intervene with federal agents. The brothers came to the fight reluctantly because they didn't want to piss off the southern Democrats, still the mainstay of the Democratic Party. Now that they were in, Bobby suggested voter registration would be a better way to go."

"Is that when you first met Bobby Kennedy?" Dave asked.

"No, that would come later. I was in prison when my colleagues met with him, and he suggested switching our focus to voter registration. Should we get out the vote or should we march? Should we work on voter registration or ride freedom buses? Not many movement leaders agreed with shifting the emphasis from protests and demonstrations to elections and voting, but the offer of administration support carried the day."

"When did you first meet Bobby?"

"Summer of '63. They chose me to lead the group of student activists known as the Student Nonviolent Coordinating Committee, and everyone called us "Snick." We had been at the forefront of the lunch counter sit-ins and Freedom Riders. We were too radical for many of the more established civil rights organizations with our aggressive, confrontational approach even though we were strictly non-violent. The Kennedys invited us to the White House, along with other organizations, and I attended as the Snick representative. At one point, Bobby pulled me aside and said 'John, now I understand. The young people, the students have educated me. You have changed me.' The courage of the freedom riders in the face of violence clearly moved him. Both the president and the attorney general had optimistic, can-do personalities, but civil rights was far down their list of priorities in the first years of the administration. If our purpose in marching and protesting and riding the freedom buses was to let the people see the scum under the rug and thereby change hearts and minds, it worked all the way up to and including the Kennedy brothers, the president and attorney general. Bobby Kennedy listened. He learned. He changed. He grew. He gained my respect and that of our entire movement."

John paused and stared out the hotel room window. Just when Dave thought he was through for the night, John turned around and sat down in a chair in the corner, gathering his thoughts. John seldom showed emotion, but Dave detected a quivering chin as John picked up the story.

"Events came together and exploded on a fateful day in the summer of '63. Alabama Governor George Wallace made a show of blocking black students from registering at the University of Alabama before backing down to federal authorities. On the same day, Dr. King announced a massive march on Washington. After midnight, a sniper assassinated civil rights worker Medgar Evans in his driveway as he carried an armload of "Jim Crow Must Go" T-shirts. But, earlier that evening, President Kennedy addressed the nation on national television. I'll never forget watching him and hearing him say these words:"

We face, therefore, a moral crisis as a country and a people. It cannot be met by repressive police action. It cannot be left to increased demonstrations in the streets. It cannot be quieted by token moves or talks. It is time to act in the Congress, in your state and local legislative bodies, in all of our daily lives.

"The Kennedys' support for civil rights was now out in the open, and there was no turning back."

John looked at his watch. "Hey, it's past midnight. Let's pick this up later."

The next morning, April 4th, Senator Kennedy flew north to speak at the University of Notre Dame and Ball State University. After dropping him off at the airport, Dave returned to ferry John around the city to make final arrangements for Kennedy's speech that evening to a black audience in the heart of the black section of Indianapolis.

"When are you going to get your own driver's license," Dave asked.

"Why would I do that when I have a boy like you to drive me around?"

Both men smiled at John's ironic humor.

Dave picked up the conversation from the prior evening as they drove around Indianapolis.

"You spoke at the March on Washington, didn't you? How old were you?"

"In August of '63, I was 23-year-old. Probably in over my head. Probably a bit angry, and there were some who didn't want me to speak. In the minutes leading up to my speech, I was behind the Lincoln Memorial arguing over the words. I made slight revisions, but my tone of impatience with the pace of change still came through. Afterwards, we were invited to the White House, and the Kennedys were elated with how it all turned out, especially since there was no violence. Of course, Dr. King's 'I have a dream" speech was a fitting climax to the day."

"Tell me about Dr. King."

Just then, Dave slammed on the brakes as he nearly missed a red light. The car stopped partly in the intersection, and a chorus of honking horns let Dave know. After he backed up, he repeated his question.

"Tell me about Dr. King. Do you know him well?"

"Well, we crossed paths now and again, and our student group modeled our non-violence after his example. He is the unquestioned leader of the civil rights movement, but there are some who are envious and resent him for that. He is in constant demand to support this march or that one. This protest or that one. He must choose his battles, and he sometimes leaves folks disappointed because he can't say yes to everyone. Right now, his focus is on Memphis and the sanitation worker's strike that threatens to spiral out of control into violence. He's there to keep the marches peaceful and non-violent. Others disagree with the non-violent approach. Malcolm X comes to mind, and one of my former colleagues, Stokely Carmichael, with *Black Power* ideas. Stokely said, 'The major enemy is the honky and his institutions of racism.' While that may be true, such brash talk is not going to help move forward with change for the better. H. Rap Brown called to 'move from resistance to aggression, from revolt to revolution.' I fear the Black Power movement will be the death of the civil rights movement, especially as it tilts toward violence."

Dave pulled the car up against the curb of Broadway Street near the intersection with 17th. Bobby would speak outside the Broadway Christian Center located there later in the day. John didn't immediately hop out. He had more to say about Dr. King.

"After the assassination of President Kennedy, Martin became a close ally of President Johnson as they worked together to pass the 1964 Civil Rights Act followed by the 1965 Voting Rights Act and the rest of the 'Great Society' legislation during LBJ's first years, and some resent him for working with the administration. Of course, Martin broke with LBJ over Vietnam, and he is now one of the loudest voices in opposition to the war. He feels the money and effort in Vietnam sidetracks from the commitments made by civil rights legislation and dilutes the war on poverty. He wonders how black and white soldiers can fight and die together but they can't sit together in the same schools or live in the same neighborhood. More than anything, he fears loss of the moral high ground as America abandons the spirit of self-determination for brown-skin folks in the third world.

"How did you come to join the Kennedy campaign?"

John drew a deep breath and exhaled slowly.

"Long story. After living and breathing and bleeding for the movement for over six years, I got fired. Well, maybe that's a bit harsh, but as the movement grew, it changed, and not for the better, and my replacement as the head of Snick epitomized the change. At first, we were tight knit and of one mind, and that mind was non-violent. We believed in the beloved community of white and black living in harmony. We believed in working within the system."

"As the movement grew, so did black consciousness and black pride—good things—but with the side effect of mistrust of our white brothers and sisters who had worked with us and shed their blood, too."

"Disillusionment followed the 1964 Democratic National Convention when black delegates attempted to replace the segregationists who were chosen through the official party apparatus in Mississippi. Although nominally Democrats, the official Mississippi delegates were for Goldwater! President Johnson put his finger on the scale and urged a compromise that neither side wanted or accepted. The official delegates walked out, and the black delegates were frustrated after shedding blood that summer to register and work within the system. LBJ feared that seating the black delegates would cause him to lose the south. Well, it turned out that he had already lost the south followin' the passage of the Civil Rights Act that summer, even though it may have aided his landslide victory elsewhere. Party realignment in the south moved faster than even Johnson, the savvy politician, anticipated."

"Frustration, impatience, and cynicism led to rising black nationalism, black power, and Black Panthers. Within Snick, we debated. Were we gonna be an interracial movement or a separatist movement? Violent or nonviolent? Community or conflict? As the leader, I was seen as too cozy with the administration, too defensive of Bobby Kennedy, too respectful of Dr. King, and I was defeated for re-election—put out to pasture because I was the old guard. I was only 26! I took a job in New York City and Atlanta working for a non-profit, but when Bobby Kennedy called last month, I jumped at the chance to get back in the game. I believe he is the leader who can bring people together."

After John finished and he departed to make final arrangements for the speech that evening, Dave returned to campaign headquarters to kill time. Dave was to pick the Senator up at the airport when he returned and drive him straight to the Indianapolis event that John had arranged, and Dave lolled about the campaign headquarters as he waited. Late in the day, Mr. Doherty received a phone call. Dave heard half the conversation.

"Yes, Mr. Mayor, he is scheduled to speak in the inner-city tonight. Yes, 17th and Broadway. Yes, we know it's a black neighborhood."

Suddenly, all the color drained from Mr. Doherty's face, and he slumped into a chair.

"Yes."

"Yes."

"He's flying right now, but I'll speak to him as soon as he lands."

He hung up the phone and took a moment to gather himself before he turned to Dave with tears streaming down his face.

"They assassinated Martin Luther King in Memphis, and Mayor Richard Lugar advises the campaign to cancel the speech. There may be violence."

Doherty rode with Dave to the airport. After hearing that King had died, the Senator didn't flinch. He went to the scheduled event in the inner city, scribbling notes on an envelope in the back of the car for an impromptu speech. He climbed atop a flatbed truck to speak and broke the news to the crowd as a chilly wind hummed into his microphone.

I have bad news for you, for all of our fellow citizens, and people who love peace all over the world, and that is that Martin Luther King was shot and killed tonight.

Kennedy hesitated as the crowd shrieked and wailed. After the shock wore down, he continued:

Martin Luther King dedicated his life to love and to justice for his fellow human beings, and he died because of that effort.

In this difficult day, in this difficult time for the United States, it is perhaps well to ask what kind of a nation we are and what direction we want to move in. For those of you who are black--considering the evidence there evidently is that there were white people who were responsible--you can be filled with bitterness, with hatred, and a desire for revenge. We can move in that direction as a country, in great polarization--black people amongst black, white people amongst white, filled with hatred toward one another.

Or we can make an effort, as Martin Luther King did, to understand and to comprehend, and to replace that violence, that stain of bloodshed that has spread across our land, with an effort to understand with compassion and love.

For those of you who are black and are tempted to be filled with hatred and distrust at the injustice of such an act, against all white people, I can only say that I feel in my own heart the same kind of feeling. I had a member of my family killed, but he was killed by a white man. But we have to make an effort in the United States, we have to make an effort to understand, to go beyond these rather difficult times.

My favorite poet was Aeschylus. He wrote: "In our sleep, pain which cannot forget falls drop by drop upon the heart until, in our own despair, against our will, comes wisdom through the awful grace of God."

What we need in the United States is not division; what we need in the United States is not hatred; what we need in the United States is not violence or lawlessness; but love and wisdom, and compassion toward one another, and a feeling of justice toward those who still suffer within our country, whether they be white or they be black.

So I shall ask you tonight to return home, to say a prayer for the family of Martin Luther King, that's true, but more importantly to say a prayer for our own country, which all of us love--a prayer for understanding and that compassion of which I spoke.

We can do well in this country. We will have difficult times; we've had difficult times in the past; we will have difficult times in the future. It is not the end of violence; it is not the end of lawlessness; it is not the end of disorder.

But the vast majority of white people and the vast majority of black people in this country want to live together, want to improve the quality of our life, and want justice for all human beings who abide in our land.

Let us dedicate ourselves to what the Greeks wrote so many years ago: to tame the savageness of man and make gentle the life of this world.

Let us dedicate ourselves to that and say a prayer for our country and for our people.

A black child stood near Dave, clutching his sobbing mother's hand, but his brown eyes remained fixed on Dave in a wide-eyed stare.

"M, M, Mister," he stammered. He glanced quickly at his mother seeking courage and then back at Dave. "Mister, why do white folks hate us?"

Chapter Eleven

The shadows of three Huey slicks flitted over the rocks and
eddies of a swift stream. Beans kicked his dangling legs,
but his shadow didn't disturb the pools. Did fish dart away
at the passing of war birds overhead? One by one, the
choppers swooped over the gurgling water and sand bars to
softly set down on a flat and wide LZ with short tufts of
Bermuda-like grass rather than head-high elephant grass.
Sometimes LZs in the bush were thick with punji sticks like
the quills on a porcupine's back, sometimes they were a
postage stamp opening amongst tall trees, sometimes they
hung along a steep mountain slope, but this one was as easy
as landing on a golf course back home.

The river formed the eastern edge of the LZ; a grove of
banana trees fixed the far west end; and gentle, brushy
slopes defined the north and south edges.

The soft landing allowed three recon squads to step off
rather than jump. The first team scrambled into the bush
and up the hill to the north. The second team climbed the
ridge to the south. Beans' team came in third, and they
hustled into a thick stand of bamboo on the south side to set
up their November Lima right in the corner of the jungle
overlooking the grassy LZ and the river.

After setting up and filling their bellies with C-rations,
the rhythm of the river soothed frayed nerves as pale-
yellow dusk seeped into the jungle. During the last hour of
daylight, a cacophony of croaking frogs joined the sounds
of gurgling water. As night fell, a bright-orange moon lifted
over the ridgeline across the river.

Beans would pull the fourth and final two-hour watch, so he wrapped himself in his poncho liner and soon dreamt of catching smallmouth bass in a Canadian stream. Just a few springs earlier, his Pa took Beans on a Canadian fishing trip to celebrate Beans' graduation from high school. They trudged through the Canadian forest following a fast-flowing stream to a small waterfall, and they caught chunky bronze backs with every cast of their frog-tipped hooks into eddies behind the rocks, and then his dream returned him to the farm yard of the home place, and Pa was shaking his hand, hard, and he saw mist in his eyes for the first time ever as they said their goodbyes before Beans was off to the jet plane that would carry him to Fort Lewis and then onto Vietnam. Beans awoke and listened for the frogs, but they had quieted, so he watched wispy clouds drift across the moon face before sleep again claimed him.

The recon mission settled into four days of solitude, suddenly interrupted by the radio voice of the team on the north ridge. Beans' team listened closely as their sense of alert spiked.

"A gook just walked by us," the radio crackled.

"Next time, grab him," came the response from base. "Remember, teams get an in-country three-day R&R for capturing a POW."

Since the primary purpose of the scout teams was recon and intelligence gathering, it made sense that a captured NVA soldier would be a plum source of valuable information. That's when the three teams started blathering with each other over their radios about snatching a prisoner and the good times in Vung Tau, a city on the seacoast near Saigon--three days of beaches, booze, and babes. Every swinging dick in Vietnam would get one week of Rest and Recuperation (R&R) out of country in places like Australia, Bangkok, and Hong Kong--or Hawaii for the married dudes and their wives--but an in-country three-day R&R in Vung Tau was a rare incentive prize.

The POW conversation lasted the rest of the afternoon but died down as evening approached.

Beans dozed off while leaning against his ruck, but his eyes blinked wide open when Frankie's hand covered his mouth to keep him quiet. Frankie nodded his head toward the river.

On the opposite side, about forty meters away, a man stood knee deep in the flowage, right at river's edge. He occasionally leaned over and doused his hands in the current. Was he washing himself? Was he washing dishes? Washing clothes? He wore only shorts or a loin cloth, not the lumpy green fatigues or pith helmet of the NVA. Gray tinged his shock of unkempt black hair. Did he have a weapon lying on the bank?

Suddenly, he was gone. He disappeared as silently and mysteriously as he appeared. Beans' team collectively exhaled and looked at each other with puzzled expressions. "Who was that? What was that all about? Was that the cook for an NVA camp on the other side?"

Two younger men suddenly materialized in the same spot across the river, but they didn't remain stationary. They also wore short pants plus loose-fitting shirts, and they carried woven baskets as they crossed the river, unaware of American eyes fixed like cats eyeing a mouse. They didn't appear to be carrying any weapons, but who knew what might be tucked away in the folds of their baggy shirts? They seemed completely at ease as they climbed the riverbank about fifteen meters in front of the muzzles of M-16s that followed their every step. They disappeared across the broad meadow of the LZ in the direction of the banana grove on the far end.

"We should grab one of those sons-of-bitches."

POW talk bubbled up again; base encouraged the team, and Frankie quickly hatched a plan. Beans and Frankie crawled out of their hidey hole in the bamboo to lie in wait in the brush tucked into the riverbank to snatch the two young men when they returned. Minutes passed slowly, and Beans was about to return to the bamboo patch as darkness settled in. Just then, Dozer gave the signal, and soon Beans heard muffled voices approaching.

The hand-to-hand combat lessons learned in Tiger Village at Fort Polk served Beans well. From behind, he threw his right arm around his quarry's neck, jamming his forearm into the Adam's apple while simultaneously punching his left fist into the kidney area of the lower left corner of the man's back. The man's basket of bananas tumbled into the river and bobbed as the current swept it down stream. Beans hauled his victim to the ground as Frankie did the same with the second young male, and the rest of the squad poured out of the bamboo thicket and jabbed the muzzles of their weapons into the faces of the captives, discouraging any resistance.

"What do we have to bind their hands?" Beans asked.

"I have antenna wire," Poncho said.

"Search them first," Frankie said, but a quick pat down didn't reveal any weapons.

Helicopters rarely flew at night and only in extreme circumstances, but the squad and their captives needed extraction and now. The wide, flat LZ played to their benefit. Landing in close quarters with barely visible tall trees snatching at the rotors would rattle even savvy pilots. Word soon came from base that a chopper was in the air, and the team assembled in the center of the LZ with Dozer and Poncho ready with flashing strobe lights to guide the bird in; soon they were all safely in the air.

In the dim light emitted by the pilot's control panel, Beans discerned three things in the face of his captive: he was young, perhaps fifteen or so; he was scared, obviously; and he was not ethnic Vietnamese. He was a Montagnard. The mountain people were *supposed* to relocate from the jungle to resettlement camps near military bases and Vietnamese cities. Was the gray-haired man they spotted across the river his grandfather? How many others remained in their jungle huts just across that river? These mountain people were non-combatants who disliked the North Vietnamese and the Americans equally, both invaders of their mountain domain. What intelligence could he offer to the interrogators he would soon face? When and how would he ever be reunited with his kinfolk? Selfishly, Beans wondered if the team would qualify for R&R since their captive was not NVA.

Not to worry, the team was soon on a C-130 flight to Tan Son Nhut Airport near Saigon and then a bus to the sandy beaches along the coast.

Three idyllic days passed too quickly.

Beans dozed off in the sun and sand, despite the babble of hundreds of others frolicking in the surf on the beach of Vung Tau. Most were American males, but Australian and New Zealanders mixed in, and there were plenty of Vietnamese women. Even in swimsuits, you could identify the officers—a little older and often in the company of American women.

His half bottle of beer warmed in the late afternoon sun.

"Hey, shithead, let's scram before the sun fries you to a crisp."

Beans lazily rose to his feet.

"Let's take a dip and rinse off the sand," Frankie said as he began to jog toward the surf.

Beans came to life and sprinted past him before high stepping into the lapping waves and diving into the surf. After a few plunges into breaking waves, they returned to the beach and gathered their belongings. With towels draped over shoulders, they headed toward a grove of tall trees whose splayed branches provided welcome shade for tables and chairs centered around a thatched roof beach bar. They joined the rest of their squad chewing the fat with a few desk jockeys who had not tasted combat, but the rear-echelon warriors devoured the adventures of the combat-savvy veterans, garnished with savory details of life in the bush. Somehow, the Montagnard captives had become high-ranking officers of the North Vietnamese army captured with reams of critical intelligence documents, and the Remington Raiders bought rounds to honor the brave captors.

One short E-4 with coke-bottle eyeglasses was especially fired up about the capture adventure.

"You shoulda pushed one of those slant eyes outa the chopper while flying back to base. That woulda made the other one sing like a canary."

Beans looked at Frankie and rolled his eyes. He wondered how the clerk with questionable eyesight managed to pass his induction physical. Maybe he tried to enlist multiple times until he found a compliant MD willing to overlook his vision exams, but even then, they wouldn't allow him into the infantry, and he was relegated to clerking at a desk. There was a wannabe quality to his starched uniform, slicked-down hair, glorification of conflict, and demonization of the enemy.

"He'd shit his pants if he went into the bush with us," Frankie mumbled under his breath so only Beans could hear him.

"Back in the world," the clerk continued, "it wouldn't hurt if a few fuckin' hippies got dropped from the sky. Mebbe spray a little napalm on a college campus. That would show those commie-lovin' faggots."

The men of Alpha Company seldom discussed the politics of the war. Maybe a little and maybe there were differing opinions, but that didn't matter much. They were here, and there wasn't a damn thing they could do about it. The war was not to be dissected or analyzed but simply endured. Just do it, and tomorrow will take care of itself. "Life is crazy," Frankie would say with a laugh, *La vida loca*, and that would end the political conversations. This asshole clerk was an outlier, but then again, many of Beans' buddies felt betrayed by news of the war protests back home, and there wasn't any love lost for the campus crowd.

Beans turned and looked back at the beach as they departed for the last time. He wondered again at the small island just offshore lined with bunkers that looked like pill boxes straight from WWII and Normandy cliffs. His own Fourth Infantry Division had played a major role by establishing a critical beachhead on Utah Beach at Normandy, a generation of warriors earlier. His uncle Jerry waded ashore under fire at Omaha Beach, but he seldom talked about it. Nevertheless, Uncle Jerry marched with the American Legion during the Kalmar Memorial Day parade and fired blanks into the air for the ceremonial 21-gun salute. Beans and others scrambled to pick up the empty shell casings from the city park lawn where the firing took place. It all seemed admirable and appropriate.

Beans envied the moral clarity of D Day. Fighting the Germans seemed right and just and heroic, but he had seen the NVA soldiers up close, too close, and he hadn't sensed they were evil like Hitler and the Nazis. He thought often of the man whose death he hastened, of the men smokin' and a jokin' as they passed in front of the claymore mines, and now the wide-eyed, frightened young Montagnards whose capture had resulted in the reward of this R&R. Somehow things seemed off kilter, and the shifting line separating good and evil hard to see.

Bars adorned with mixed English and Vietnamese names lined the streets of Vung Tau with bar girls hanging in the doorways soliciting business. Dodging tiny motor cars, mopeds, bicycles, horse-drawn carriages, military police jeeps, and the ever-present three-wheeled Lambros-a motor bike with covered passenger seating behind the driver--Beans' squad returned to their favorite bar and dined on burgers of questionable beef. Afterwards, a couple of the guys wandered the strip of bars and bar girls, but Beans was pensive, not horny. As the sun set over the harbor, he sucked on Kools and nursed a few beers while reflecting on three days away from the war.

The striking absence of fear while enjoying Vung Tau led to the realization of how frightened he was, day and night, while doing his duty in the Central Highlands. He did his duty, sure enough, and he did it well, but it was duty to his comrades and himself, the duty to survive, to make it home, to live another day, to have a life with a wife and kids and cousins, to hold a job, to grow old and spoil grandkids, to die a natural death in his sleep when friends and family would gather at his funeral and say, "he was a good man, and he lived a good life."

He never shared the gung-ho fervor of the outspoken clerk and others who bought into the army's bullshit as justification for the GIs' forced sacrifice. News of the protests and peaceniks back home really pissed them off. Others reveled in the sorry truths captured on the back of Zippo lighters. *We the unwilling, led by the unqualified, to kill the unfortunate, and die for the ungrateful.* Graveyard humor helped as a coping mechanism, often expressed in helmet graffiti. *I'm still here. Make war not love. Kill a commie for Christ. Don't follow me, I'm lost. Jesus is my point man.* Some inked their anticipated DEROS (date of expected return from overseas) on the cloth liners of their steel pots or crossed off the passing months. Peace signs were popular helmet adornments, and the two-fingered V sign became a standard greeting whether signifying peace or victory. Someday, perhaps, the senselessness of their imposed sacrifice would haunt the hapless combatants, but now it was just a matter of putting one muddy boot in front of the other without thinking too hard. Survival is like that.

Even as he argued with the Perfesser at his going away party, his internal doubts had nagged at him, and now they came to full bloom. Somehow, the realization that this war was different, that it was not about God and country, not about making the world safe for democracy, not about resistance to fascism and imperialism, but merely about survival, a hollow burden to be borne before earning a return to normalcy, calmed him and gave him purpose. Not the ambivalent chimera of resisting godless Communism, of propping up dominos to keep them from falling, but a purpose to prevail against the odds and survive—for himself, his family, and his future.

He resented the Perfesser, not because he shirked his duty but because he had figured out the lie. Beans should be angry, he mused, but he had no time for that now, nor self-pity. If this was the price to be paid to pursue the American dream, he would pay, no matter how unfair. If the cause was not grand, he would nevertheless joust with fate; with wit, courage, and luck, he might prevail. He owed it to himself to do his damnedest.

Chapter Twelve

Dave barely noticed the subdued voices in the back of the auto as he drove back to the hotel headquarters following the Senator's speech to the wailing black audience in Indianapolis. An epiphany washed over him, and he understood that his personal, political transformation was complete. Opposition to the war first brought him to the Democrats, to be sure, but it was also the case that the Democrats owned the war in the persons of LBJ, Dean Rusk, and Robert McNamara. It was not war policy that defined the distinction between the parties. Not yet anyway. It would be Gene McCarthy or Robert Kennedy or Wendy Cragun or the Clean Gene Brigade who would change the party first and then the country. If opposition to the war first brought him to Democratic Senator McCarthy and then to Democratic Senator Kennedy, it was the stark difference between the parties regarding racial injustice that rendered him solidly and comfortably a Democrat.

Lessons learned from John Lewis, his roommate, informed and confirmed his transformation, but there was irony in his transformation as well. The values he learned from his parents were the reason he abandoned their political party. He learned tolerance in his own home. His parents had imbued him with a sense of the inherent worth of all human beings. His folks were Republican liberals, or at least moderates, whose politics aligned with those of Governor George Romney of Michigan or Governor Nelson Rockefeller of New York. They were proud to belong to the party of Lincoln who freed the slaves. When

Romney suggested that Republicans should turn their backs on the "Southern-rural-white" drift of the party, Dave's folks said "amen," but they were swimming upstream, and Dave saw that even if they didn't.

The political ground had shifted beneath America's feet, imperceptibly at first but suddenly and recently. The Grand Old Party, the party of Dave's parents, was no longer the party of Lincoln, and the Democratic Party was no longer the party of the "solid south" of Jim Crow and segregation. The recent enactment of the Civil Rights Act, the Voting Rights Act, the expansion of Medicare and the creation of Medicaid were part of the Democratic vision for a "Great Society," but they were all opposed by the Republican party, and black America remembered. If African Americans overwhelmingly supported the Democrats, what did that say? Duh!

Dave slept alone in his hotel room for a few days as John Lewis departed to assist with the planning and organizing of the King funeral. Instead of the nightly discussions between Dave and John, Dave devoured the Kerner Commission Report that John gave him weeks earlier. The bestseller was a real eye-opener. Commissioned by LBJ in '67 to analyze the reasons for black rioting in the cities, even after and despite the enactment of the Civil Rights Act and the Voting Rights Act, the report was a scathing indictment of institutional racism, and laid the blame right at the feet of white America and not on an organized black conspiracy:

Our nation is moving toward two societies, one black, one white—separate and unequal…What white Americans

*have never fully understood — but what the Negro can
never forget — is that white society is deeply implicated in
the ghetto. White institutions created it, white institutions
maintain it, and white society condones it…The press has
too long basked in a white world looking out of it, if at all,
with white men's eyes and white perspective.*

Dave had a hard time with the network news reports of
urban violence, but like witnessing a car wreck, he couldn't
watch, but he couldn't not watch.

Harry Reasoner on CBS: "Washington, Chicago,
Detroit, Boston, New York—these are a just a few of the
cities in which the Negro anguish expressed itself in violent
destruction."

The MLK assassination ignited a powder keg of street
violence. Grief and outrage. Was the Great Society an
illusion? A hollow promise? Disappointment turned to
despair turned to destruction. America was on fire.
Washington DC appeared to be a war zone with smoke
rising from dozens of burning buildings within two blocks
of the White House. Troops guarded the steps of the
Capitol. Rioting and looting consumed Baltimore,
Cincinnati, Detroit, Pittsburgh, and dozens of inner cities
around the country. Governors activated National Guard
units in many states. Across the country, dozens died, and
thousands were injured—almost always African
Americans.

Action, reaction, counteraction, overreaction, backlash.
Black frustration and white angst.

White America was frightened. Maryland Governor
Spiro Agnew called in a hundred black leaders and
chastised them on television for failing to control their

constituents; Agnew's racial rebuke caught the scheming eye of presidential candidate Richard Nixon. California Governor Ronald Reagan blamed an increasingly permissive culture. South Carolina Senator Strom Thurmond, who heralded the transition of southern politicians from Democrat to Republican years earlier as a "Dixiecrat," blamed the civil rights movement as a whirlwind put in motion years ago. Although segregationist Governor George Wallace lamented King's death, nevertheless his dog whistle "law and order" presidential campaign took hold. Once again, Richard Nixon paid attention.

President Johnson declared a National Day of Mourning, and flags around the country flew at half-mast. The segregationist governor of Georgia, Lester Maddox, resisted and refused to allow King's body to lie in state, calling King "an enemy of the country." Bobby Kennedy and Richard Nixon attended a private funeral at Ebenezer Baptist Church in Atlanta. Pastor Ralph Abernathy, who often marched with King, offered the sermon, calling King's death "one of the darkest hours of mankind." From there, a funeral cortege carried the casket to a public ceremony at Morehouse College, King's alma mater. National TV aired the activities. A hundred thousand mourners lined the route. Dave spied his friend, John Lewis, at the head of the procession along with other civil rights luminaries. Dave and thousands of others around the country cried as Mahalia Jackson sang a slow rendition of *Take My Hand, Precious Lord.*

The day after the funeral, Dave turned the TV channel to the Academy Awards, rescheduled due to the assassination. Actor Gregory Peck offered a moving tribute to King at the outset. Coincidentally, two of the films nominated for Best Picture wrestled with racial themes. Black actor Sidney Poitier starred in both. *Guess Who's Coming to Dinner* grappled with interracial marriage. The Best Picture Award winner, *In the Heat of the Night*, featured Poitier playing a Philadelphia detective investigating a murder in the Jim Crow south. He was strong, intelligent, and unyielding in stark contrast to the stumbling Sambo character that had long been Hollywood's black stereotype. "They call me MISTER TIBBS."

When John returned from the funeral, his face visibly expressed his grief with a hangdog look, and his voice was barely a whisper.

"Mrs. King and her kids lost a husband and a father. Movement activists lost a colleague and their leader. I lost a friend and mentor, but I fear America has lost the dream and perhaps her soul. Is it two steps forward and one step back or vice versa?"

After a cup of coffee, he perked up a bit.

"We still have Bobby Kennedy," John said as if to convince himself. "We still have hope."

Weeks after the assassination, Dave drove the Senator fifty miles to the University of Indiana Medical School for a campaign speech to the med students. One of the students challenged Kennedy's proposals for expanding social programs.

"Where are you going to get the money?"

Under present circumstances, the Senator wasn't putting up with any bullshit. Without hesitation, he spoke truth to privilege.

"From you."

Stunned med students squirmed in their seats as Kennedy continued.

"I look around this room and I don't see many black faces who will become doctors. I don't see many people coming here from the slums, or off Indian reservations. You are the privileged people. You sit here as a white medical student, while black people carry the burden of fighting in Vietnam."

Chapter Thirteen

"Saddle up. We're going TDY to the 1st Cav to rescue Marines holed up near the DMZ," Frankie relayed the orders he received from TOP, the company First Sergeant.

"What the hell?" Beans replied. "Since when do the Marines need the Army to rescue them?"

"Sounds like a big friggin' deal, and they need bodies," Frankie said. "This is the way TOP explained it to me. Alpha Company and half a dozen other 4th Division units are being assigned to Temporary Duty with the 1st Cavalry Division, and we'll be airlifted north to clear supply routes into Khe Sanh where thousands of Marines are under siege from heavy concentrations of North Vietnamese regulars and constant artillery, rocket, and mortar bombardment."

"For Chrissake," Poncho said. "Back in the states, the press is calling Khe Sanh the American version of Dien Bien Phu, the shit show where the French got their asses kicked."

Beans nodded. Heading north toward the Demilitarized Zone in Vietnam was never good news.

At first light the next morning, the men of Alpha Company climbed aboard deuce-and-a-halfs for the first leg of their journey. First stop, Camp Radcliff near An Khe along Highway 19 heading east from Pleiku.

QL19 wasn't exactly a freeway, but it was the main east-west roadway running from Pleiku and Camp Enari, connecting to An Khe and Camp Radcliff and the seaport of Qui Nhon beyond that. Troop and supply convoys moved back and forth regularly during the day, but the night belonged to the NVA and the Viet Cong. Well before nightfall each day, American troops holed up in firebases strung along the highway.

The steep slopes rising on either side of the winding road seemed peaceful enough as the convoy ascended through the infamous Mang Yang Pass.

"Lock and load, *mis hermanos*," Frankie said.

Beans and the others slammed full magazines into their M-16s and chambered a round with muzzles poking up from the back of the trucks like porcupine quills. The jungle had been razed along the roadway, which hadn't been the case when the Viet Minh ambushed the French here fourteen years earlier. Everyone knew the story. The 1954 Viet Minh ambush of the French moving through the pass from An Khe to Pleiku was a major defeat for the French and the last battle before the French quit the battlefield. Three weeks later, the French government signed the Geneva Accords, dividing the country and recognizing the legitimacy of the government of North Vietnam. Soon, the French moved out of South Vietnam, and American advisors moved in, and the rest is history, as they say.

After traversing the down slope on the back side of the mountain pass, the convoy halted for half an hour while a land mine, placed the night before, was cleared from the roadway. A plume of smoke spiraled upward from a hole in the roadway where the explosive burned off. Some troops had the daily duty of sweeping the highway for mines, and burning off the mines they discovered was old hat.

The convoy arrived at sprawling Camp Radcliff by early afternoon. Radcliff had been the base camp for the 1st

Cavalry Division and their four hundred helicopters. Nicknamed "the golf course," flatland surrounded a single, steep-sloped rocky outcropping smack in the center of the base camp that towered over the An Khe plateau, a landmark visible from miles around called Hon Cong Mountain. Atop the mountain, radar installations and an array of radio towers and antennas jutted skyward amidst the hooches where signals specialists holed up. A huge, yellow 1st Cav patch adorned the side of Hon Cong Mountain.

"Yer on yer own for the rest of the day," Top said, "but stay out of trouble. We'll board a C-130 transport plane first thing in the morning for an airlift north."

Many of the men napped, others found their way to the NCO club, but neither appealed to Frankie. He looked at the sun, still high in the sky, pointed at the mountain and said to Beans,

"To the top. *La vida loca.*"

The Spanish phrase was something Frankie the Puerto Rican said often. There was warmth in it but also a wild and fierce pursuit of adventure, of experience, of all the savage vagaries of life. He travelled a journey with many detours, twists, and turns, but he never retreated or stood still. He swallowed big gulps from a firehose.

When asked, "Do you have a girlfriend back home?"

He would reply, "Not just one. Many." And somehow you knew that he loved each one passionately.

He was also unique when the shooting started: fearless, detached, brave. He fought with the same fierceness of existence but without cause other than to live in the moment. There were no political bones in his body nor animus toward the enemy. It was combat for no greater purpose than it was his fate in that instant, merely *la vida loca,* and he would blitz the moment with savage exuberance.

Frankie and Beans decided to hike the twisting trail to the installations atop Hon Cong Mountain. Part way up, they hitched a ride with a jeep heading to the top.

The flat top of the rock housed communication teams and their equipment. Every unit stationed in the base camp had their own commo team atop the mountain along with the technicians to maintain the radar and other signals equipment. A village apart.

As Beans and Frankie stepped down from the jeep, a stooped-over, gangly black dude sporting sandals, fatigue cutoffs, and a black shirt--the same type worn by local peasants—flashed the two-fingered peace sign. A skull cap offered no protection from the sun for his beak nose and beady red eyes. His cutoff fatigues revealed spindly legs and bony knees.

"My name is Josiah Johnson, but the guys call me Bird."

Of course, they do. "Crow" would work as well. Or "Raven."

"Don't often get real soldiers up here. Let me show you around," and he did with the short tour ending in his hooch.

Bird cracked open a couple of cold ones from his fridge. As froth dripped down Bean's wrist, Bird invited the men up a rickety ladder onto his flat roof of corrugated tin. He lit a thick OJ with a dark stain and passed it around.

An OJ was a marijuana joint with liquid opium dribbled onto the cigarette rolling paper.

Bird spread his arms wide, embracing the wide vistas in all directions from his mountaintop hut. As a shit-eating grin spread across his face, he repeated his well-rehearsed line that he uttered on all such occasions.

"You're now the highest sons of bitches in all of Vietnam."

Stoned as hell, Beans and Frankie slowly paced around the rooftop edges, surveying the landscape and the hazy horizon in each direction. For a speck of time, Beans and Frankie escaped the jungles and the overgrown grasslands they looked down on that seemed damned peaceful now.

Strains of a Beatles tune lifted from the stereo in the hooch below. Something about a blackbird flying away. It all made perfect sense. This mountaintop was a crow's nest with a bird's eye view of the world and a safe haven above the creatures prowling below. A raven's roost. Damn smart birds, the crows. Crafty. So long as they did their job, Bird and the others lived a safe and low stress existence up here with a small mess tent and personalized hooches outfitted with stereos, fridges, and beach chairs purchased at the PX. Plenty of down time with little hassle from lifers and far above the din of war. The Beatles lyrics about blackbirds flying away made perfect sense.

After flying north for barely an hour, the C-130 carrying Alpha Company touched down at LZ Stud, a recently constructed camp at Ca Lu that would serve as the jumping off point for Operation Pegasus, the name assigned to the rescue mission based on the mythical flying stallion. The thousands of Marines at Khe Sanh had been cut off from ground supply and depended upon parachute drops and touch and go airlifts. The NVA controlled Highway 9, the only roadway heading west to Khe Sanh with a river on one side and steep slopes on the other that created a natural ambush point where the enemy could hit and run back into the jungle. Bridges had been blown, and the roadway was in a sorry state of disuse and disrepair. The planners of Operation Pegasus intended to clear the hills and jungle of any enemy presence and allow combat engineers to reconstruct Highway 9 all the way to Khe Sanh.

Alpha Company offloaded from the C-130 and retreated to the tents assigned to them. Beans made a beeline to the crapper. The six holes of the latrine lined up over recycled steel drums cut in half. The task of removing the barrels, dousing with kerosene, and burning the crap fell to local *mama sans* hired for camp cleanup.

Beans was alone until someone burst in, mumbling. The two stars on his baseball cap said Beans was in the presence of a major general.

"Don't you quote me, Son, but Westy's got his head up his ass. He figured the NVA would storm Khe Sanh en masse, and our firepower would obliterate them, but they ain't that stupid. They laid back and lobbed mortars and fired artillery, and now it's our Marines that are taking it in the ass."

After Beans finished his business and exited the latrine, he turned to the private who waited outside, apparently the general's aide.

"Who the hell is that?" Beans asked.

"That's our commanding officer, General Tolson."

"He sure as hell is pissed about something."

"He ain't none too happy about General Westmoreland's handling of Khe Sanh, but probably no more so than the Marines themselves who see little reason for being there and incurring the shit piled on by the NVA."

Pegasus was quite a show of force, with the Army, Navy, Air Force, and Marines all contributing. B-52 bombers lit up the countryside, and Navy fighter bombers from an aircraft carrier floating in the nearby South China Sea flew dozens of sorties. The bombing, along with a barrage of artillery shelling, softened potential enemy resistance.

It turned out that the TDY assignment of Alpha Company would merely be to join the troops providing security for the combat engineers reconstructing the roadway. While the men of Alpha Company never objected to less-hazardous duty, they also sensed disrespect toward the Fourth Infantry from the higher ups of the 1st Cav, as if they didn't really belong here, as if they weren't worthy front-line soldiers, as if they couldn't handle themselves if combat flared hot. To each their own.

The next morning, Marines and the 1st Cav ground troops headed out at 0700 along each side of Highway 9 with the intention of searching and destroying any NVA lying in wait. Early reports said they encountered little resistance. Morning fog delayed the airborne helicopter assaults intended to leapfrog forward of the ground troops, but the winged warriors lifted off by early afternoon. The worker bees of the combat engineers moved quickly without resistance. By day's end, the engineers had rebuilt

Highway 9 a click and a half forward with their tractors, bulldozers, road graders, and other heavy equipment.

The assault troops set up night locations and remained in place, but Alpha Company and the engineers returned to LZ Stud, which was a beehive of activity with C-130s and Chinook helicopters bringing in thousands of troops with dozens of slicks coming and going.

Frankie returned from a briefing. "Fifteen fucking thousand men deployed in less than a week. Seems like Uncle Sam has his shit together this time."

Day two brought more of the same: easy advances by the assault troops and nearly three clicks of road building by the engineers, with a couple of bridges added for good measure. Day three continued the rapid advance. The Air Cav continued to leapfrog forward establishing new positions. It appeared that the NVA had hauled ass in the face of the advancing American assault. In fact, they left tons of munitions and materiel behind to be captured by the advancing troops.

Providing security for the engineers proved to be downright boring, and Beans and his buddies *almost* wished for a little more action, especially in light of the rapid advances of the assault troops on the ground and in the air. Almost.

"At least they ain't assigned us to shit-burning detail," Poncho said.

Late in the day, Captain Connally addressed the men of Alpha Company in his Texas drawl.

"Y'all listen up. Marines from Khe Sanh performed their own offensive operation today and chaaysed the enemy away from strategic high ground just south of the

Khe Sanh perimeter. Choppers are fixin' to pick us up, and we'll be helicoptered in to provide reinforcements to hold Hill 471 in caayse the enemy comes back. With the waay the NVA is retreatin' all around, Ah'm not expectin' any action, but what the hell, at least we'll be done eatin' bulldozer dust.

Marines crawled all over Hill 471 digging bunkers and slashing brush as the choppers delivered Alpha Company late in the day. There were already fortifications there from the repeated capture and abandonment of the hill, but they could be booby trapped by the departing NVA. Captain Connally did his share of digging with an entrenching tool, and the rest of Alpha Company followed his example. By the time the troops stood down and chowed on C-rations and enjoyed a smoke, bunkers encircled the perimeter as dusk settled over the peaceful hilltop even as far off explosions continued.

Somehow, Beans ended up sitting atop a bunker with half a dozen Marines who had been holed up at Khe Sanh but who broke out and pushed the NVA off this strategic hill. The Marines would be his bunker mates for the night.

"You're welcome here, but we really don't need any help from the Army. We been fighting off the NVA for months, and now we're starting to push 'em back."

The Marine Lance Corporal failed to credit the thousands of sorties flown by Air Force, Marine, and Naval aircraft over a period of months. Bombing the shit out of the massive buildup of NVA forces surrounding Khe Sanh kept the enemy at bay.

"What the hell were we doin' in Khe Sanh in the first place?" The Marine asked, not expecting Beans to answer. "Enemy mortar, rockets, and artillery bombardment rained down on us every day and every night. For all our technical advantage, their artillery had longer range than ours and fired from a distance that our guns couldn't reach. Hundreds of incoming rounds pounded, pounded, pounded the red soil every fucking day. I ain't had a good night's sleep in months, mostly curled up in my poncho like a cocoon. It wasn't logical but somehow, I felt safe, or at least, safer, wrapped in my poncho as the ground shook all around. I probably woulda gone nuts if'n I didn't have that cocoon 'roun' me."

"Mebbe you'll sleep tonight," Beans said.

"Yep, mebbe tonight," the Marine replied.

The Marine zonked out immediately, filling the bunker with Z's. When it came time to roust him for his spell on guard duty, Beans let him snore away. After enduring two months of constant shelling, the poor bastard ought to enjoy some sweet dreams.

Dawn came early, accompanied by crackling small arms fire from a whole goddammed battalion of hardened NVA regulars charging up the hill and assaulting the freshly dug defensive fortifications of the Marines and Alpha Company. Beans shook his new Marine friend awake, and they joined the others in laying down small arms fire holding off the assaulting enemy until close-in artillery and aerial bombardment pummeled the NVA troops caught out in the open on the hillside. At times, all Beans had to do was cover his ears at the thunderous explosions and keep his head down as shrapnel ripped through the treetops.

Sometimes, the enemy gets too much credit amidst criticism of your own side, but on this morning, it was the officers of the NVA battalion who screwed up, causing the deaths of hundreds of their own soldiers before retreating. The harmony between air, artillery, and ground operations tuned over the first days of Operation Pegasus struck the downbeat and routed the attackers.

Operation Pegasus was a resounding success, pushing back the enemy around Khe Sanh and reopening the Highway 9 overland supply route. The opening salvos of the Tet Offensive marked the beginning of the siege of Khe Sanh, and months later Operation Pegasus ended it. As with Tet itself, the Americans won the battle but may have lost the war. After Alpha Company returned to its own area of operations with the rest of the 4th Infantry Division in the Central Highlands, after months of heavy fighting, thousands of aircraft sorties, tons of bombs and artillery shells, hundreds of American casualties, and thousands of Vietnamese casualties, the Marines abandoned the Khe Sanh camp where rivers of blood had flowed, and North Vietnam declared victory.

Chapter Fourteen

"Good morning, Senator," Dave said as he held the rear car door open.

"I'll sit in front with you, if you don't mind," the candidate replied.

Several senior advisors usually accompanied Senator Kennedy, but today he was alone.

"You seem bright-eyed and bushy-tailed this morning," Kennedy said as Dave slid behind the wheel in his continuing role as the Senator's chauffeur.

"Yes sir, I guess I've got a little spring in my step. My girlfriend is flying in to join the party tomorrow night. I'm sure it'll be a victory celebration."

"Don't jinx us now, young man."

A week earlier, Angie mentioned the invitation to her mother after building up her courage for a day.

"Mom, Dave invited me to Indianapolis for the celebration on primary night. He tells me the campaign is very enthusiastic and expects to win."

"Really? You're going to go hang out with Bobby Kennedy?"

"Course not. I'll be with Dave, and we'll probably see the Senator give a speech, but hang out with him? Really, Mom, don't be sarcastic."

Joyce Olson had known Dave Karlstad since he was born, and she liked him. He was a young man with smarts and ambition, but he was swimming in deep water working for the Kennedy campaign. Joyce and her deceased husband, Ben, always voted Republican, but who knew what might happen this year. She was pleased that Dave and Angie finally figured out what she knew all along— that they were meant for each other. Still, she was skeptical about sending her only child, an innocent high school girl, to a big city and a national political event without a chaperone.

"Is that wise?"

"I'm so bored, and Senator Kennedy's victory party sounds exciting. I need a pick-me-up, Mom."

"Maybe I should go with you. I could use some cheering up, too."

She teased, but her smug smile and tone gave her away. Joyce and Angie Olson had always been close; after Ben's death, Angie was a fatherless only child, and Joyce was a widow, and they grew closer. Joyce looked much the way she did when she was Angie's age. Joyce and Angie could be mistaken for sisters rather than mother-daughter. Yet, in the weeks since her husband's death, Joyce's face began to bear the markings of middle age with fatigued and tiny wrinkles beneath her eyes and stray strands of gray sprinkling her blonde hair, but when she teased Angie about partying with her at the Senator's victory party, the cheery, animated countenance of a jaunty teenager returned. The day would come when she would date again, and her good looks and financial security with Ben's life insurance proceeds would render her an attractive partner.

"Mostly, I miss Dave." Angie said.

Joyce's tone turned skeptical again. "Of course, you do, but where will you stay?"

Angie shrugged her shoulders, "I don't know. With Dave, I guess."

"Are you ready for that?"

Angie didn't answer but scowled at her mother.

Joyce inhaled a deep breath and let it out slowly. "I'm not going to say no, but please think it through before deciding."

On May 4th, Angie attended the prom without a date. The 1968 spring social highlight was an anti-climactic drag. Marching in the processional to Elvis crooning Blue Hawaii, the prom theme, was even worse. Beans' letters encouraged her to join him in Hawaii for his R&R. Angie and Dave agreed to keep their secret until they could speak to Beans face to face--no Dear John letter would do—but Hawaii was not going to happen. So, Dave and Angie's relationship remained a secret to all except Joyce Olson and Dave's folks, Harv and Meg Karlstad.

Angie slipped away from the Hawaiian shores early, declining invitations to post-prom parties. Angie's entire spring seemed out of sorts following her father's death. She was so ready to be done with high school. Dave's phone calls offered short-lived interludes, and his invitation to join him in Indianapolis buoyed her spirits.

On Sunday after the Saturday night prom, Joyce helped Angie pack for the Monday morning flight to Indianapolis. She handed Angie a paper bag from a drugstore.

"Mom!" Angie said when she looked at the contents.

"I'm not saying anything or encouraging or condoning, but I want you to be responsible. So, if … I mean, you need to protect yourself."

Angie arrived at buzzing campaign headquarters at 11:30 on Monday morning. Soggy sandwiches appeared, and Dave downed several, chased with a Coke, but Angie barely touched hers. Dave called over one friend after another for introductions, but it all seemed a fog for Angie.

"We've still got campaigning to do," Dave said. "It'll be fun."

Awe-struck Angie rode in the passenger seat of a sleek red convertible with Dave at the helm. Bobby and Ethel Kennedy rode in the backseats, sitting up high and waving to the adoring crowds.

"Of course, you should ride along," Ethel said. "We need to show that McCarthy isn't the only one with energetic young supporters. Both of Bobby's opponents for the nomination are from Minnesota, so we would love to have two clean-cut Minnesotans riding in the front seat. I think the irony is delicious."

Dave and others watched the televised speech of Vice-President Hubert Horatio Humphrey ten days earlier when he made the much-expected announcement that he would seek the nomination. Humphrey boasted that his campaign was "the way politics ought to be ... the politics of happiness, the politics of purpose, the politics of joy." Governor Branigin, the Indiana favorite son, intended to be a proxy for President Johnson, but when LBJ dropped out, the party apparatus in Indiana and across the country favored Humphrey. Prior to the vice-presidency, Humphrey had been the senior Senator from Minnesota with McCarthy as the junior Senator. The Kennedy campaign now saw Humphrey as the prime opposition, but McCarthy's dedicated "Clean Gene" brigade of loyal and enthusiastic supporters wasn't about to surrender.

Newsweek Magazine didn't even include McCarthy in their Indiana poll that day that showed Kennedy swamping

Branigin as Humphrey's surrogate 61% to 39%. No wonder the campaign was optimistic.

Late in the evening, they made their way to Dave's room. John Lewis moved out that morning, with a wink, so Angie could move in.

"Finally," Angie said as the door closed behind them. She threw her arms around him, and they tightly embraced, swaying back and forth, and then they kissed.

"Which bed do you want?" Dave asked.

"Which one do you sleep in?"

"That one," Dave said with a slight nod of his head.

"Then I'll take that one, too," she said.

With a mischievous laugh, Angie released him and opened her suitcase and handed him the drugstore bag containing condoms. "Mom sent a present for you. Do you believe it?"

She hugged him again, and they tumbled onto the bed. Soon, giggles gave way to heavy breathing. It was her first time, and she didn't suspect it wasn't his.

Kennedy's victory was assured early the next evening. Word out of the Branigin headquarters said he understood the initial returns. "I got whipped," he acknowledged. "I got taken to the woodshed."

McCarthy and his supporters remained defiant even though the final tally would show a distant third place finish: Kennedy 42%; Branigin 31%; and McCarthy 26%.

Late in the celebration, word came to Dave that the Senator wanted to see him.

"Ethel and I haven't eaten a thing, and we need to find someplace that is open this time of night."

Someone suggested that the airport would have a twenty-four-hour cafe, so Dave and Angie drove the Senator and his wife to the airport to eat. On the way, the Senator groused:

"Senator McCarthy says it's just another step in a series of steps, and this isn't a defeat. Well, I don't know whether people think it's so good to be second or third. That's not the way I was brought up. I was always taught that it was much better to win. I learned that when I was about two."

A pair of youthful McCarthy supporters sat on the floor in an empty concourse alongside their suitcases. The college kids had missed their flight and appeared tired and deflated. The woman sat with a McCarthy straw hat tilted over her cropped red hair, and a couple of McCarthy buttons adorned the jacket of the man. Kennedy approached them and invited them to share a bite to eat.

"All right," the young woman said, aware but not impressed with the candidate who invited her to a late-night meal. She placed her McCarthy hat on Kennedy's head.

For the next two hours, Kennedy engaged the college kids, and he was obviously frustrated at their defiant support for their man, but there was also grudging respect. He really tried to understand what made them click, and, by extension, McCarthy's whole "Clean Gene" brigade.

"We're going to stay with Gene," she said. "Most of them will. The ones who like McCarthy don't want you."

Kennedy seemed less annoyed by the rejection than quizzical. On the return trip to the hotel, Kennedy turned his questions to Dave.

"Why do the kids stick with Gene? What's the attraction? They seem damn smart, don't they see that he can't win the nomination, much less win the election?"

It was a question that Dave had already been pondering ever since New Hampshire, and with a shrug of his shoulders, he voiced his well-thought-out answer.

"It's the tyranny of the new," Dave said. "McCarthy is a clean slate for them, and he is a projection of their ideals, without a significant track record to contradict the image he willingly cultivates."

Dave surprised himself with his 3:00 am insights.

"You've been in the top echelon of leadership, and that's a black mark for those who believe the system needs to be turned upside down. Your opposition to this war is no less than his, but you're seen as part of the system, and he's not. It's easier to sit on the back bench as a purist than take hard positions of leadership."

Dave took a deep breath and continued. "The injustice of this war and the injustice of the draft are not pie-in-the-sky abstractions for my generation. This shit is real for us."

Dave glanced in the rear-view mirror to see if Ethel was offended by his swear word. She wasn't.

"Senator McCarthy touts this single issue, and it is the thing that pricks a visceral repulsion toward the war. He leads a movement, and movements are often borne more by emotion than logic."

Dave was rolling now.

"Did you see the reaction in those two tonight when you brought up race relations? It was like they didn't even know about your strong civil rights record compared to McCarthy. For them, Vietnam is the one and only issue."

"Dave, I think your talents are wasted as my chauffeur," the Senator said.

"What are your thoughts, Angie?" the Senator asked.

Angie looked at Dave for help but quickly realized this was on her.

"They were rude,' she said. "Putting that silly straw hat on your head. Honestly."

She drew a breath and dared to continue. "I'm not nearly as up on this stuff as Dave, but a lot of folks are put off by the condescending tone of the McCarthy crowd. Maybe they have studied this stuff, but they don't need to be smart alecks about it."

"I agree," Ethel Kennedy said. "Yes, they were idealistic but rather self-righteous and smug, I thought."

Dave drove on in silence. As he turned the car into the Marriott parking lot, Kennedy had the last word:

"I have a lot of respect for those two who held fast to their support for the Senator tonight. That's what we need in this campaign. Are you with me, Dave? Will you continue with the campaign as we move west?"

Chapter Fifteen

Beans stared at the newspaper clipping he received in a letter from Big Jimmie Overskei back home in Kalmar. He turned it over and looked at the back side and then the front again, as if the picture would fade away, but the black and white image became starker the longer he glared at it. Somehow the local rag, the Kalmar Chronicle, picked up a newswire story with a picture of a long convertible carrying Senator Robert Kennedy and his wife, Ethel. Although the driver and front seat passenger weren't named in the wire story, there was no doubt for the editor of the Chronicle who put names to faces and soon all of Kalmar buzzed.

Boot camp drill sergeants teased that "Jody's gonna get your girl." Jody was the composite of the soldier's worst nightmare. The one who stayed home and shirked his patriotic duty; the one who would steal in and console your girl simply because he was there, and you weren't; the one who would take your place in your girl's arms and her heart.

Beans should have suspected something was up. Angie's letters had slowed down, and their tone had changed. She put off his request that they meet in Hawaii for his R&R. What he didn't expect was that Jody's real name was Dave, a sonofabitch who was no longer Beans' friend. Somehow, the fact that his girl had been kidnapped into the campaign of Kennedy, the anti-war asshole, seemed cruel yet predictable irony. The echoes of marching boots tramping to the cadence of a boot camp ditty roiled his thoughts.

Beans threw the letter and the clipping in the garbage. He slung his rucksack onto his back and headed toward a waiting deuce-and-a-half. A convoy of trucks would carry his platoon to their next mission. He threw the ruck onto the back end of the truck and started to climb aboard, but he had a change of heart and bolted back to the garbage can in the barracks. He smoothed out the clipping, folded it carefully, and tucked it into his shirt.

Beans' platoon bounced along in the back of a deuce-and-a-half for the hour-long ride along Highway 19 from Camp Enari to a roadside firebase. They travelled with a convoy through high plains, rolling hills, and the occasional village toward a rugged mountain range and the infamous Mang Yang pass. The convoy would continue through the pass, but the trucks carrying the 1st platoon would peel off at a firebase on the western edge of the mountain range to deliver Beans and the rest of his platoon. The platoon's next mission would be to provide security for the firebase, and that would be a cakewalk compared to humping in the boonies. Every couple of miles, they passed a tank guarding the roadway. Helicopter gunships circled the convoy. Charlie would be damned stupid to try an ambush, and Beans and the others felt safe and in a party mood. Somebody passed around a whiskey bottle and a couple of joints appeared.

Along with the gunships, a Light Observation Helicopter (LOH) circled. When the loach swung low over the deuce-and-a-half, someone on the truck flashed the two-fingered peace sign but when Frankie flipped the finger, everyone joined in. The convoy moved another mile or so and then it stopped. Up ahead, the LOH had landed alongside the road, some muckety muck general climbed off, and Lieutenant Wolsey, the platoon leader, stood stiffly at attention as the general chewed his ass. As the convoy moved out, word came back for everyone to don their steel pots and show respect for buzzing helicopters. Lieutenant Wolsey took one for the team, and they enjoyed it.

They arrived at the firebase in time for a hot lunch, followed by endless games of eight ball around a pair of pool tables. Dozer, Jonesy, Sam, and others sacked out in a bunk inside their barracks. They would pull the eight to midnight shift. Beans would be on the third shift of the night from 4:00 am until 8:00 am.

Three tanks motored into the base in time for supper after pulling roadside guard duty during the day. The off-duty tanker crews would party in the evening and sleep through the night before returning to their roadside duties the next morning.

By the time Beans arrived at his east-facing post, the moon had set. On a starry, cloudless night, the dark outline of a brooding mountain range loomed over the cut known as the Mang Yang pass.

The rising sun poured through the pass and soon the mountains turned green with jungle. It was picturesque and deceptively peaceful. The jungle fingered down along ridges toward the plain with one ridge extending nearly to the edge of the firebase. If trouble was to come, that's where it would come from, and then Lieutenant Wolsey decided to seek it out.

By now, Wolsey had been promoted to 1st Lieutenant, but that was merely based on time in-country rather than merit. The men of the 1st platoon under his command considered him to be an incompetent asshole. When company commander Connally had announced the promotion, he was as embarrassed as the men, but not Wolsey who promptly had a silver bar sewn on his uniforms to replace the yellow bar, and he strutted around like a fucking peacock. Part of his incompetence was that he didn't realize he was incompetent.

After three uneventful nights at the firebase, Lieutenant Wolsey assigned the eight men of Frankie's squad to head up the ridge, into the bush, to provide advance listening posts for any enemy activity heading toward the base, not that there was any reason to expect unwanted guests. An hour before nightfall, the men headed out with ponchos, radios, and their normal weaponry. Half a click up the ridge in thick brush, the squad split in two. Beans, Poncho, Dozer, and Sam would set up their November Lima here, and Frankie, Jonesy, Will, and a FNG would keep going for another half click up the ridge and set up there.

When the sun dropped beneath the western horizon, and before a full moon ascended over the mountains to the east, pitch blackness enveloped the men. Except for croaking lizards, all was quiet.

"Fuck you. Fuck you."

Poncho mimicked the sounds of the lizards, and the men stifled laughs. Sure enough, with Poncho planting the suggestion, the high-pitched chirps sounded exactly like the lizards were swearing at the human interlopers.

An hour after the moon peaked over the mountains and moonlight cast shadows all around, Beans heard Frankie whisper on the PRC-25.

"Base, this is Alpha team two. We've got movement."

For nearly a minute, there was dead silence, and then Frankie whispered again into the radio.

"Base, do you copy? We heard something in the bush."

"Roger that. Wait one."

Another minute passed.

"Alpha team two. Do you read.?"

"I read you. Something's in the bush. Maybe it's just a fucking racoon. Are there racoons in Vietnam?"

Another minute passed. That asshole Wolsey back in the firebase was in over his head and couldn't decide what to do.

"Team two, we're sending reinforcements. One of the tanks is on the way."

Fucking A. A tank in the dark, in the brush, manned by a crew with a snootful. That'll take care of that goddammed rodent. Soon, Beans heard the grinding diesel engine of the tank and the clatter of the tracks moving up the ridge toward his position. It was an odd juxtaposition of stealth meeting brute force.

"No, it wasn't us," Beans said to the tanker driver. "It's the second team farther up the ridge."

With a jaunty salute from the glassy-eyed driver, the tank was off, crunching through the brush. The noise gradually wore down, followed by several minutes of silence.

RAT A TAT. RAT A TAT.

Several bursts of the tank's heavy machine gun split the night.

"Cease fire! Cease fire!" Frankie's frantic voice filled the radio waves.

"Cease fire, God damn it. You're shooting at us!"

The firing stopped, but the panicky radio traffic continued.

Will and the FNG had been hit. The tanker crew and Frankie's team joined up. The tank headed back, carrying Frankie, Jonesy, and the wounded. Beans' team hoofed it out, following the tank. The FNG sat upright holding a bloody shoulder, but Will was laid out over the track, unconscious. By the time they reached the firebase, a medivac helicopter was already on station waiting to carry the wounded to the hospital at Camp Enari.

Beans picked at his scrambled eggs and sipped cold coffee. Nobody had anything to say. Frankie couldn't explain what went wrong.

"They just started firing," he said. "What more can I say?"

Waiting. Waiting for word. Was no news good news? Did silence mean they were still alive, still being operated on, still receiving transfusions, still … What the fuck. Who could know?

Beans had barely met the FNG, and now he couldn't even remember his name, but Will had been part of Frankie's squad all along. Will was a quiet guy. Beans replayed the recent conversation he had with Will. Will grew chatty when he showed Beans the picture of his wife and two-year old son.

"See, he's got my curly hair."

Will's dad owned a hardware store in some small berg in upstate New York. It would be Will's store one day.

"Me and the wife and kids will run that store. She's six months pregnant, you know. We had our good times when I was home on leave before shipping out for over here," he said with a smile and a wink.

Beans showed him a picture of Angie, but that was before. Before Big Jimmie sent him the picture with Angie and Dave and fucking Senator Kennedy.

The tanker crews departed for their daytime roadside duty. On their way out, Beans caught a glimpse of the bleary-eyed tanker driver from the night before. His cheeks were red and damp from weeping.

It was around 11:00 am when Frankie took the call. Lieutenant Wolsey sulked in a back corner. Frankie didn't say anything; he just listened. The whole platoon gathered round. Frankie's hand shook as he put down the land line phone.

"Will didn't make it," was all he could say.

Beans knew the routine. In a week or so, an army vehicle would pull up to a house in upstate New York, and a young officer--his dress uniform spotless, the creases in his pants and shirt sharp, the black leather gear and shoes shined to a mirror finish—would knock on the door.

"I regret to inform you that your husband was killed by friendly fire."

The woman would clutch at the baby in her belly and wail, and her two-year-old would cling to her dress pleading, "What's wrong, Mama."

For sure, the young wife and mother wouldn't say, "Thank God, it was only friendly fire."

Friendly fire. What a goddammed sack of shit.

Chapter Sixteen

From the railway platform of Portland's Union Station, the snow-capped peak of Mount Hood glistened in the sunrise. Dave drew deep breaths of the cool, humid air. Returning to the campaign trail invigorated him. He carried a paper bag with a couple of blueberry muffins in one hand and steaming coffee in a Styrofoam cup in the other as he boarded the southbound train. A brochure with details about the locales they would pass through jutted from his pocket.

"Good morning. Good morning. Good morning."

Greetings all around as the Kennedy campaign staff boarded with many faces familiar to Dave but many new faces as well. A sizable press contingent filled several railway cars.

His folks back in Minnesota, and Angie, too, disagreed with his decision to continue to work with the Kennedy campaign.

For Angie, it was about being sensible and practical. For her, it was apple-pie Americana vs pie-in-the-sky foolishness.

"I don't see what this has to do with us," she said. "Or, school, career, family. Do you feel like a bigshot? Come down to earth and get on with your life. Our lives."

Dave drank deeply of the heady brew of politics. Maybe it was an ego thing being so close to the action, breaking bread with Senator Kennedy and the campaign pols, but he believed his tiny role was important enough to put his education on hold. Less front of mind for twenty-year old Dave was the feeling of being rushed and smothered by Angie's "us" talk. He meant it when he said he loved her, but still. Rejoining the campaign felt liberating.

For his father, it was a Republican vs Democrat thing, but especially a deviation from Harv's expectations for his son. Maybe Dave wanted to impress his dad, or maybe he wanted to piss him off.

His mother didn't understand dropping out of school.

"This will look great on my resume someday," he assured her.

Dave caught the infectious fervor of activism from Wendy Cragun, John Lewis, and the rest of the Kennedy campaign crew. The more he learned about the war, the more he saw the wrong-headedness; the more he learned about race relations, the more he believed in John Lewis' beloved community. Inspired by McCarthy and now Kennedy, Dave felt momentum for systemic change swelling from New Hampshire to Indiana and now to Oregon.

As the train started forward with a lurch, Dave enjoyed the shop talk he overheard from campaign workers.

"We've got the momentum after Indiana and clobbering McCarthy in Nebraska."

"Did you see the latest Gallup poll? The combined insurgent support for Bobby and McCarthy nearly doubles Humphrey's."

Someone passed around a recent copy of Time Magazine with a pop-artist's conception of Kennedy as a comic book superhero on the front cover.

Dave's coffee had barely cooled enough to drink when the engineer blasted his air horn, signaling arrival at Oregon City. Dave wolfed down the muffins and fed the scraps to the dog in his charge. In a throwback to old-style whistle-stop campaigning, the Kennedy entourage rode the six-car "Beaver State Special" down the Willamette River Valley south from Portland, Oregon.

From the brochure Dave followed, he learned that Oregon City, once the end of the line for the prairie schooners of the Oregon Trail and a former Hudson's Bay Company outpost, became the first incorporated city west of the Rockies. Before that, the local waterfall in the Willamette River provided abundant year-round fishing grounds for several tribes of native Americans. The hydroelectric plant constructed late in the nineteenth century provided electricity over a fourteen-mile transmission line to Portland.

An early morning mist rose from the churning water at the base of the falls as Senator Kennedy moved to the platform at the back end of the trailing car. Loudspeakers affixed to the roof of the car carried his stump speech to the curious crowd of onlookers, many sipping their own coffee. The middling crowd offered polite applause. Still waking up, Dave thought.

Next stop, the capitol city of Salem. An influx of students from Willamette University injected more life in the crowd, but it still was not large or boisterous.

As the train pulled out, the dog sharing a seat with Dave attracted the attention of a young woman who had just climbed aboard the train.

"What a sweet puppy," she said as she slid into the seat across from Dave. "Can I pet him?"

"Of course," Dave said. "His name is Freckles. He belongs to the Senator."

"My name is Jesse," she said as she eagerly scratched the springer spaniel behind his ears.

"Welcome aboard. I'm guessing you're a Willamette coed?"

"Yep. I'm the organizer for the campus students for Kennedy. And you are?"

For the first time, her brown eyes set in a tanned, oval face looked up from the dog to Dave.

"I'm Dave from the University of Minnesota," he said extending his hand. "I joined the campaign in Indiana."

"So, you're the official dog sitter?" she said.

Dave ignored the tease.

"What do you think of my state?" Jesse asked as the train passed through small plots of brilliant blooming flowers, filbert trees, and hops.

"Is it always this lush?"

Jesse shrugged. "Guess so."

She apparently wasn't interested in horticulture-cum-agriculture.

"We had a great night last night before 1,300 screaming high school students, but they're not voters." Dave said. "What's the mood on campus?"

"I'll be honest," Jesse said. "McCarthy is very strong."

"I'm nervous," Dave said. "The polls are too damn close. LBJ is still on the ballot and that scares me. A vote for Johnson is a lost vote for Kennedy."

"How so?"

"In an odd twist, Johnson is now the surrogate for Humphrey, so he'll get votes even though he's not in the race. If Johnson wasn't on the ballot, those voters would likely vote for our candidate because they see McCarthy as too big a risk. Kennedy, not McCarthy, would be their second choice."

Jesse silently mulled Dave's insights.

"I don't mean to be critical of Oregon," Dave continued. "It is what it is, but it seems like a great, white, middle-class suburb. The crowds are lily white and reasonably well off. In Indiana, the crowds were more diverse, and that's Kennedy's strength."

"Busted," she said with a shrug. "I'm about as white middle class as you can get. My dad's a lawyer in a two-lawyer shop, and Mom's a schoolteacher."

"Democrat or Republican?"

"Rigid Republicans, at least my dad. He'll vote for B movie actor turned California governor, Ronald Reagan, in the primary. When Reagan blames big government, Dad laps it up. When Reagan assails lenient judges, liberal elites, and leftist protesters, Dad claps his hands. I don't think my dad has ever had as much as a five-minute conversation with a negro, and he doesn't think he's racist, but when Reagan says the welfare system is the problem and not the solution in urban ghettos, Dad nods his head. I've heard Dad say, more than once, 'What those colored folks need is not a handout but a bit of gumption and self-reliance.' The thing I find most disarming about Reagan is that he says mean-spirited things with a smile rather than a scowl. He's a natural showman with a pleasant style that masks his gloomy substance."

"Don't know about Mom. She doesn't say, but sometimes I see more in her glance than she means to let on, and it wouldn't surprise me if her quiet independence shows up in the privacy of the voting booth."

"Would she vote for Bobby in the general election if it comes down to him against Nixon?"

"Maybe, but I doubt it," she said, shrugging her shoulders.

"I think she agrees with what our Republican governor said about the anti-war movement forcing the commander-in-chief to lay down his sword in the middle of a war. She may harbor doubts about the war, but since we're there, she believes America should be united in supporting the troops. I find it odd and disingenuous that somehow 'support for the troops' has become code for supporting war policy."

"It sure as hell looks like Nixon will sashay his way into the nomination," Dave said. "First, he knocked off Governor George Romney, and now he'll likely end the token opposition from Rockefeller and Reagan. You know, I crossed paths with Romney people in New Hampshire when I was knocking on doors for McCarthy. Although Romney had been a media darling for a time, he sealed his fate when he said he had been 'brainwashed' about Vietnam."

"No shit. You worked for McCarthy? I thought once you were on his team you were too pure to sully yourself with anyone else. The McCarthy crowd on campus thinks Kennedy is a brazen opportunist joining the race after McCarthy did the heavy lifting."

"I get that, but the Senator himself told me that he had already decided to join the race *before* McCarthy kicked

Johnson's ass in the New Hampshire primary. True or not, that's what he said, and I believe him."

Just then, a long air horn blast signaled the next stop.

"I sure hope the crowds pick up," Dave said.

"Were you here for his Portland State speech?"

"No,' Dave said, unsure what she was talking about.

Jesse seemed pleased to one up Dave.

"Soon after the Senator announced his candidacy in March, he spoke to a delirious college crowd in Portland. The Senator gave a great speech, and the crowd swooned. Afterwards, the students swarmed him, tousling his hair, and I heard they tore off his cuff links. Oregon crowds aren't as restrained as you think."

"Hope so," Dave said as the train pulled into the Albany station.

Dave and Jesse stepped off the train to walk Freckles and to mingle with the Albany crowd for the Senator's speech.

"I told you so. Does this crowd satisfy you?"

Dave nodded, the crowd was much bigger than earlier, and enthusiastic, too.

"Buy you a cone?" Jesse asked, pointing at a nearby Dairy Queen.

"Sure. Sounds good."

Dave's eyes followed her as she walked away. She was petite but shapely in snug jeans.

Jesse soon returned and handed Dave his cone. The swirl on top already sagged, and melted soft serve dribbled down his chin. With one hand on Freckle's leash and the other holding the cone, his hands were full, and Jesse dabbed at his chin with a napkin. Their eyes met, but the moment immediately felt awkward to both, and they quickly looked away and paid attention to the Senator's speech.

As was typical, Senator Kennedy criticized Humphrey without mentioning McCarthy.

"If he wants your votes, I think he should come here and campaign for them. I bring my candidacy to the people and not the backroom power brokers."

True enough, but his hopes for winning the nomination depended upon wheeling and dealing at the convention since he would not have most of delegates committed to him at the outset. Winning the last few primaries would sway the delegates—at least, that was the hope and the plan.

Back on the train, Dave and Jesse sat silently. With the dab on his cheek, a threshold had been crossed.

The crowds swelled in size and enthusiasm at each whistle stop as the train continued south toward Eugene and to a climactic end to the day. An estimated two thousand greeted Kennedy at the Eugene train station, more than that crowded the streets as the entourage travelled toward the University of Oregon campus, and more than that again when he addressed the crowd assembled on Hayward Field in a near riot of enthusiasm.

"Can you dig it?" Jesse asked as the adoring crowd mobbed the Senator.

The Senator enjoyed the adulation, and a few staffers provided some measure of control, but there was no Secret Service protection.

After the crowd dissipated, the campaign entourage split up. The Senator and his closest staff flew to California for a few days of campaigning before a planned return to Oregon four days later for a final sprint to the primary on the 28th. Other staff and surrogates would remain in Oregon. Dave would overnight in Eugene before flying to Minnesota in the morning for Angie's High School graduation.

"Grab a burger?" Dave asked.

"You bet," Jesse said. "I'm famished."

Neither said much, and Dave stared past her at the Cascade Range to the east. All day the mountains followed their journey down the river valley as if curious at the political spectacle below.

"Where are you staying," Jesse asked as she picked at her fries.

"I forget. I'll have to check my notes."

"And you? You heading back to Salem tonight?"

"That's the plan," she said. Her wide brown eyes under thick eyelashes fixed on Dave's eyes. "Unless you want me to stay."

It was still dark when Dave awoke hours before his scheduled departure. He filled a glass with water from the sink in the hotel bathroom and returned to sit on the edge of his empty bed. He did the right thing walking Jesse back to the train station after they finished their burgers, but that didn't allow him to sleep any easier.

After Dave exited the plane following the short hop from Eugene to San Francisco, he searched the Departures screen to find his gate for the onward flight to Minneapolis. The sign blinked *CANCELLED*.

"Nothing more today, Hon," the uniformed gate agent with black hair pinched into a bun said. "We'll get you out first thing tomorrow."

Dave fingered the vouchers for meals and a hotel room. How to spend the day in the Bay Area? The restaurants of Fisherman's Wharf? Nah, his vouchers would do him no good there. Carol Doda and her oversized breasts at the Condor Club on Broadway? She was the first topless dancer who started a revolution that "spun as fast as twirling tassels." Salacious, but no.

With his suitcase in one hand and a paper bag carrying a sub sandwich and a coke in the other, Dave hailed a cab and embarked on a pilgrimage into the heart of the city and the Haight Ashbury District. For a bright shining moment, the Haight was the *de facto* capital of hippie counterculture featuring music—Janis Joplin, Jefferson Starship, The Grateful Dead and others--while dabbling in free thought, free love, free meals, free clothes, and free health care all inspired by drug-induced consciousness. Yep, the hippie anthem about going to San Francisco was right on. The folks you meet there are pretty laid back, or "far out, groovy, flower children" as they would say.

Dave chomped down his sandwich while seated on a park bench looking across Stanyan Street and down Haight Street.

"Ya wanna be a hippie?" A raspy voice intruded. "Yer too late. The real hippies have come and gone."

The speaker sat on the adjacent park bench. It was hard to tell how old he was: gaunt, with disheveled oily dark hair streaked with gray hanging over a face with deep set eyes and whiskers that barely covered hollow cheeks. Dave crumpled his bag, tossed it in a garbage basket, and sat down next to the town crier.

"Tell me how it was," Dave said.

He looked Dave up and down with skepticism. Dave wore a sport jacket over an open-collar dress shirt.

"Them was groovy times, for sure, but it was more. It was a commune in the city. The drugs offered an alternate form of consciousness, but the Haight was also an alternate form of living. Ya wanna change the world? First ya gotta change yer mind, the way ya think. Trip out, man. Take a magic carpet ride to a revolution of thought, of consciousness, of spirit. Don't need no money. No rich or poor. No violence. We meant it when we said, 'make love, not war.' We lived it too."

He smiled and added, "Plenty of pussy."

A tourist bus pulled up across the street, and middle-aged folks exited. With cameras dangling around their necks, they headed down Haight Street, stopping to listen to a couple chanting as if in a trance. After snapping pictures, the tourists moved on after leaving bills in a hat.

Dave's companion shook his head. "Shit, those two ain't hippies, them's capitalists."

"It ain't like it was last year in the summer of love and before that. It was just a happening that happened. Now, the drugs are bad, and people no longer come here to give but to take. Lotta takers. The Diggers are gone who just gave shit away because it was their thing. Schemers not searchers nowadays. No flower children to put a flower in yer hair but someone selling a flower they probably swiped. Real revolutionaries walked these streets and not just punks who get punked by the street hustlers. Worse yet are the tourist-voyeurs who come expectin' to see real life rather than livin' their own."

The men sat silently watching pigeons patrol the sidewalk. The man reached into his pocket and pulled out a bag of seeds, and he fanned a handful for the birds.

"Ya wanna do a number?"

"Ah, no thanks," Dave said and stood up to leave. "Well, what the hell," and he sat down and shared a joint with the burned-out devotee of Timothy Leary's dictum to "turn on, tune in, drop out" while his boom box played Jerry Garcia and The Grateful Dead with lyrics suggesting nothing matters.

The next morning, Dave had time to kill before boarding his flight home to Minnesota, and he devoured his airport scrambled eggs, bacon, and toast with jelly while he pored over the San Francisco Chronicle. He dwelled on two related but unrelated stories.

Nine Catholics, led by priests Daniel and Philip Berrigan, broke into the files of a Selective Service Office in Catonsville, Maryland. They gathered nearly 400 records into wire bins. After sprinkling their own blood on the draft records and then homemade napalm, they ignited the bins in the parking lot and prayed while they awaited arrest. The "Catonsville Nine" refused bail and issued a statement as they began a fast:

We shed our blood willingly and gratefully in what we hope is a sacrificial and constructive act. We pour it upon these files to illustrate that with them and with these offices begins the pitiful waste of American and Vietnamese blood 10,000 miles away.

This was beyond dissent to resistance. They reasoned that America needed a wakeup call through disruptive attacks against the war machine.

The second news story reported the opening of the trial of "The Boston Five," headlined by Dr. Benjamin Spock and Yale University chaplain William Sloane Coffin, Jr. Dr. Spock, a pediatrician, penned *the* book on parenting and childcare that influenced millions of American mothers and contributed to the wellbeing of the post-war children of the baby boom. Dave wondered whether his mother, Meg, used the book as a guide for his own upbringing.

The defendants led protests and encouraged draft age men to refuse to serve in the Vietnam War and to demonstrate their unwillingness by burning or turning in their draft cards. Once again, protests turned into active resistance. Burning draft cards was not merely a symbolic act; it was illegal. In October 1967, thousands gathered on the Boston Commons for protests led by Spock and the others. Hundreds of young men heeded the call to burn their cards, but rather than prosecute the draft-age men, the feds indicted the celebrity defendants who encouraged the resistance.

In January, the Justice Department handed down indictments charging the Boston Five with conspiring to "counsel, aid, and abet Selective Service registrants to evade military service and refuse to carry draft cards." The defendants and their movement welcomed the indictments as an opportunity to put the government's war policies on trial. As the trial approached, the defendants continued to give anti-war, draft resistance speeches, and they received significant press attention.

Dave poured the last of his coffee pot into his cup and continued to read. The Chronicle reported that the trial had now begun, but the trial judge refused to allow the defendants to raise a defense based upon the illegality of the war and the draft.

Dave folded up the newspaper, opened his billfold, and pulled out his own draft registration card, which he carried with him as the law required. It was a simple card with his name, home address, phone number, and occupation as a student listed. It also had his dad's name and address listed as someone who would always know his whereabouts. If he went into hiding, not that he would, he wondered if his dad would turn him in.

He pulled out two additional cards called "Notice of Classification." Both cards bore the signature of a member of his local draft board and denoted a 2-S draft deferment, indicating a full-time student making satisfactory progress in a field of study. The deferment protected him from the draft so long as he continued to receive an annual renewal, but post-graduate student deferments were questionable, and General Lewis Hershey, the Director of the Selective Service, encouraged local draft boards to revoke student deferments for anti-war activities. All classification decisions were at the discretion of local draft boards. Some were strict; some were lenient. Sometimes it mattered who you knew.

Dave's first classification card was dated October of 1966, which he received after entering the University of Minnesota as a full-time student in the fall after his graduation from Kalmar High School that spring. The second was dated October of 1967, which indicated a renewal of his student deferment status. Dave never thought much about his student deferment. He enrolled in college after high school as a matter of course. A college education had always been a given, and the deferment was just incidental to college plans—never the primary or even secondary motivation. The deferment was a privilege that he took for granted.

Dave returned the cards to his billfold, leaned back in his chair, and drained the last of his coffee that had cooled. Travelers scurried past. Many wore Class A military dress uniforms. Each one travelled alone, never in a group. The nearby Oakland Army base served as a major transit hub for military personnel departing to or returning from Vietnam, and the San Francisco airport connected these military travelers with cities across the US. The Vietnam bound recent graduates of boot camp tended to have shorter hair and lower ranks than the returnees, but the faces of both sets betrayed stress borne of fright at what lay ahead or trauma from what lay behind.

Selective Service. With a few exceptions, these anxious souls didn't choose to serve. They were selected. *Give me your tired, your poor.*

Chapter Seventeen

The incoming mortar fire was more an aggravation than a danger, but because it *could* be dangerous, it was an aggravation.

Beans and the 1st platoon continued to provide security for the firebase on the western edge of a mountain range after the friendly fire incident with the tank. One night, half a dozen mortars landing near the perimeter got everyone's attention and messed up their sleep as they crawled into sandbagged bunkers. The second night was more of the same, and on the third night they abandoned the bunks in the barracks at the outset in favor of sleeping in the bunkers, listening to the *kerplunk* of mortar rounds exiting their launch tube and counting down until the high arching explosive detonated on impact thirty seconds to a minute after launching.

The asshole lieutenant Wolsey requested helicopter reconnaissance over the nearby ridges and valleys during the daytime, but as Beans and the others who had humped jungle terrain knew, that was pure bullshit. From the sky, Charlie was invisible in his jungle domain. Then Wolsey made another command decision. He ordered a recon patrol. He studied his map intently and picked a ridge about three clicks into the mountains. The ridge came to a point overlooking a vast valley in three directions. He figured that observers on the high ground could pinpoint any enemy activity in that valley.

The next morning, Frankie's squad headed out after dousing their bloused pant legs and faces with standard issue bug juice full of DEET. The bug juice offered a couple of benefits in addition to acting as a mosquito repellent. Back home in Minnesota, Beans knew about the nasty black creatures called blood suckers that attached to your body when swimming in certain bodies of water, but the Vietnam leeches could latch on anywhere in the grass. Keeping pant legs bloused tight over combat boots helped protect against the irritating little bastards, but sprinkling the bug juice on pant legs cinched it. Secondly, the green and black face paint used when stealth required camouflage was difficult to smear on without an initial layer of bug juice to act as a solvent.

Beans walked point. In slow motion, he lifted his combat boot over a rotting branch and gingerly stepped to the soft ground on the opposite side. Momentarily straddling the fallen limb, he scanned the brush from left to right before dropping his gaze to the forest floor ahead to plan for his next footfall. When he was satisfied, he shifted his weight forward and lifted his trailing foot over the branch. Again, and again, Beans repeated the methodical process as he silently crept through tall ferns, low-hanging vines, and suspended air plants of a rugged valley. Behind him in five to ten-yard intervals, his six teammates mimicked his actions.

In the branches above, a noisy flock of flycatchers bobbed and weaved for bugs, while the seed-eating finches flitted here and there in the low grass and brush; the birds didn't notice the intruders. Birdsongs and chattering squirrels said all was well; silence would sound an alarm.

In an hour, they traveled a click up the slope and into the bush. With hand gestures, they came together in a thick patch of underbrush to pore over their map. Which way was the point of that damn ridge? Stretching out again, they ascended toward higher ground. Soon, the greenery of the valley gave way to brown savannah, and they moved from jungle to tall, elephant grass.

Leaving the heavy cover of the rainforest, they moved from one thicket to the next and avoided open spaces, but then they came to barren ground. The next patch was twenty to thirty meters ahead. While Beans paused to think it through, he saw the tall grass across the way shudder even though there was no breeze. Instinctively, he squatted and held up his hand to freeze the others, eyes fixated on the clump where he had seen movement, but the leaves of grass were now still. Too still. There were no songbirds and no chattering rodents, only Beans' pounding heart. A reddish-brown hawk with a tufted crown peered down from a perch on a dead branch of a tall thorn tree, jerking its head back and forth as if following the performers in the morality play unfolding in the brush below. Beans wished he could see with the eyes of the raptor.

They retreated in reverse order with Frankie now in front. Beans brought up the rear, walking backwards, not daring to release the grassy patch from sight. They circled around and within half an hour they were back on course, and Beans convinced himself that he hadn't seen anything. It was strange for him not to be on point. As the drag man, he covered their rear, and with each step forward he turned slowly and scanned 180 degrees behind them. Perhaps it was the unusual sensation of walking drag, but Beans felt like they were being followed even though he never saw anything to feed his foreboding.

When they reached the spine of the mountain ridge, they turned west to follow the sun. They figured the plateau with the sharp point with steep declines into the valley on three sides was just ahead, and they were right. When they arrived at their destination, the sun glowed orange in the western sky in the direction of the firebase.

Perfect.

They enjoyed a vantage point over a vast swath of the valley. They would easily spot any smoke curling up through the canopy from enemy campfires. They would monitor the grassy patches with binoculars. Artillery batteries, helicopter gunships, even fighter jets and bombers awaited their instructions, for they were now forward observers, and they could call in death and destruction upon their dominion. Maybe the asshole lieutenant wasn't as stupid as they thought.

Better yet, this was a safe position. They could scramble down steep slopes if it came to that, but no wandering NVA would attempt to scale the incline. The only direction of danger was the same way they had come, but who would follow the mountain spine to a dead-end drop off?

Perfect.

They bunched Claymores mines, pointing them up the spine. Since the approach to their November Lima was so narrow, they stretched thin wire from tree to tree six inches above the ground and affixed white phosphorous grenades--illumination flares--to the ends. Even a couple of frag grenades. Any enemy traffic traveling along the ridge toward them would be funneled right into their booby traps.

Perfect.

By the time they finished their meal of C-rations, the western sky was a palette of pinks and purples. Beans enjoyed a languorous last smoke, and when he snuffed out his Kool, the first pale-yellow stars had appeared.

That's when the music startled them. It came from the valley, to be sure, but where?

"Call it in! Call it in!"

Frankie shrugged his shoulders.

"What do I say? There are dinks in the jungle. No shit."

Frankie was right. Unless they could pinpoint the source, there was nothing to do. Sometimes the music seemed near and then far. Sometimes to their left and then to their right. So, they did nothing except to lean back against their rucks and listen to the simple stringed instrument plucked by an unseen hand. Occasionally, there would be a clang of a tinny drum or gong or other undefined percussion instrument. It was local music with an oriental sound, strange and dissonant to their western ears.

Then a plaintive female voice startled them by joining the stringed instrument, and the siren's song wafted through the heavy night air. At first, Beans thought it must be a radio or cassette player because there could be no woman in the jungle, but she seemed real and alive and here and now. And alluring. And intoxicating.

Beans woke with a start and realized a chorus of croaking frogs had replaced the now silent siren. His six teammates slept soundly, and Beans was embarrassed that he had drifted off because he had taken the first watch.

Strict protocol required that one of them remain awake through the night but staying alert for a full two-hour shift often proved difficult.

Beans put both hands on the ground and pushed himself up into a seated position, leaning against his ruck. He picked up his M-16 and checked the safety, as he always did, then laid the weapon across his thighs. He checked his sleeping teammates to his left; even with his eyes accustomed to the night, they were invisible in the dark, but he heard them breathing.

Beans glanced at the dark sky; a cloud bank had rolled in because he saw no moon or stars. He sure could use a smoke, but the burning ember would shine like a torch. He pulled back his sleeve and checked his watch. In the smothering blackness, the fluorescent dial glowed like a green beacon, and he quickly pulled the sleeve down.

He thought about that music again, trying to figure who the woman was behind that beguiling voice. Was she just a cassette player? An NVA soldier? Or was there a hooch down in the valley with a family living there that had refused to leave the jungle like the army ordered? A "free-fire zone" they called it. Since they cleared out all the friendlies, whether they liked it or not, the only ones there had to be unfriendlies--at least according to the army--and liable to get shot. A convenient and simple morality, but Beans always wondered. And, what about the Montagnards, the primitive mountain people who knew no life other than the jungle? How many Yards remained on their home turf, despising both the NVA and the Americans?

Beans was itching to look at his watch again, to hurry it along so he could wake the next guy, then go to sleep.

And that's when he sensed it.

Movement. Beans didn't know if he heard something; he sure as hell didn't see it; but he sensed it. Something was there, and it was goddammed close. Somehow, something penetrated their perimeter. Past the trip wires. What the fuck? Like flipping a switch, Beans was suddenly wide awake and scared shitless. Danger was practically on top of him; if he reached out into the sinister blackness, he could touch it, or at least it seemed that close.

His M-16 lay across his lap, and he leaned forward to reach for it, but when he did, the movement stopped.

Beans stopped.

It started.

Beans reached again.

It stopped.

Beans stopped.

Seven men lay in a row, head to toe. The other six lay to Beans left, toward the west. To his right, to the east, the ridge funneled into their November Lima, where the trip wires were set up to warn of intruders, but somehow, something penetrated their perimeter. Somehow, the movement slipped past their booby traps. Somehow, the movement was damned near on top of him, there to his right, about to stumble into him.

It started again, circling north, moving along his legs, moving toward his feet. For the third time, Beans leaned forward to reach his rifle just inches from his fingertips, but as soon as he did, the movement stopped again.

Movement. What the hell is movement? Beans didn't know, and he was fucking scared, but every time he tried to reach for his weapon, it stopped. *Movement* is what you reported to base when something unseen, something unknown, but something sure as hell unfriendly and after your ass was moving around and scaring the shit out of you. *Movement* was death: lurking, stalking, waiting its chance. Somehow *movement* avoided their trip wires, and it was damn near in his lap, and he couldn't reach his goddammed rifle, and it was moving again.

Now it was past his feet, still moving north. It was dark, so dark he couldn't see his M-16 laying across his legs, but he could feel the weapon just like he could feel the movement that he couldn't see. It was there, and it was the only reality that mattered, and that's when it made a left turn and headed toward the west, beneath his feet, and in front of the only patch of sky visible in the heavens, and then he saw it, the full silhouette of a great cat.

A fucking tiger.

It stopped, right there in front of him, and turned its head toward him, and Beans saw white fangs when it canted its head and let out the most god-awful roar that shook the trees and probably awoke all the dinks in the jungle and sure as hell roused his six buddies, who jumped around and yelled and scrambled, but it was gone.

Beans didn't see it leave; he didn't know where it went; it was just gone.

Beans had heard stories of other patrols not so fortunate--of guys waking in the morning to find one missing and a bloody drag trail leading into the brush and a half-eaten body at the end of it. The tiger scratched away the recon team's pretense and subterfuge. They fancied themselves to be jungle cats prowling around the jungle, but the real feline called them liars and exposed them. They trespassed in the tiger's lair, but their stealth couldn't save them, nor their perfect hiding spot, nor even the firepower a radio call away, waiting to be loosed from afar.

That's when the music started again. They heard the plucked strings, and they waited for the female voice, but it never came.

Chapter Eighteen

Two years can be a long time or an eye blink. Times change and times stay the same.

Memories from the Kalmar High School gym washed over Dave: the Phy Ed classes that honed his competitiveness; the delirious crowd for a Friday night basketball game; the concerts; the plays; and the assemblies. The old gym looked the same: bleachers on the sides; folding chairs set in rows on the hardwood floor; the Kalmar High band tucked into the left-front corner; and the elevated stage on one end.

When the director gave the downbeat and the band struck up Elgar's familiar *Pomp and Circumstance March* for the processional, Dave remembered his own graduation ceremony two years earlier when he delivered the valedictory. How full of himself he was then and how trivial his speech was. He hoped he wasn't the same smart-ass, but he conceded that was unlikely. Certainly, his worldview had evolved. Yes, the world was a bigger place than Kalmar, but Kalmar would always be the core of his being. Never mind that Kalmar now seemed insular and provincial.

The first seniors ascended the steps to the stage and took their places standing in front of the back row of chairs when Angie appeared toward the rear of the procession with the other honor students. The tasseled cap didn't diminish her wavy, blonde hair. The blue gown accented her glowing, milk-white face with a touch of pink on her cheeks. A hint of a smile tugged at her lips, revealing her dimples.

There were speeches, a reading of the class will, and musical selections, including a female trio, led by Angie, offering their rendition of *What the World Needs Now is Love.* The trite message of the pop tune somehow seemed apropos in the moment to the listening ears of the Kalmar High School crowd.

After the School Board Chairman handed Angie her diploma and shook her hand, she emphatically flipped the tassel on her cap from right to left.

After the ceremony, well-wishers congratulated the graduates. Dave stood at the edge of the throng that clustered around Angie. Amazing what a picture in the paper can do. Even the Republican-leaning citizens of Kalmar were impressed.

"Did you really meet the Senator?"

"How did you arrange that?"

"You put Kalmar on the map."

"Your father would be so proud."

"Is the Senator tall?"

"What's his wife like? Ethel is her name, right?"

Eventually, the commencement crowd broke up, and Dave rode with his parents to Joyce Olson's house for Angie's party. Dear friends and mere acquaintances kept arriving to rub elbows with Kalmar's newfound celebrity.

"Goodness, I'm going to run out of cake!" Joyce whispered to Meg Karlstad. Meg departed and returned with chocolate chip cookies from her cookie jar.

Dave repeatedly circled with coffee and Kool Aid but avoided conversation and deferred to Angie as much as possible. This was her night.

The Karlstads were the last to leave. The next morning, Dave slept in and returned to Angie's house around noon.

"You kids go," Joyce said. "I'm still cleaning up, and then I need a nap."

Joyce and Angie had planned to do spring cleaning at their nearby lake cabin. Opening the cabin was an annual rite of spring, but Ben Olson had always been in charge. He supervised putting in the dock, activating the water and sewer systems, and raking the yard while Joyce cleaned inside.

Dave was not a handy man, and it took them a while to figure out which valves to open and where to find the switch that would turn on the well pump, but they got it done. The roll-in dock was heavy, and they needed to wade into the chill water that had been ice covered just a month ago. They got that done, also, but Angie and her bikini proved to be more than a distraction, and soon they tore open the plastic garbage bag they carried from town with linens and blankets for the bed.

"Wake up! Someone's here," Angie nudged Dave.

She heard the crunch of rubber on gravel and the muted squeal of worn brakes coming to rest.

They had dozed off after sex. Dave pulled on his jeans and T shirt and went outside barefoot. Big Jimmie Overskei stood at the end of the dock looking for sunfish in the shallows. Dave joined him there, but Jimmie didn't look up as he approached.

"Hey Jimmie. How they hanging?"

"Not so bad. How 'bout you?" he replied, looking past Dave toward Angie who was just then exiting the cabin.

"Hey Ang."

"How have you been, Jimmie?" Angie asked. "I don't see much of you these days."

"Livin' in St. Cloud, ya know. Usually make it up on weekends."

"Still working in your cousin's body shop?" Dave asked.

"Not for long. When I heard from my draft board with my 1-A classification, I enlisted for four years. By signing up, I get to go to auto mechanic school. Mebbe I'll end up in the Nam like Beans, but at least it'll be in the motor pool and not totin' an M-16 in the rice paddies."

"Probably a good decision," Dave said. "I hear Little Jimmie Nelson joined the Navy for similar reasons.

Jimmie appeared pleased that Dave gave his blessing to his plans.

"Yep, and my cousin's gonna be a weekend warrior in the National Guard."

Dave flipped a pebble into the water, and the sunfish scurried.

"Say, what about you? If'n yer galivanting all over the country, what about yer student deferment? Ain't you liable for the draft?"

Angie cast a worried glance at Dave, looking for reassurance.

"I'll be back in school soon enough. I'll sign up for summer school at the U when I get around to it."

Jimmie stomped on the dock with one foot as if to test its stability. "I'd a helped, if you asked."

"Yeah, we shoulda asked," Dave replied. "We managed, but it was a hassle."

"Been on the water, yet?" Jimmie asked, lifting his eyes toward the overturned canoe on the shore.

"Maybe later."

"I hear the crappies are biting."

"You been out?"

"No. I just heard."

Jimmie turned away and looked across the lake.

"Saw the paper," Jimmie said. "That's a big friggin deal."

"Yes, it was an adventure I'll never forget," Angie replied.

"Don't figure Beans will neither."

Conk-la-ree!

A Red-winged Blackbird swayed on a dead cattail reed. Eager to find a mate, the bird spread his tail feathers, fluffed his bright red shoulders, and filled the silence.

Conk-la-ree!

Jimmie turned back and looked directly at Angie.

"Listen, I don't mind you guys hooking up. I ain't surprised, neither, but I worry about Beans, being over there and all."

"Of course," Angie said, "We worry, too. We're still wrestling with what to say, but we're going to say it together, face-to-face. We owe him that."

"What? You ain't told him? Sheeit."

"We have to tell him now," Angie said, and Dave reluctantly agreed.

He wasn't sure how to reveal or describe their relationship. Were they dating? Going steady? Was she pinned? When Angie chided Dave over flying off to participate in the Kennedy campaign, she spoke of "settling down," "family," and "our future." He was twenty, and she was only eighteen, for chrissake.

On Dave's last night in Minnesota, he and Angie labored over a delicate letter to Beans.

"We don't mean to hurt you."

"We didn't plan this."

"We still care deeply for you."

"We still want you to be part of our lives."

None of it was right. Every sentence they wrote seemed wrong. The finished product pleased neither of them, but it was what it was, and they both signed it. There just wasn't a good way to say, "Dear John."

Chapter Nineteen

The tiger never returned, and Frankie's recon squad spent four idle days at the point of the ridge overlooking the verdant treetops of the jungle below. Nor did the siren of the valley reprise her night song. On the morning of the last day, the eastern sun filtered through the treetops and warmed Beans' sleeping face. He was the first to awaken except for Dozer who pulled the dawn watch. Beans rubbed the sleep from his eyes and began to heat water in his canteen cup for instant coffee. A used can from a pack of C-rations made for a good stove fueled by a lump of combustible C-4 plastic explosive.

"I heard a loudspeaker in the valley," Dozer whispered.

Beans lifted a sleepy eye in his direction. He was dubious. Charlie was secretive, and a loudspeaker in the jungle seemed unlikely. Plus, Dozer was the guy who always claimed loud explosions damaged his hearing. Beans leaned against his ruck as he sipped hot coffee with long pulls on a Kool.

"Not just once, but several times," Dozer claimed.

The other guys stirred and came to life. Soon, seven guys listened with pricked ears trying to hear what Dozer heard.

Beans realized how much he could hear when he listened intentionally. The wind rushing through quaking leaves, dozens of unique bird calls, occasional shrieks from an unknown creature, but no goddammed loudspeaker. The squad listened hard for the next hour, and their doubts swelled, and with each new bird call, they screwed up their faces with looks that asked Dozer, "Was that it? Was that what you heard?"

The more they doubted, the more Dozer's faith grew. Finally, he said, "I'm calling it in."

A few shrugs, but nobody objected. Better to overreact.

The squad had front row seats for the entertainment that followed. First to arrive was a fixed wing "bird dog," a small plane that circled overhead and communicated first with the squad to identify the target and then with the Phantom fighter/bomber jets on station to launch rockets into the valley. The first jet to arrive scared the shit out of the squad. They didn't see it coming, and their first notice was the roar of the jet engine that shook the trees as the jet screeched out the far end of the valley. After that, they watched closely as the Phantoms approached from the west. From their lofty perch high on the ridge, they looked down on the jets as they roared through the valley in a split second on their strafing runs.

For good measure, a pair of WWII vintage fighter aircraft, probably hellcats, arrived after the Phantoms departed. Each of the retired champions, still frisky and anxious to stretch their legs, made a few runs through the valley with guns blazing.

Beans figured the official records noted a great victory, but he suspected the bombing merely knocked over a bunch of trees and killed a swarm of jungle critters. Maybe a tiger.

After the fireworks, the whir of Cobra gunship rotors sounded in the distance, faster and higher pitched than the *wump-wump* of the slicks that ferried the troops. The Cobra pilot hailed the team on their radio frequency.

"Recon team, this is Elijah five-oh," the Cobra said. "We're hunting in your neighborhood, and we'll be close by if you need help."

The team packed up and headed out to return to the firebase the way they came. Frankie walked point, and Beans walked drag. On the way in, they were studiously stealthy, picking their way step by step, but now they moved quickly and casually through the shoulder height savannah grass atop the ridge, slowing and becoming cautious when an open patch appeared.

"Shit!" Frankie muttered and hit the ground, and the others instinctively followed suit.

In an instant, Frankie flipped his safety to rock and roll, and he emptied his magazine in three quick bursts. The squad was damn lucky Frankie saw the approaching NVA soldiers before they saw him. Within seconds, the rest of the squad opened fire.

Except for Beans. He grabbed the handset to his PRC-25 radio and began to shout over the crackling gunfire.

"Contact! Contact! Recon Team in contact!"

While his teammates continued to lay down small-arms fire, Beans maintained radio contact with the firebase, and that's when the Cobra again came on their frequency.

"Recon team, this is Elijah. We're two minutes away," said a friendly voice.

Beans detached a smoke grenade from his rucksack and awaited the request from the gunship to pop smoke. After receiving the request, Beans would pull the pin on the grenade and allow colored smoke to waft upward through the brush. Normal SOP would require the Cobra to report sighting of the smoke and its color--"I've got goofy grape"—which Beans would confirm. The process would mark the spot where the gunship *shouldn't* fire. Colored smoke wafting upward toward the heavens would be the signal, the plea, the prayer, "for Chrissake, don't shoot here!"

The request to pop smoke never came.

There is no sound like the chainsaw groan of the six-thousand-round-per-minute miniguns of the Cobra. With one pass over a football field, a Cobra sprayed M-60 machine gun rounds into every square foot, or so they said, but now the son-of-a-bitch piloting that killing machine opened fire before waiting for Beans to pop smoke.

"They shot my fucking legs off!" Dozer moaned as the Cobra gunship screamed by, barely clearing the treetops over their heads.

Why had the Cobra gunship failed to follow SOP?

Without lifting his head, Beans gator crawled over to Dozer, expecting to find his life ebbing away in spurts of blood.

"You dumb son-of-a-bitch," Beans said. "You ain't shot."

Instead of finding a pile of mangled flesh, all Beans saw was a spent shell that fell from the sky as the Cobra passed over, and it burned a brown spot on the back of Dozer's pant leg.

The firefight was over as quickly as it started, and the squad escaped unscathed, except for that burn on the back of Dozer's leg. Then came the wait. Echoes of gun fire and the whir of helicopter rotors died quickly, and the sounds of the jungle returned. Beans chain smoked Kools, waiting for the inbound slicks carrying a rapid response team. Not much for the grunts to do now except count the bodies. The higher ups would like what they would find. Beans scanned the ridge the army now owned, bought for the right price-- enemy blood--but by evening, the scrub brush and savannah grass would be returned to the creatures of the jungle, be they NVA or tigers.

When the rapid response infantry unit finally arrived and offloaded, Frankie's squad replaced them on the slicks that returned them the short distance to the firebase. It had been a great and terrible day. Fear and anger gave way to giddy exhilaration when the slick deposited them back at the firebase. Dozer laughed harder than the rest of them when they told the story of the legs that weren't shot off. Life is grand when you think you're dead, but you discover you're alive.

Back in their own hooch, they learned why the gunship fired without waiting for the SOP smoke signal. It seems that a platoon of North Vietnamese soldiers, about thirty men, unwittingly walked head on into the scout team walking in the opposite direction. When the firing started, the NVA panicked and ran, unaware that the firing came from only seven men. The Cobra didn't wait for smoke because the pilot saw the khaki clad men in pith helmets scattering through the savannah grass, and the Cobra miniguns mowed them down.

Beans wondered if the army had a strategy beyond accumulating a body count. That's what mattered. How many of them versus how many of us? Get the numbers up. By that standard, today had been a great victory. None of us, plenty of them.

After a hot meal and a shower, Beans cracked open a can of Hamm's and waited his turn for a game of eight ball as a tropical rainstorm pelted the tin roof. As he waited, his mood darkened, probably about the time the adrenalin wore off. The exhilaration of escaping death clouded over with the truth that others died.

His thoughts wandered off to a story Harv Karlstad, Dave's dad, once told the boys. Harv served on a Navy destroyer in the Pacific in WWII, a sleek and speedy escort that operated on the edge of the fleet, chasing Japanese subs and providing the first line of defense for air attacks. Harv recounted the excitement the crew felt one day when they pursued a Japanese submarine. They followed it on sonar back and forth, cat and mouse, and they dropped depth charges several times to no avail, as the thrill of the hunt heightened. Finally, when a smear of diesel fuel rose to the surface, the crew cheered their victory, as did Harv. Only later did Harv feel the full impact of what had happened, of dead men in a sunk submarine, and he heaved his breakfast over the side of the ship.

Beans didn't appreciate the story then, but now he understood. Beans and his team were timeless warriors caught in the amoral fate of soldiers to kill or be killed. On this day, he was the one to live while others died; the absurdity closed in on him, and he struggled to catch his breath.

"You guys play," he said dropping his pool cue on the table. "I gotta get outta here."

The screen door slammed behind him as Beans disappeared into the driving rain.

Chapter Twenty

From thirty-five thousand feet, the snow-capped Rocky Mountains appeared white and majestic as Dave jetted from Minnesota to California. He silently hummed *America the Beautiful*, wondering why the lyrics painted the mountains purple. Despite Senator Kennedy's narrow defeat in the Oregon primary, Dave was upbeat, and he was confident that California would cement the Senator's standing as *the* alternative to Vice President Humphrey. A victory in California, the most populous state with the most votes in the electoral college, would go a long way toward convincing August conventioneers that Bobby was the voter's choice with the best chance to defeat Nixon in November.

Oregon was mostly white, but California was diverse—Senator Kennedy's natural constituency of impoverished African Americans and disenfranchised Hispanic farmworkers. Dave remained confident of the promise of Kennedy's candidacy: to heal a nation torn by the Vietnam War and divided by race and class.

And crown thy good with brotherhood
From sea to shining sea!

Dave was proud of his own insignificant role in the experiment in democracy that was America: chauffeur in Indiana, dog sitter in Oregon. He was pleased that the voters rewarded Kennedy's hopeful campaign with a string of victories and a close second in Oregon. He was optimistic about California, the August national convention, and the November election. Yes, the nation had lost its way in Vietnam, but that too would change, and soon.

America! America!

"My, my, you're a chipper young man," the gray-haired woman in the middle seat said.

"Does it show? I'm really in a good mood this morning."

"Are you a college student?"

"Yes, but I'm on my way to join friends in the Senator Kennedy campaign."

The man with a buzzcut in the aisle seat tensed up, and the woman took several deep breaths. That was the end of the conversation.

Later, as the plane began its initial descent into the Los Angeles airport, the stewardess made an announcement.

"Ladies and gentlemen. We have special passengers on board today. They are gold star grandparents of Marine Corporal Joshua Albing who died serving his country in Vietnam. They are with us today as they fly to his funeral. After we land, please remain seated to allow Mr. and Mrs. Albing to exit first."

The lady in the middle seat dabbed at her eyes and then clutched her husband's hand.

"Are, are you Mr. and Mrs. Albing?" Dave stammered.

She nodded.

"I don't have the words. I apologize if I seemed glib earlier."

"You seem like an earnest young man. No need to apologize for that, and you are also a lucky man. Good for you, but don't take anything for granted. Appreciate your privilege to attend college. Joshua, our grandson, planned to use the GI Bill to pay for college when his service was done. We know that Senator Kennedy wants to quit the war, and I assume you feel the same but respect our grandson's sacrifice. Don't dishonor the troops."

The husband then had his say, "Peace yes, but with honor, that what's Nixon says, and I'll vote for him, that's for damn sure."

Dave applauded with the other passengers as the Albings made their way up the aisle.

The Albings humbled him. For him, the war was an abstraction; for the Albings and thousands of other families, it was a gut punch. Nor had he appreciated his own privilege. College was natural for him, but not for everyone, and that shielded him from the draft but exposed others. Most Vietnam casualties were minorities and/or from low-income families. Did Corporal Albing *want* to go to Vietnam? Did Beans? Perhaps. Dave didn't doubt that there were true believers, trusting that America was doing the right thing, but he was equally sure that many served not out of conviction but of circumstance.

Dave paid the cabby and eagerly entered the lobby of the Ambassador Hotel. Compared to the simple suite and meager staff in Indiana, the California campaign headquarters swelled with staffers and volunteers who bristled with energy and enthusiasm. When he arrived in Indiana, the joke was that as a Scandinavian Lutheran, he added diversity to an otherwise Irish Catholic campaign, but this campaign community was as colorful as the ghettos of the Watts neighborhood and the farm fields of the Central Valley.

"Me llamo Esteban," a greeter said, brown eyes sparkling under a mop of curly, black hair. "But you can call me Steve."

That's how Dave met his roommate at the Ambassador Hotel. Esteban Rodriguez hailed from East Los Angeles, but he was on scholarship as a freshman at UCLA. He showed Dave the ropes and brought him up to speed while introducing him to other campaign workers.

"Senor Chavez," Steve called out to the well-known leader of the United Farm Workers and introduced him to Dave.

Dave knew Cesar Chavez by reputation. Earlier that year, his hunger strike in support of non-violent protest made national headlines. Senator Kennedy had been the guest of honor at the fast-breaking event, and that's when the Senator confided in Chavez and others that he would soon enter the race for the presidency. Dave wished he had announced right then and there, two days *before* Senator McCarthy's showing in the New Hampshire primary, which would have blunted the complaints of the Clean Gene brigade that Kennedy was a Johnny-come-lately who only joined the race *after* McCarthy paved the way.

Cesar Chavez and Dolores Huerta, organizers of the farmworkers' union, sent warm bodies to register voters and get the vote out. Dave could see it in the faces of the Hispanic campaign workers; their excitement was infectious. Black Olympic champion and local hero Rafer Johnson was a constant presence. Dave was a long way from the homogenous northern European community of Kalmar; he was in greater America.

Across the lobby, Dave saw his dear friend John Lewis. They waved but John was whisked away by others, and they never got a chance to talk.

"Well, look who's here," the Senator said when he saw Dave. "We missed you in Oregon. Can't call you a leprechaun—what's the Swedish equivalent? A troll? You're my lucky troll."

Under a thick mop of hair, Bobby's blue eyes sparkled in a tanned and healthy face, but the bags under his eyes revealed fatigue. When he shook Dave's hand, Dave noticed scratches on his hands and forearms from people reaching out to him during campaign motorcades.

Ethel Kennedy nodded and pecked Dave on the cheek.

"How was the graduation for Miss Apple Pie?" The Senator asked.

Ethel grimaced. "Her name is Angie, in case you forgot."

The Senator ignored her. As he moved to greet another staffer, he reminded Dave over his shoulder, "We're set for another train ride tomorrow. Be sure you're there."

Following the tracks of the Southern Pacific, the campaign train traversed the San Joaquin Valley from Fresno to Madera to Merced to Modesto to Stockton and finally reached the state capitol of Sacramento. Dust devils kicked up from the fields and the orchards as the late May temperature spiked to 90 degrees. The crowds didn't mind. "Viva Kennedy" reverberated through the rapturous throngs of Hispanic farm workers. When he reached down into the adoring crowds, his cuff links disappeared, and his hands became red with scratch marks. All for a touch of the messianic hero.

At every stop, the Senator spoke of peace, justice, and inequality and how much America needed her farmers and how the farmers needed a champion in the White House. Each speech concluded with the George Bernard Shaw quote, "Some men see things as they are and ask why. I see things that never were and ask why not."

Later in the week, Dave reprised his role as chauffeur, piloting a big red convertible through the Los Angeles crowds with the candidate standing in the back. Aides held his legs as he leaned into the throng to allow his adoring followers to touch his hands. The rapturous crowds cheered and laughed and visibly shed tears. Disheveled young women with lipstick smeared and hair mussed jogged alongside the convertible.

With hindsight, Bobby's Oregon strategy of campaigning against Humphrey while ignoring McCarthy had been a mistake. By narrowly winning, McCarthy's candidacy survived, and the sense of Kennedy invincibility tarnished. Reluctantly, the Kennedy campaign in California agreed to a televised debate with McCarthy. Although Bobby did great with the personal touch of the crowd, Gene's strength was his dignified and cerebral television presence. He appeared calm, and he spoke coherently, appealing to reason rather than emotion. Thus, it was risky for Bobby to agree to a televised debate.

Half a dozen volunteers crowded into Dave's hotel room to watch nervously. When the moderator asked McCarthy about domestic issues, he stumbled.

"Fucking A, Man," someone gushed. "He's only a one-pony candidate, and he just pissed himself."

Even when given an opening to criticize Kennedy, McCarthy balked.

"See, he's weak. Nixon would crucify him. People will see he isn't a serious candidate."

Post-debate polling agreed. The pollsters and the pundits suggested a clear Kennedy win, and momentum was on his side as election day neared.

Dave and Esteban watched the early returns from their hotel room. McCarthy took the early lead.

"Where are these returns coming from?" Dave asked, pacing the room, but as the ballot counting continued, Bobby moved into the lead.

"Hey, look that!" Esteban said, clapping his hands.

The results of the South Dakota primary scrolled across the screen showing a smashing victory for Kennedy over both McCarthy and LBJ, who now served as the Humphrey surrogate.

"That's the state where Humphrey was born," Dave said. "I'll take this as an omen."

A TV reporter approached a young woman in the crowd at McCarthy headquarters. With a microphone in his right hand, he held his earpiece in his ear with the forefinger of his left hand and spoke over the murmur of the crowd; he asked her:

"If McCarthy loses, what happens to your political life?"

"Well, if Gene McCarthy loses," she said with a grudging smile. "I'll have to vote for Kennedy."

"Yes!" Dave bellowed. "That's it exactly. That's how the convention delegates will see it. They have to."

When the vote count reached 50%, Kennedy maintained his lead.

"If we can hold on, that's four out the five primaries Bobby competed in, besting McCarthy and Humphrey surrogates in each one," Dave said. "Damn, I wish we could have pulled it out in Oregon. It would be over."

The vote count reached 60%, and the solid Kennedy lead persisted.

"I'm going down," Dave said. "I'm going to check the crowd in the ballroom." Esteban followed.

The TV showed a festive crowd, brimming with anticipation, but the television cameras failed to catch the pulsating energy. With each new vote count displayed on the screen the intensity grew. The ballroom rocked as optimism swelled.

"Let's go upstairs and see how it's going with the big shots," Esteban shouted into Dave's ear. Dave nodded.

The Kennedy suite was already full, and Dave and Esteban crowded in. Bobby sat calmly waiting, but with a broad smile. For the last few days, the faces of senior aides barely masked their anxiety, but now they all appeared relieved. Finally, around midnight, the networks called the race. It was close, but Bobby won. They had done it. Bobby had done it. The nomination was clearly in their grasp and beyond that the presidency. When Bobby stood up, the Red Sea parted, and he exited the room to make his way to the ballroom and his victory speech. The aides followed with Dave and Esteban in the rear.

From the back edge of the podium next to the door to the kitchen, Dave sensed the fever pitch of unrestrained joy in the ballroom crowd of rich and poor; old and young;

white, brown, and black; male and female. It was John Lewis' beloved community. It was as if the riots and looting, the police beatings and the violence of white racists, the poverty, the racial prejudice, the disaster of the war, even the assassination of MLK were behind them. History pointed toward this moment. A new dawn was breaking. It felt like the promise of America, the ideals of America, the hopes of America came true in this instant, a singular, rapturous moment in time.

Cries of "RFK, RFK, RFK" reverberated off the ceiling. Bobby finished his speech by flashing thumbs up and a peace sign.

"Thanks to all of you, and on to Chicago and let's win there."

****

Prehistoric apes lumbered around the movie screen as a Richard Strauss musical score filled the crowded theater in a scene that came to be known as "the dawn of man." Driven by pounding timpani, the music crescendoed as an ape discovered the use of a dry bone as a weapon; when the primate committed the first murder, a man in the audience stood and wailed with shoulders convulsing. Soon, attendants removed the man and the woman at his side who could not console him.

Angie thought the summertime blockbuster movie, *2001: A Space Odyssey*, would be a diversion for Dave, a respite from his melancholy. It was therapeutic but not as she expected. She hoped for gentle healing, but she got a cathartic explosion.

"They murdered him," he sobbed.

"I know, sweet boy, I know."

"He won the California primary, and he was going to be president, but he died."

"Yes, Yes," she said, running her hands through his hair and wiping away his tears.

Gradually, he calmed, and then he talked for the first time since the blood of Senator Kennedy splattered over him in the kitchen of the Ambassador Hotel.

"Chaos erupted," Dave said, looking away. "Blood everywhere. Shouts and screams."

A silent moment passed as Angie squeezed his hand.

"I have this dream, every night," he continued as he sucked in deep breaths. "I see a pistol in the crowd, and I lunge for the faceless man with the gun, tackling him to the floor before he could squeeze off a shot. I pummel him in the face, and my bloody knuckles match the bleeding face of the gunman."

"Bobby Kennedy slides his hands under my armpits and lifts me to my feet. 'Thank you, my lucky young troll,' he says. 'You saved my life.'"

"'It was an honor, Mr. President,' I say as I notice the blood all over my shirt."

He choked on his words and then turned to face Angie.

"And then I awake, confused and despairing. What is truth and what is fantasy? The adulation of the crowd, cheering a decisive victory that opened the door to the nomination and election as president? That was just a bitter memory, and tomorrow will not be as hope promised."

As the sun set and the last glitter of sun on roughened water faded, they lingered in the driveway at the lake cabin,

Dave was talked out, and they sat silently in the car, soaking in the dusk.

Chapter Twenty-one

Beans pinched the motorcade clipping sent by Big Jimmie between his thumb and pointing finger. He set it afire with his Zippo lighter, holding it until the flame burned his fingers. He did the same with the Dear Beans letter from Angie and the Perfesser. He canceled his request for Hawaii and put in for R&R in Bangkok, Thailand, the favorite destination for a week of boozing and whoring. Processing his request would take at least a month.

Meanwhile, Beans' platoon continued to provide security for the roadside firebase. Two-man teams would climb a ladder to one of three elevated guard towers around the perimeter in a monotonous pattern of four hours on and eight hours off. Sandbag walls under a sheet metal roof provided ample space for radio, M-60 machine gun, and ammo. Truth be told, the watchtowers were little more than observation platforms overlooking fencing, concertina wire, and several hundred meters of open ground cleared of trees and brush. The elevated towers would be easy targets for shoulder-fired rocket propelled grenades, but there was no strategic reason for the NVA to attack the roadside firebase, and that, more than anything, kept the firebase safe.

At 0800, Dozer and Jonesy climbed the ladder to replace Beans and Frankie.

"Hurry up, and you can still catch breakfast."

Frankie went straight to the mess tent, but Beans carried their M-16s and other gear to deposit in their barracks. The daily poker game was getting organized, and

Jimi Hendrix wailed *All along the Watchtower* in the background.

The weathervane atop the mess tent caught his eye. He hadn't really noticed it before, and it took a couple of glances to figure out that the ornament was a joker, like you would see in a deck of cards, and the joker's wand pointed toward the wind. He watched that joker dance and spin. First the wand pointed west. Then the damn thing spun around and pointed north.

"Take yer medicine," the medic said standing at the doorway to the mess tent, handing out the daily dose of malaria pills.

Beans kept one eye on that spinning joker while he tossed down a little pellet and a tablet the size of a horse pill. A dust devil kicked up sand that stung his face, and when he wiped his eyes, the joker now pointed east. The wind blew where it would, and Beans was still puzzling over that joker when the mess crew filled his tray with scrambled eggs and bacon, but with the first sips of steaming black coffee, his mind moved on.

"There's still a seat open," someone at the card table invited him when he returned to the barracks.

Beans decided to join the poker game instead of crawling into his bunk for a nap. Hard to sleep with Hendrix blaring from a Panasonic cassette player.

Some days, luck is against you, and you'd be better off just walking away, but how do you know when that is? What if your luck is about to turn? Beans had been playing for about an hour and his chips were slowly dwindling, but this hand looked damn good, and he figured this was his chance to get ahead.

The game was five-card stud, and Beans' hole card was the ace of spades. The dealer dealt the ace of clubs for his up card giving him a pair of bullets.

"High card bets," the dealer said, looking at Beans.

House rules for the running poker game in the barracks allowed two-dollar limits and three raises per round. If Beans bet two bucks, he guessed he would win the pot right there, but it needed to grow a bit first. He didn't want to chase everyone out.

"Open for fifty cents," Beans said, and he flipped in a red chip.

"Fold."

"Fold."

The two guys to his left dropped out.

"Call," the next guy flipped in a red chip. His up card was the six of diamonds.

"Raise," said a stranger to Beans, a new arrival at the firebase, and he tossed in a red chip for the original bet and two blue chips for a two-dollar raise.

Judging by the peach fuzz on his cheeks, the fucking new guy (FNG) hadn't shaved in a couple of days, but he could probably manage a few more without any problems. He wore fatigue pants bloused over combat boots, but no shirt covered his pale, hairless chest or the dog tags that dangled from his neck. He had been winning that day, but it seemed to Beans that he overplayed his cards, and the jaunty tilt of his bush hat said he was prepared to gamble. The deuce of spades that was his up card wasn't very impressive. Why'd he raise? Must have a pair of deuces, but that wouldn't beat Beans' aces.

"I'm out," the next guy around the table said, and the bet moved to the dealer.

"I fold," the dealer said as he flipped over his up card, the deuce of diamonds, which was a key card if Beans' hunch was right that the FNG held a pair of deuces.

It was back to Beans, and he thought about re-raising, but he slow played that sucker and just called, and the six of diamonds called also. Three players remained in the hand.

"Eight, no help," the dealer said as he dealt the eight of clubs to go with Beans' face-up ace. He offered running commentary as he dealt the cards.

"Ten, no help."

"Nine, no help," the dealer said as he dealt the nine of hearts to go with the FNG's black deuce.

"Your ace is still high card. Ace bets," the dealer said to Beans.

"Two bucks," Beans said, throwing in a pair of blue chips. If they both folded now, that would be alright.

"I'm out," the six of diamonds said as he turned over his up cards.

"Make it four," the FNG said.

Beans was surprised when the FNG raised him again. With a deuce and a nine off suit showing, he had diddly, but he raised anyway. His ass was grass.

"Make it six," Beans said.

"Might as well make it eight."

The FNG made the last raise of the round.

On Fourth Street, another face-up card, Beans drew the nine of diamonds, and the FNG drew a jack, but it didn't matter; he kept raising Beans' raises as if he had a joker in the hole, but they didn't play with jokers. It was again an eight-dollar round.

The last card was dealt down, and Beans drew the eight of spades giving him two pair, aces over eights, the so-called dead man's hand. They say that was the hand Wild Bill Hickok was holding in Deadwood when he got shot in the back, but Beans was happy to draw that eight. The only way the FNG could beat him would be to suck out, and that's just what he did. His luck continued to run hot and Beans' cold.

Just like Beans suspected, the FNG had been raising all along on a fucking pair of deuces. A third deuce had been face-up in the dealer's hand so there was only one deuce left in the deck. Only the case deuce could win the hand for him, but that's what the FNG drew. The goddammed deuce of clubs! His trip deuces beat Beans' two pair.

Beans lost about fifty bucks in a little over an hour, most of it on that hand, and he walked away from the game. It wasn't Beans' day. Christ almighty, a pair of fucking deuces.

Beans had been sitting on a footlocker with his back against the wall, and the FNG was straight across, with his back to the aisle, and the guys had to stand up to let Beans out. Playing cards plastered the barracks wall behind him; every time a new deck was opened, someone pinned the jokers onto the barracks wall. As Beans stood up, one of the figures caught his eye. It was the same goddammed joker of the weathervane atop the mess tent; up close Beans could see the hideous laugh pasted on the sprite's face. It seemed like that son-of-a-bitch pointed his wand straight at Beans.

"I need a beer," Beans said as the Jimi Hendrix Watchtower song recycled over and over.

The card game was in the center of the barracks between a pair of bunks that butted up against the wall. It was an extra wide space where the running poker game went on day after day. Players would come and go, but the game rolled on.

Beans poked his head into an adjacent AO, the "area of operations" shared by three permanent residents of the firebase. They had arranged their bunks to create a room, two bunks perpendicular to the wall and one parallel to it along the outside of the AO. The mosquito netting that draped down over the bunks provided walls and a little privacy. Courtesy of the PX at Camp Enari, they boasted a minifridge, a Panasonic cassette player, and a couple of beach chairs, all lined up against the barracks wall. Beans plopped a dollar down on the fridge and cracked open a cold one, and the suds ran down his hand and dripped in the dust. One of the guys was reading the Bible, and he had the annoying habit of mouthing the words out loud. "No one has power over the wind to restrain the wind, or power over the day of death; there is no discharge from the battle ... all is vanity and a chasing after wind."

Just then, an M-16 burst rang out from one of the watchtowers, and everyone scrambled, but word soon came that a guard merely shot a passing dog. The card game rolled on, and Jimi Hendrix continued to wail about jokers, thieves, and howling wind.

The FNG continued playing his cards aggressively and continued winning. Some days are like that, when luck is on your side, and you played it for all it was worth because it could turn on you just like that.

Around noon, most of the crowd departed for chow at the mess hall, including a couple of guys at the poker table, but others joined the game, and the FNG stayed in place. His luck hadn't turned yet, and no way would he surrender the charmed seat.

Damn, it was hot. It was always sweltering in the central highlands of Vietnam, but it seemed especially prickly that noonday. Like a stalking beast holding its breath, the wind that couldn't make up its mind all day now hesitated altogether, and no breeze filtered through the screen windows of the mess hall. Tall clear glasses filled with ice and cherry Kool-Aid sweated droplets of water that looked like blood streaking down the sides. Beans lifted the cold surface to his forehead, and then he sucked on an ice cube. By the time he finished the macaroni and cheese and boiled hot dogs slathered in mustard, Dozer and Jonesy arrived after their guard shift.

"What the fuck, Dozer?" someone jeered. "You afraid of stray mutts?"

"Hell, yes, it was me what lit up that fuckin' mongrel," Dozer admitted, still carrying his M-16. "I thought it was a wolf."

"Shit, ain't no wolves in the Nam."

Beans returned to the barracks, and laid down in his bunk, but sleep didn't come. Loud voices announced that Dozer returned to the barracks and was taking shit for shooting that hound. Beans poked his head out and looked toward the poker game. Dozer was there, talking loud and fast, gesturing with his M-16 held by the pistol grip in one hand as he defended gunning down the wandering canine that wasn't a wolf.

A gust of wind blasted through the barracks from the open door on one end and slammed the door on the other, and Beans felt a chill as the breeze rushed past. Suddenly, his gut told him something wasn't right. A colored stencil pasted on the black stock of the forward hand guard of Dozer's M-16 pulled Beans' eyes in. What he saw told him that the luck of the poker playing FNG was about to run out, and Beans' jaw dropped open to shout a warning. The stenciled joker with the haunting grin danced on that stock as Dozer carelessly waved the M-16 muzzle right behind the head of the FNG. In that moment, Beans knew that the M-16 was loaded with a full clip; in that moment, he knew that the safety was switched to rock and roll; in that moment, he knew that his adrenaline-intoxicated buddy was about to accidentally squeeze the trigger; but Beans' scream was drowned out by the burst of four or five rounds.

The FNG slumped forward onto the poker table, and red, white, and blue poker chips scattered. The back of his head was gone, and his blood splattered the jokers tacked to the far wall.

Some asshole said, "War is hell." True enough, but it's also absurd, cruel, and unforgiving. And ironic. Dozer thought he saw a wolf, shot a dog, but it was a comrade whose head was blown off. The FNG is dead, and Dozer's soul is forever wounded.

For several hours, the barracks swelled with the comings and goings of higher-ups, medics, MPs who escorted Dozer away, and who knows who, but Beans cleared out. He grabbed his poncho, poncho liner, a beach chair, a carton of Kools, a jug of Kentucky whiskey, and a transistor radio. He intended to spend the night under the stars in the patch of tall grass outside the barracks, but there were no stars, only dull gray clouds scudding across the sky, roiled by a growling wind. He sucked on Kools chased with slugs of bourbon and listened to his blaring transistor radio.

In the middle of the night, the clouds spit out a sprinkle, and he pulled his poncho over his head and slouched down in the beach chair and fell asleep. When the rising sun warmed his stiff body, and the sky glowed yellow in the east, he trudged back to the barracks for another hour of sleep before roll call.

Chapter Twenty-two

Dave never registered for summer classes, and he was short of cash. Much like the previous summer, he took a job painting houses for Frank Nelson, the local painter in Kalmar. At least the cathartic experience of *2001: A Space Odyssey* raised Dave out of the dumps enough to go to work for Frank, but he sure wasn't his normal upbeat self. Listless. His mother hid her worry, but his dad was openly critical. Although he should have been pleased that Dave had returned to work, he offered a sarcastic dig.

"House painter, huh? I guess your flirtation with the Democrats has sapped your ambition. I never expected you'd be a college dropout after only a year and a half. Maybe it's time to rethink your priorities and your friends."

Dave didn't respond; he lacked the energy to engage his father. He simply walked through the living room and climbed the stairs to his bedroom. He flipped on his transistor radio, plopped onto his bed, and stared at the ceiling.

"Come down for supper." Meg called to her son, and he joined his parents at the kitchen table. They ate in silence.

When Dave finished, he asked, "Can I borrow your car? I'm going to pick up Angie and shoot some hoops in the gym."

His dad merely grunted, but his mom said, "Take your father's Oldsmobile and fill it with gas. Your dad is heading to Minneapolis first thing in the morning before the station opens."

"Shit! That's Beans' dad," Angie said as Dave pulled the Oldsmobile up to the pumps. A red pickup with the hood up was on the opposite side. Angie slouched down.

Clarence Pfeffer owned a meager farm, but except for a few hogs and chickens, he no longer farmed the land, renting it out instead. He earned a living by trucking livestock to the slaughterhouses on the banks of the Mississippi just south of St. Paul where meat packers sliced up over a thousand head of hogs, cattle, and sheep an hour, turning out beef steaks, lard, canned chili, mutton, hides, or fertilizer. The stockyards put burgers and bacon on American plates.

An advertising jingle from Armour Meat Packing, one of the major stockyards of South St. Paul, flashed across Dave's consciousness. He couldn't help it. Seeing Clarence Pfeffer always triggered the ear worm about all the kids who eat Armour hot dogs.

Clarence Pfeffer was tall and angular like his son, but with gray hair peeking from beneath a faded Minnesota Twins baseball cap and salt and pepper stubble over a square jaw. He had apparently finished his daily job as a livestock truck driver to a South St. Paul stockyard as he wore coveralls stained with cattle manure. The stench of the slaughterhouse clung to him and so too the rough culture of the cowboys, packers, and stockmen.

Clarence poked the metal spout through the lid of a quart of motor oil and inserted it into the oil pan opening. After the quart can glugged empty, he replaced the cap, pulled the spout out of the can, and threw the can in the garbage. Only then did he glance at Dave.

"Hello, Clarence," Dave said.

Dave always got along ok with Beans' dad. Dave's first overnight at a friend's house in grade school had been at the Pfeffer farmstead. It was an uncomfortable night because Dave had to pee, but there was only an outdoor biffy and no bathroom in the house, and the chamber pot at the head of the stairs intimidated young Dave.

Mr. Pfeffer barely nodded.

"Seems I need to fill this old beater with oil more regularly than I need to fill up with gas," Clarence said as he wiped his hands with a paper towel.

He gestured by lifting his chin toward the Oldsmobile. "Don't s'pose you have that problem with that fancy Olds."

"Say, what's your Republican dad say about you galivanting around with the Democrats? Don't matter to me. There's not a dime's worth of difference between the two parties. What 'merica needs is someone who says what's on everyone's mind. Fuck the war. Fuck the n ... s. Fuck the pointy-headed liberals in Washington."

His eye slits narrowed and focused on Dave. "Fuck the hippies. Especially, fuck the hippies."

He tossed the paper towel in the garbage. "The guvmint needs to stop wasting our goddammed tax dollars worrying about slanty eyes overseas. It's just pissing money down a rat hole."

Dave could tell that Mr. Pfeffer was riled up about Beans and the war, but that was just the starting point for his grievances. Dave didn't take the bait. Best to cut and run before Clarence got around to Beans and Angie and all that.

"Good to see you, Clarence. I gotta go."

Clarence slammed the hood shut and then the door behind him as he ascended to the driver's seat. The engine fired up with a raucous splutter, and Clarence ground the gears before speeding away, as much as the old Ford could do.

"George Wallace? Isn't he the redneck governor from down south?" Angie asked as she pointed to the sticker attached to the rear bumper of the red pickup.

"Sheeit!" Dave exhaled a deep breath. "He's a racist presidential candidate from Georgia or Mississippi; no, I think Alabama. Why he's running for president, I don't know. He's got no chance."

As Dave put the Olds in gear and turned toward the high school, he wondered out loud, "Why the hell does Clarence have a George Wallace bumper sticker on his pickup?"

The basketball felt familiar and reassuring in his hands. He was alone in the cavernous old gym, and each bounce echoed off the cement block walls. His first shot fell a couple of feet short of the rim. Two years of rust since he had starred as a high school basketballer on this court. It didn't take long to recalibrate, and soon his jump shot was falling.

Swish. Swish.

He dribbled hard and fast from one end to the other and laid the ball softly off the glass before sprinting back to the other end. In his sleep, he often dreamt a dream, a flying fantasy where he soared high and slammed the ball two-handed through the rim, something he could never do for real. Dreaming of dunking the basketball was control, order, and well-being.

He hadn't dreamt that dream lately.

"See that basket, see that rim, come on Dave, roll it in!"

Angie teased from the bleachers. She repeated the ditty the cheerleaders chanted when Dave or a teammate dribbled the ball at the free throw line, gathering themselves and finding their rhythm for their shot. Breathing, bouncing, bending the knees. 1966 made sense then. Harmony, Equilibrium. Congruence. Hope. Optimism. Were better days ahead or merely behind? 1968 wasn't sure.

Dave took one final shot before departing with Angie. *Clank.*

Frank Nelson the house painter was an alcoholic, and that cost him a career as a college professor. Born and raised in Chicago, he came to Kalmar many years earlier to live with his grandparents and to dry out after he lost his professorship in the political science department of Northwestern University. His grandfather taught him house painting; it suited him, and he remained sober over the years, most of the time. He became somewhat of an elder statesman in the community and a white-haired eminence at Kalmar Lutheran Church. The Sunday School kids called him the "candy man" because he handed out hard candy wrapped in cellophane in exchange for a smile. An ardent fan of the high school teams, Dave was a favorite.

Cocking his bushy right eyebrow, he looked sideways at Dave as they drove to the jobsite.

"You gonna watch the Republican Convention?" Frank asked.

"Maybe. My dad has been pushing it. He thinks he can convert me back to the Republicans—at least to Governor Rockefeller. Rocky's in, he's out, and then he's in again. Despite my dad's hope, he doesn't really have a chance, does he?"

"You could do worse, but you're probably right, he won't get the nomination even though his poll numbers are good. He's more popular with Democrats than Republicans. He's a throwback, the last of a dying breed of liberal Republicans. It's like he's running a protest campaign, a last-ditch effort to preserve the party of Lincoln that is slipping into subtle and sometimes overt racism. Instead of succumbing to the inclination to use civil rights as a wedge issue, Rockefeller doubled down on LBJ's Great Society. Rockefeller proposed *increasing* the commitment to rebuilding American cities. As Nixon cries law and order, Rocky replies 'To keep law and order there must be justice and opportunity.'"

"If my dad believes that, why can't he shake his Republican label and join the Democrats?"

"Tribalism. Your dad understands the Republicans to be the home team, his team, but cut him some slack about his attitude toward the war."

Dave wrinkled his brow and looked quizzically at Frank. "What?"

"Your folks' generation did a brave and noble thing by defeating the Nazis and the Japanese warlords at great personal and national sacrifice. Your Mom's brother died in *their* war as I'm sure you know. There was great moral certainty about *their* war. Coming out of WWII, America viewed itself optimistically as can-do and self-sacrificing— a generous and compassionate leader of the world and protector of democracy. Add to that the threats posed by the totalitarian Soviets and the loss by our friends, the Chinese Nationalists, to the Chinese Communists, and you can understand the pre-conceived notions that folks of their generation bring to the current questions surrounding *your* war."

Dave shook his head. "I thought you were against *my* war."

"Of course, I am, but you need to understand how others think, including your dad. As *your* Mr. Dylan says, 'the times they are a-changin'. Don't be too hard on your dad and others who don't see the change as you and I do."

A few miles passed under the tires on Frank's pickup before Dave spoke again.

"Tell me about Nixon," Dave finally asked. "What makes him tick?"

"Tricky Dick is shrewd and devious. He senses fear and turns that to his advantage. Ever heard the word 'pinko?' It was a scary word, for a time, that Nixon used to gin up fear."

Frank drummed his fingers on the steering wheel, delighting in the conversation; he knew that Dave would be a safe audience to hear his liberal views, which wasn't always the case in the Kalmar community. He may have lost his professorship years earlier, but his keen interest in history and politics never waned.

"After the Second World War, fear of the Soviet Union and communist infiltration of American institutions bordered on hysteria. Senator Joe McCarthy was the extreme example with his red-baiting speeches in which he bragged he had a list of communists in the State Department. The House Un-American Activities Committee ruined lives and careers with their trumped-up witch hunts into left-leaning Hollywood types. In 1948, Nixon kicked off his political career by appealing to the same fears, and he won election to Congress by falsely accusing his opponent, an incumbent Democratic Congressman, of communist ties. When he ran for the Senate two years later, it was even worse, adding misogyny and antisemitism to his redbaiting by calling his female opponent who was married to a Jew the 'Pink Lady right down to her underwear.' That 1950 campaign was one of the most hate-filled in history. Nixon learned how to effectively use dirty tricks to hype up the fears people had of Jews, of women leaders, of Soviet and Chinese Communism, and the liberals that he demonized as 'pinkos.'"

Frank chuckled and added, "During the 1960 campaign, the public perceived Kennedy to be stronger against communism. Nixon was galled as hell."

Frank turned into a driveway and parked next to the scaffolding raised earlier.

"Fear of being seen as weak on communism explains the mess we're in. Cold War inertia. For two decades, the Democrats bristled at being labelled as soft on communism. During his first term as a US Senator from Texas a generation earlier, LBJ witnessed first-hand the beatdown President Truman suffered when China fell to Mao and the communists. LBJ was determined not to lose Southeast

Asia to the communists, and he expanded the war effort rather than cutting and running when it became obvious that the corrupt South Vietnamese government was unable and unwilling to go it alone."

Dave climbed atop the scaffolding. Frank muttered to himself as he mixed paint in the back of the pickup. From the neck up, Frank looked the part of an academic with a full mop of thick, white hair over steely blue eyes framed by wire-rimmed glasses, but the white, paint-stained, bib overalls belied his poli sci background. He was *sui generis,* Kalmar's one of a kind painter-academic who seldom, but occasionally, went on a bender.

The day passed quickly. For the first time in weeks, Dave's mind turned over and over with thoughts of politics, and he was anxious to hear more from the former poli sci professor during the return drive at the end of the day. Frank was also eager to continue the discussion, and he started right off as he wheeled the pickup out of the driveway and onto the highway.

"I know your generation may not want to hear it but let me put in a good word for President Johnson. He's a tragic figure straight out of Shakespeare with domestic accomplishments to rival Lincoln and FDR but whose political fate and legacy will be defined by his wrong-headed decisions in Vietnam. He took a great risk leading up to the 1964 election by pushing civil rights. He succeeded in passing the Civil Rights Act of 1964 that prohibits discrimination on the basis of race, color, religion, sex or national origin. It was monumental legislation, followed by his landslide victory over Goldwater that fall and the Voting Rights Act of 1965, an equally monumental piece of legislation. If Lincoln freed the slaves, LBJ got black Americans the right to vote. If FDR got us Social Security, LBJ got us Medicare and Medicaid. If FDR got working folks home loan guarantees through the FHA, Johnson got the Fair Housing Act that eliminated discrimination in home ownership and in loan applications. He worked hand and glove with the leaders of the civil rights movement, especially Martin Luther King, Jr., and they rightly saw him as the greatest White House ally of black Americans since Abraham Lincoln. Tragically, the flawed hero who braved the wrath of his own southern Democrats over civil rights, succumbed to crippling fear of red-baiting foreign policy hawks. Of course, King broke with Johnson over Vietnam, and that exemplifies the tragic turn when LBJ reluctantly acceded to the request of Commanding General Westmoreland to send ground troops to Vietnam. Once that was done, the course was set, and the generals wanted more and more. Johnson supposedly said he hoped that he had better generals than Lincoln did in the Civil War, but history will show the bitter hollowness in the advice he received from Westmoreland and the upper echelon of the military, Secretary of State Dean Rusk, and Secretary of Defense Robert McNamara."

Dave vaguely knew all that, and it was true that his generation demonized Johnson over Vietnam. *Hey, hey, LBJ, how many kids did you kill today.*

"Unless McCarthy works a miracle, Vice President Humphrey will be the candidate of the Democrats," Frank said, changing the subject. "What will be the biggest campaign issue between now and November?"

Dave shrugged. "The war?"

"If that's the case, what are the conflicting policy positions?"

Dave shrugged again.

"Right answer. Who knows? The Johnson administration, and therefore Humphrey, are pushing the peace talks in Paris, and Nixon promises an honorable end to the war, whatever the hell that means. Even more ambiguously, he claims a secret plan to end the war. Neither side wants to appear weak but both parties are also aware that the American public is fed up with the war."

"At least the Democrats are trying to get the Paris peace talks underway. I'm not so sure Nixon has the same hopes for the negotiations. The worst thing that could happen to the Nixon campaign is that peace breaks out before the election."

Dave stared out the window at the passing corn fields with stalks higher than a tall man. The healthy tassels on top suggested a strong harvest, but he barely noticed. He was listening intently to Frank.

"Don't get me wrong," Frank said. "The war is *the* issue in the sense that voters will punish the Democratic incumbency because the public is dissatisfied, but the war will not be an issue based upon competing policy positions of the parties. The election's effect on the future conduct of the war is uncertain. Twenty years of anti-Communist momentum will continue to carry us forward on the same path until someone figures out how to lose while declaring victory. My guess is that a Humphrey victory will lead to stepped up peace talks but with an uncertain outcome and war continuing in the meantime, while a Nixon victory will mean more of the same. A Nixon victory will be ironic—

the electorate wants the war to end and may oust the incumbent Democrats because it hasn't, but a Nixon victory will only prolong the foolishness."

Frank's voice dropped to a whisper. "Let me tell you a secret. The consequential issue this year is race."

Dave turned to face Frank with a "tell-me-more" look, and suddenly his conversations with John Lewis flooded into his thoughts.

"Will America continue down the path toward racial justice, or will there be retrenchment against the Civil Rights Act, the Voting Rights Act, and the Fair Housing Act--the singular accomplishments of the Johnson administration? Nixon, the evil genius, senses fear in white America following summertime ghetto riots, and he'll use that fear to his advantage. George Wallace will be Nixon's useful idiot. He'll gin up white fears. He'll threaten to drive a car over protesters. He'll rant, 'segregation today . . . segregation tomorrow . . . segregation forever.' But in the end, white moderates will reject Wallace's overt racism and prefer the veiled dog whistle of Nixon. The most important political slogan this year will be 'law and order,' and white America will hear that as clamping down on black unrest."

The image of the Wallace bumper sticker on Clarence Pfeffer's rusty red pickup jumped into his thoughts, but Dave still wondered why Clarence would follow a southern segregationist. Race issues certainly weren't an issue in lily-white Kalmar.

"You know," Dave said, "my roommate in Indianapolis was a veteran of civil rights skirmishes in the south, and he bemoaned the violent turn of civil rights protests. His name was John Lewis. Maybe you've heard of him?"

"I think so. Wasn't he the young man who got his head smashed leading the Selma march?"

"That's him. Like Dr. King, John believes in non-violence, and he fears the rise of militant black protest will be counterproductive."

"Do you remember the Watts riots?" Frank asked.

"Not really. Summer of '65, right? Heading into my senior year, my mind was definitely somewhere else."

"It started with a traffic stop of a black man for drunk driving in a black slum of Los Angeles. When he resisted, a fight with the police broke out. Six days later, dozens were dead, thousands were arrested, property was looted and burned, and thousands of national guardsmen were called in to quell the violence. Without considering the black frustration over unemployment or poverty, the LA police chief slammed the "young hoodlums" who broke the law. White America largely agreed. Suddenly, LBJ's "Great Society" didn't look so great."

Frank wheeled his pickup into the Karlstad driveway.

"But Watts was merely a foretaste of what was to come. After King's assassination, violence in black ghettos played out on TV screens across America. Baltimore. Washington DC. Cincinnati. Kansas City. Protesting led to rioting. Rioting led to looting and vandalism. Shops on fire. National Guard troops mobilized. White Americans scared shitless. Gun sales skyrocketing."

The drive was over, and Frank dropped Dave at his parent's house. The Perfesser thanked the professor for an enlightening conversation, and then he encountered his father in the living room.

"Look at this crap," Harv said, pointing at the TV screen and the Cronkite news on CBS.

Not only did the war in Vietnam play out on the evening news, so did the gun battle in a black neighborhood in Cleveland. For four hours on a hot summer night, black nationalists exchanged gunfire with the Cleveland Police Department. Three policemen, three suspects, and a bystander were killed. Over a dozen others were wounded. It didn't help public reaction that the recently elected Cleveland mayor was a black man.

The ink was barely dry on momentous legislation: civil rights, voting rights, housing rights. The War on Poverty and the Great Society. Martin Luther King Jr. died a violent death. Bobby Kennedy, too. America's embrace of civil rights was also on life support, grievously wounded in a black LA slum and now a hail of bullets flying between black nationalists and a white police force.

Irony can be cruel. A white racist murdered the leader of the civil rights movement, sparking a chain of events that elevated race-baiting politicians. For every action, there is a reaction. And then a counter action. After King's assassination, black ghettos burst aflame, kindling fears in white Americans. Politicians like Nixon and Wallace fanned the flames. The conflagration threatened to consume the civil rights movement, liberals, hippies, homosexuals, and bra-burning feminists.

Law and order.

Dave passed through the living room and went straight to his bedroom. He stripped, showered, and put on clean clothes. He awaited supper laying on his bed and listening to his transistor radio.

Earlier that afternoon, Harv slathered mustard and mayo on white bread sandwiched around thick slices of Meg's leftover ham and yellow American cheese singles. In too great a hurry, he popped the cap of a bottle of Grain Belt Premium, and he licked the suds that overflowed onto his wrist. Meg attended a ladies' circle meeting at the Kalmar Lutheran Church, and Dave hadn't returned from a long day painting houses with Frank. Harv switched on the TV and settled into his easy chair to savor the Republican Convention in Miami Beach. He was hopeful but not optimistic for moderate New York Governor Nelson Rockefeller on the left; dismissive of conservative California Governor Ronald Reagan on the right; and resigned to the warmed-over "New Nixon" in the middle. An acquaintance from Lion's Club conventions served with the Minnesota delegation, and he assured Harv that the Minnesota delegation would be supportive of late-comer Rockefeller who joined the race after Michigan Governor George Romney's candidacy flamed out.

When Dave passed through an hour later, he commented, "I don't see any color in a crowd of pasty-faced folks with straight teeth."

Talking heads speculated that Rockefeller and Reagan would make strange bed fellows in an effort to keep Nixon from securing the nomination on the first ballot, but when it was apparent that the strong man from the south, Senator Strom Thurmond from South Carolina, would carry water for Nixon, it was all over except for the balloon drop and Nixon's acceptance speech. Thurmond was the same man who led the "Dixiecrats" out of the 1948 Democratic Convention twenty years earlier in response to Minneapolis Mayor Hubert Humphrey's civil rights speech. On the third night of the convention, the Minnesota delegation voted slightly in favor of Rockefeller over Nixon on the first ballot, but Harv's favorite finished a distant second and Reagan even farther back as Nixon squeezed out his coveted first ballot victory.

The midnight hour had passed when the votes were tallied, and Nixon ascended the podium to claim his victory by speaking to "the forgotten Americans—the non-shouters, the non-demonstrators. They are not racist or sick; they are not guilty of the crimes that plague the land."

His listeners understood who the shouters were, the demonstrators, the ones who whined about racism, the criminals behind ghetto riots. Be afraid. Be very afraid of those others.

Chapter Twenty-three

Another day, same old shit, only different.

The shadow of a low-flying helicopter skittered across flatland scrub brush, elephant grass, rice paddies, and water buffalo ranging around waterholes. Riding in a Huey with his ass on the steel floor and his feet dangling was old hat for Beans. He kicked his legs, and the ground shadow responded in kind. This ride lacked the adrenalin-laced tension of an insertion or the giddy relief of an extraction. The chopper merely provided transit from one firebase to another. The slick gradually tilted upward, leaving the plain and climbing across mountains, ravines, and triple canopy jungle. Funny, Beans never appreciated the rugged beauty of the harsh landscape until just now.

After providing security for the roadside firebase along Highway 19, Beans' platoon boarded three Huey helicopters for an airlift into the mountains where they would join the rest of Alpha Company on a remote hilltop firebase near the borders with Laos and Cambodia. As the birds approached their landing, the under-construction firebase appeared as a smear of reddish-brown mud surrounded by lush greenery. Ant-like humans scurried about their anthill chewing up the vegetation with chain saws.

After landing, Beans' platoon joined the rest of the company in defensive positions providing security for combat engineers, the worker ants. The engineers worked quickly to create an outpost in the wilderness. A grunting bulldozer plowed trenches for deep bunkers: defensive firing positions around the perimeter, a tactical operations center (headquarters), a communications center, and an aid station staffed by medics. Eventually, tents with low-lying sandbag walls would house a mess hall and barracks with rows of side-by-side bunks. Flying crane helicopters that looked like giant mosquitos with muscular rotors and an onboard crane capable of hoisting tons had delivered the bulldozer and continued offloading heavy material. The final delivery would be a battery of six 105 MM howitzers, light artillery weapons capable of reaching miles into the hidden valleys where the NVA slipped in men and material along the Ho Chi Minh trail.

The firebase along heavily travelled highway 19 boasted high civilization compared to this remote location deep in the mountains; nevertheless, Beans' platoon and the rest of Alpha Company expected continuing light guard duty with hot meals, a tent to keep the rain out, a bunk to sleep in, and hours of boring downtime. Boring is good.

The enlisted men of Beans' platoon eagerly assessed their new leader, a 2nd lieutenant to replace the asshole who had commanded the platoon previously. The enlisted men stayed together for a full tour of duty, but the officers rotated to rear echelon positions after a few months in the field. Lieutenant Farnsworth was a college grad with an officer's commission via ROTC. Even officers are FNG when they arrive in-country, but Farnsworth appeared to have his shit together.

"Hey, Beans," Frankie said. "The LT wants to see you."

"I've got a couple of orders for you, Pfeffer," Lieutenant Farnsworth said. "First, you've been promoted to E-5. Congratulations, Sergeant."

Sergeant. Sergeant Pfeffer. Had a nice ring to it.

"Second, your R&R to Bangkok has come through. You're scheduled to fly from Cam Ranh Bay next week. We'll put you on a slick back to base camp, and you'll have a couple days to get cleaned up and get your ass down to Cam Ranh Bay."

For several millennia, cavalry shock troops rode horses into battle. Soldiers mounted on fast, agile horses swept across battlefields, and scouts on horseback explored broad swaths of terrain. By the twentieth century, the day of the horse cavalry was over, replaced by ever more efficient armored vehicles—tanks and mechanized infantry. German Panzers and blitzkrieg tactics overran Europe, and the allies countered with Russian T34 tanks and American Sherman tanks. For Beans' war, the rugged terrain of the central highlands of Vietnam with a lack of clear battle lines inhibited the use of armor except in defensive modes.

Enter the ubiquitous Huey helicopter. Manned by a pilot, copilot, and a pair of door gunners on either side, the slicks had room for half a dozen foot soldiers with their rucksacks and weapons, even if it meant the men dangled their feet over the side as the countryside slipped below. Flying in formation, a dozen or more Hueys airlifted whole infantry companies into remote regions for combat assaults, search and rescue, or reconnaissance. Individual Hueys inserted small scout teams of LRRPs into postage stamp landing zones deep in the mountains and jungle and extracted them when the mission was complete or sooner if exposed. Huey Medivacs bearing a red cross on their nose served as airborne ambulances transporting the wounded to base camp hospitals. The steady *wump-wump* of Huey chopper blades reassured combat soldiers in the jungle awaiting support or rescue.

Except for the crew, Beans was alone for the flight back to base camp, but the bird had barely lifted off when it banked hard to the east, and a door gunner mouthed the words, "Detour. More passengers." Although the troops usually plopped right down on the steel floor, the door gunners prepared by unfolding the seats attached to the back wall. When the slick landed at another remote firebase, four blushing Donut Dollies gingerly climbed aboard, assisted with the gentlemanly hand of the door gunner.

There was little chance for small talk over the noise of the chopper blades, and the pilot thrilled his passengers with a joyride, showing off for the women in short white dresses adorned with Red Cross badges. Cresting a mountain range, the pilot dove his bird into a valley, gravity adding to the acceleration. Huey helicopters aren't nimble, and they lumber along like airborne deuce-and-a-halfs, but the pilot put his bird through its paces. Like a swooping nighthawk, the Huey abruptly flattened out its downward plunge just above a gurgling stream. For miles, the chopper curved along the meandering blue line until it suddenly careened upward like a roller coaster in front of a wide but not too tall waterfall. The women enjoyed being frightened, and one grabbed Beans' shoulder for balance with an embarrassed smile.

After Beans showered away the sweat and grime, he headed for the Red Cross Rec Center where the smiling Donut Dollies dispensed cookies and Kool-Aid. He figured that sharing a helicopter ride made him old friends with the Dollies. Like the soldiers, the Dollies expected a one-year tour of duty. Unlike the grunts, the Dollies volunteered for Vietnam, but their plastered-on smiles barely veiled their aloofness from the horny S.O.B.s who were thinking about their panties. It was like there was a sign on the door, "Look but don't touch."

That was part of it. But even more, the Dollies didn't risk becoming close to the soldier who might not return next week. Like the other females on the base--the nurses at the hospital--the Donut Dollies saw wounds they couldn't heal, and the innocent idealism that brought them here beat a strategic retreat.

Beans didn't hang around long. None of the women from the flight were there, and Beans would soon fly to Bangkok where female companionship would be easily attainable. All GIs in Vietnam received a weeklong R&R getaway out of country for "Rest and Recuperation." For some, it was I&I—"Intercourse and Intoxication."

Click.
Click.
Click.
With each revolution, the slow-moving ceiling fan in his hotel room registered a single click. Beans peered out the third-floor window down New Phetchaburi Road, aka the American Strip of Bangkok, Thailand. Neon signs flashed up and down the strip: *Rhapsody Bar, Flamingo,*

Copa, The Nightspot, La Boheme, ABC Room, and *Bali Bar. Super Pussy* took the prize for its lack of subtlety. Military personnel in class A dress uniforms from all branches filled the sidewalks. It seemed odd to Beans to see sailors in white uniforms and white hats. American Military Police patrolled the strip. Honking cars jostled with motor bikes on the busy street.

"No drink water in room," the desk clerk warned him. "Water cooler in hall better."

Visions of non-potable water tanks flashed before Beans. He unconsciously rubbed the long-healed scar on the back of his hand from boils after drinking polluted river water.

"Where can I get something to eat? Something American?"

"*Thai Heaven* cheeseburger. Live angels, too," the clerk said with a knowing smile. "Pretty girl, five dollah."

The burger was surprisingly tasty and the tall glass of beer extremely strong. When his glass was half empty, the bar tender topped it off. It didn't take long for a buzz. Alluring angels in flowery miniskirts and bikini tops circulated. Beans guessed they ranged from fourteen to eighteen years old. A Thai band covered American rock tunes. Raucous music inspired twisting and shouting on a crowded dance floor.

Beans approached an older girl. Tall and slender with close-cropped black hair over an oval face.

"You dance?"

She nodded emphatically with a broad smile. Beans was a clumsy dancer, but she was playful and graceful. After several exuberant rock and roll tunes, the band slowed down for *Unchained Melody* by the Righteous Brothers. She snuggled in close and rested her head on his shoulder. The white jasmine blossom in her hair smelled sweet.

"I go with you?" she whispered in his ear.

Beans assumed that was the way it was done. No haggling and no mattress in a back room. They walked with arms locked around each other back to his hotel room. She stayed the whole night. Before dawn, Beans sat in a chair in the corner watching her sleep. Moonbeams filtering through a gauzy curtain cast a bluish sheen over the buttery skin of her naked body. When her brown eyes fluttered open, a dimpled smile creased her face. She rose from the bed and sat on his lap, facing him with her arms around his neck. They made love one more time in the chair. She dressed, and he placed a $5 bill in her purse, a generous sum according to the desk clerk. Without even a glance at the bill, she kissed him on the lips and turned to leave. She hesitated at the door.

"My name Malee," she said, and then she departed.

Beans returned to bed and fell into a sound sleep, deeper than he had slept in months.

Click.

Click.

Click.

His eyes opened slowly, and he listened to the rhythm of the slow-moving ceiling fan. Had she been a dream? A fantasy? The crushed jasmine flower on her pillow reminded him she was real. He picked it up and slowly breathed in the pleasant scent. The night had been physical, yes, but also emotional. Less business and more personal.

More like a courtship than a transaction. She was more than he expected and more than he was prepared for. She was wonderful but frightening.

Beans never returned to *Thai Heaven*. He feared he would see Malee again, and he dared not fall in love.

Avoiding the bar scene, Beans arranged with a taxi driver named Somsak to be a tour guide for the remainder of the week. Somsak's stilted English proved passable, and they traveled around the city in a green and white '56 Pontiac sedan. Long and sleek.

They first visited a Buddhist temple called *Wat Arun.*

"You say, 'Temple of Dawn,'" Somsak said.

The central tower of the temple reached for the sky, high as a football field is long. Four smaller towers in pagoda style surrounded the main tower. Colorful tiles and seashells adorned each tower.

After removing their shoes, they passed by large and small Buddha statues that dominated every nook. Somsak hesitated in front of a centrally located large statue and bowed. Beans awkwardly did the same, mindful of his sporadic Catholic upbringing. His mother was observant, his pa not so much.

They climbed to the central balcony and enjoyed splendid views of the city across the Chao Phyraya River. The Grand Palace and the Temple of the Emerald Buddha stood out. Skilled boatmen standing in the rear of long, slender boats plied the current with a single, long oar extending out the back.

"One day we go to floating market," Somsak said, nodding. "Very nice."

They did, and it was. While seated in a long slender boat that navigated up a narrow canal off the main river, Beans haggled under Somsak's encouragement and bought a piece of cheap jewelry, a necklace of shells that he would bring to his mother. In the meantime, he wore it himself along with his dog tags.

Everywhere they went, the locals smiled and bowed. The friendly welcome toward the American seemed genuine, something that was uncertain in Vietnam.

On his last night in Bangkok, Somsak honored him by inviting him to his home and a meal with his family. Not much more than a crowded hut, Somsak seemed proud of his humble home. Anong, his wife, smiled broadly and bowed but spoke no English. Nor did the handful of children whose names bounced off Beans' ears.

Beans feared the food. Somsak ladled the thick, orange, creamy mix of vegetables, fish, and peanuts atop a bed of rice. Beans had never tasted curry, but after his first tentative bite, he smiled. It was damn good, and he gladly accepted the offer of a second helping. With bows all around, Beans departed for his hotel.

As Beans stepped off the Huey back at the remote firebase, red mud clumped onto his jungle boots. Another day, same old shit.

Chapter Twenty-four

Cropped locks replaced red pigtails, but Wendy Cragun's saucy exuberance remained, and Dave was surprised at how pleased he was to see her. Dave and Angie bumped into Wendy while touring the University of Minnesota dorms. Angie had chosen the U over other college choices, and Dave enrolled for fall classes at the registrar's office. Dave never imagined the two women together, but now their contrasting personalities came into clear focus. It was more than Angie's apolitical disinterest compared to Wendy's hyper activism: Angie was solid, and Wendy was liquid; Angie was apple pie and ice cream while Wendy was boiled lobster; Angie was the starlit heaven, but Wendy was a meteor shower; Angie would sing *Amazing Grace* in the church choir while Wendy would rock out to *In-A-Gadda-Da-Vida* by Iron Butterfly.

Dave awkwardly introduced Angie to the woman who had introduced him to pot, sex, and politics, but, of course, he didn't mention everything in the introduction.

"Angie, this is Wendy. We worked together on Senator McCarthy's campaign in New Hampshire."

With sparkling green eyes and a broad smile, Wendy ignored Angie's extended hand and went right in for a hug.

"You've got a hot one," Wendy whispered. "Hold onto him, tight."

Angie responded with a wan smile. Somehow, another woman telling her that Dave was hot wasn't something she needed to hear.

"I'm so sorry about Senator Kennedy," Wendy said. "You must be devastated."

He was, of course, but more than he could say, and so he merely nodded.

"Have you talked to Alex our New Hampshire team leader? Maybe you'd like to help Senator McCarthy again. Some of us are headed to Chicago next week for the Democratic Convention."

Angie's eyes darkened and darted at Dave.

"Gotta go," Wendy said.

Upon departing, Wendy squeezed Angie's hands and pecked Dave on the cheek.

"I'll have Alex give you a call. Look me up if you decide to join us in Chicago."

"She was your girlfriend, wasn't she?" Angie said when they were alone.

"I wouldn't say 'girlfriend,' but yeah, we hung out together some." That was an understatement, he knew, and so did Angie.

"Someone named Alex called and left a number for you to call back," Meg said as Dave entered the kitchen after Frank Nelson dropped him off. "Said he knew you in New Hampshire."

"Hey man. This is Dave. You called?"

"Long time no see. How ya been?

"Shit happens. Been a long fuckin' summer."

"Yeah, I heard you were there when Kennedy got shot."

"Yeah," Dave said, slowly breathing out through pursed lips. That's all he could say, and the telephone line went silent for a few seconds.

"Hey, if you're ready, come to Chicago. You know I agreed with you when you said you were bolting for Kennedy, but when I got a personal call from Gene to join his travelling team--well, I guess my ego got in the way."

"Shit, I don't know," Dave said. "I'm pretty busy, and when Kennedy died, so did my political spirit."

"I hear you. You know, Gene felt the loss in a profound way. He told me that if Bobby Kennedy had declared months earlier, he would have supported him and not run himself. I guess Kennedy's death depressed everyone in the political system, even his opponents. Gene is tired all the time, and you can tell he isn't sleeping. Listless. No passion. Even though the polls showed him leading both Humphrey and Nixon this summer, his heart isn't in it. You were right, and we knew all along that Gene isn't presidential timbre. He's a great intellect and a man of impeccable character, but he's not a politician who can win because he refuses to play the game."

Alex hesitated a moment before continuing.

"Let me tell you a secret just between us girls. I don't think he wants to be president. Plus, he doesn't want to take on Humphrey in a personal way. They're friends. When they were the two Senators representing Minnesota, they carpooled to the Capitol building. The only time he shows passion is when he's pissed that Humphrey or his team takes shots at him, but he won't respond in kind. He gives speeches against the war, but he never asks people to vote for him. He says he's *willing* to be president but never that he *wants* to be president. He's just playing out the hand he was dealt. He's the face of the anti-war movement, *within the system,* and he feels the need to allow the system to give voice to the movement all the way to the convention."

"So why in hell are you still with him? Why should we go to Chicago?"

"I dunno. I guess I feel the same way as the candidate. We've come this far, and we should play it out. We've taken *the* principled stand, and we should continue to do that when all eyes turn to Chicago. The world won't end after Chicago, and neither will the war unless we keep up the drumbeat."

"I don't think so but let me talk to my girlfriend. Mebbe. Hang in there, man."

"Will that girl be there? Wendy, I mean. Is that her name? Angie asked.

"Yeah, sure. I don't need to go."

"You should go," Angie said.

Is this a test? Dave asked with imploring eyes.

"No, I mean it. You need to get back into your political activism. It animates you. I'll see you soon when you return. I'll watch for you on television."

In 1865, Chicago renamed a popular park on the northside of the city in honor of Abraham Lincoln whose reward for freeing the slaves had been to die from an assassin's bullet. The Democratic National Convention would convene on Monday, August 25th ten miles away on Chicago's southside, but Lincoln Park hosted throngs of activists on the weekend before the Convention opened.

Although Mayor Richard J. Daley and the city of Chicago had refused permits, Lincoln Park nevertheless became the *de facto* gathering place in the days leading up to the convention. Hippies were there for the good times. Yippies from the Youth International Movement were almost organized, half seriously promoting a pig for president. The better organized National Mobilization Committee to End the War in Vietnam (the MOBE) boasted success in gathering hundreds of thousands in Washington D.C. the previous fall. Most of the folks in Lincoln Park were young, middle-class kids from here, there, and everywhere.

Alex was already in Chicago with the McCarthy team headquarters in the Conrad Hilton Hotel. On Sunday, August 24th, Wendy and Dave arrived at Lincoln Park, the day before the official opening of the Convention. They wandered through impromptu yoga sessions, snake dancing, and high-spirited revelry. The aroma of marijuana lingered in the air. A large contingent of policemen in blue uniforms watched from the fringes. After a long shift, many of the men in blue leaned against trees or rested on picnic tables as fatigue mingled with resentment toward those who flashed peace signs or single finger salutes in their faces. After rock band MC-5 finished pounding out anti-establishment lyrics, many in the crowd slowly disbursed.

Had the mood of the crowds changed through the hot summer of assassinations and violence? It seemed so as Dave and Wendy slowly meandered through the park. The college kids stumping for Gene in New Hampshire had been clean-cut and serious. Poly Sci types. Student government types. The screaming Hispanics who mobbed Senator Kennedy's Los Angeles motorcade or the swooning students at his college appearances mimicked the rapturous crowd at a Beatles concert. That was then but now there was a numbed irreverence, nihilism, and a seething underbelly of pent-up anti-establishment, anti-institutional frustration and anger. The death of King. The death of Kennedy. The death of rioters and policemen in the streets. It all added up to the death of hope and trust replaced by a jaded anger. Counterculture run amok. The mood of rebellion, even revolution, was about more than the politics of the Democratic Party and more than anti-war resistance. Many saw themselves as cultural guerillas seeking to remake the world order.

"I've lost my innocence," Dave said. "Lincoln, MLK, the Kennedy brothers all dead. Europe is exploding in protest over the war and every damn thing, but repressive police just beat folks up. It seems like the world is a boiling cauldron. Every time a peace bubble or a justice bubble rises to the surface, it pops, and nothing happens except the heat rises. Will the kettle boil over? The Prague Spring with idealistic hopes for democracy within the Soviet bloc has been put down. Just this week, the Soviets and their thug allies invaded Czechoslovakia to kill the Czech liberals and quell the democracy movement. What's the point?"

"Well, we could just get high and screw all week," Wendy said.

Dave rolled his eyes and ignored her sarcasm. Yet, for many, sex, drugs, and rock and roll had become the answer, if not the antidote, to bone-numbing disappointment and disillusionment that was the detritus of a season of discontent. Get high and get laid.

"No, really, why are we here? What do we hope to accomplish?"

"Politically? Probably nothing," Wendy said with a shrug of her shoulders. "We can march and protest and carry McCarthy signs--and we will--but we both know Humphrey will be nominated and Richard Nixon will win the general election by touting law and order. We may not win the political revolution this time, but we're planting seeds, cultural seeds, that there's another way without racism and without militarism. We're reminding the nation of who and what America can be and should be if we just remember our own ideals."

They paused to listen to a black man in a skull cap arrayed in a pseudo-military green jacket. He sat on the grass, encircled by a dozen or so white kids, likely from a suburb somewhere. He reflected on the recent violence in Cleveland when black nationalists exchanged gunfire with Cleveland police.

"What was the experience of those n ... s that spawned violence? The system. The man. He beats you down when you're hungry, and you swipe an apple, but when you try to get up you tip over the whole goddammed apple cart and, the man says, 'fucking n---r spoiled it for the whole neighborhood. Ain't that too bad!' A honky assassinated Martin Luther King Jr. but when black anger spilled over, the man says, 'angry n ... s ain't qualified for the American dream. Ain't that too bad!' Do your protesting, White Bread. Go ahead and fight the system, but don't expect shit. The man always wins."

Wendy cupped Dave's hand between her own palms and pulled him away. Her eyes pleaded.

"We can't despair, and we can't give up. Yes, we may lose this time, but if we give up, we lose for all time. The stakes are too high. We're fighting for the soul of America."

They approached a well-dressed young man reminiscent of the "Clean Gene" brigade in New Hampshire, who spoke to a small crowd. Dave hoped to hear a less radical view. He was disappointed.

"When we occupied the Ivy draped halls at Columbia University this spring, city police violated us. Beaten. Kicked in the balls. Women pulled down stairways by their hair. Hundreds of us arrested. But listen to me, we achieved our goals, and the University met our demands. We were guerillas in the field of culture with visions of a radical transformation of society. Call it utopian revolution if you like. It's time to man the barricades, even if symbolic. Party politics are dead. Who gives a shit whether Tweedle Dum beats Tweedle Dee?"

Dave thought of the fading dream of his friend, John Lewis, for a participatory democracy, the beloved community of black and white, rich and poor. Was this asshole who spouted revolution right?

Then there were the media-seeking, self-promoters, Jerry Rubin and Abby Hoffman. If they weren't the leaders, they were certainly the faces of the protests, which didn't help the cause because they provided convenient targets for establishment scorn--the court jesters who promoted guerilla theater. Provocative action that invited police repression. Provocation to create visibility. Anarchy and nihilism and narcissism. Dissent to resistance to revolution.

The establishment saw it all as one, lumping all the young activists together and assuming the worst.

"We should leave," Dave said, pointing at the shift change in the police. Helmeted reinforcements in riot gear supplanted the blue uniformed officers.

"You spoiled brats," a policeman who had been heckled all day had the last word. "You think you know better than everybody else."

The words were barely out of his mouth when a cloud of tear gas wafted over Dave and Wendy. The rioting riot police broke ranks and lunged forward with excited anger, swinging batons. Chaos. Ferocity. For the police, this was their war, and the middle class kids the enemy. The police action went beyond protecting and serving to punishing. A spoiled generation deserved a good ass kicking. Most of the innocents retreated, but others fell under the blows that didn't stop after the victim cowered on the ground.

"Christ, let's move!" Dave said, but Wendy just stood and watched, and then she pointed at a TV crew.

"The world needs to see this," she said, and she moved toward the advancing police in full view of the cameras. She stood her ground, and Dave reluctantly followed, tugging at her blouse. When the police pushed her, she pushed back, but then they swarmed her, and a single, slashing baton blow across the face felled her.

"Please, please, leave her alone," Dave said, and he jumped on top of her to shield her; the police pummeled him with their night sticks before moving on to fresh meat.

Dave pulled Wendy to her feet, but she was dazed and the slash across her face oozed blood. Dave lifted her and carried her from the park.

"She needs help. Where can I find medical help?" Dave asked of no one in particular, but someone directed him to a nearby hospital emergency room.

"She needs stitches," the doctor said, "and overnight observation. Prob'ly a concussion. Her facial injury is serious, but I hope her eye isn't damaged. You need to be checked out as well, and the tear gas flushed from your eyes."

Dave caught snatches of sleep in a chair next to Wendy's hospital bed. He was alright with a headache and a few black and blue marks across his back and arms, but Wendy's face was dressed in bandages from her forehead, across her broken nose, and onto her left cheek. A padded bandage covered her left eye, and Wendy was stoic when the doctors said they couldn't predict what would happen to her eyesight.

The next morning, Dave found a lounge with a TV and stale coffee.

"Tell me more," Wendy said when he returned to her bedside. "Tell me what's happening."

"Local TV coverage is spotty," Dave said, "and pro-establishment. One commentator intentionally smeared the Yippies, calling them the 'loud-mouthed Yappies' with a sneer on his face."

Wendy sucked in a deep breath through her nose then exhaled through her mouth.

"Promoting a pig for president makes it easy to dismiss us," she said.

"Oh, they're taking us seriously," Dave replied, "but not in the way we want. It's not just that they don't *respect* us; instead, they *suspect* us. Mayor Daley announced

12,000 members of the Chicago Police Department would serve twelve-hour shifts, and 6,000 army soldiers and nearly as many national guard troops would protect the city, bolstered by military intelligence officers, the FBI, and Secret Service. Chicago is an armed camp, and the hippies and the Yippies and Wendy Cragun are the enemy."

A tall nurse dressed in a starched white dress, white cap, white nylons and white shoes entered the room.

"Young man, could you step out for a few minutes while we change the dressing and attend to your friend?"

Dave nodded. "I need some fresh air. I'll wander around the streets for a while and grab a bite. I'll be back," he said and leaned in and kissed Wendy on the non-bandaged cheek.

Dave spied the white-glazed brick exterior of a White Castle restaurant, and he entered the stainless-steel interior with an open kitchen and ordered sliders and fries with a Coke. He soon found himself back at Lincoln Park that again swarmed with young activists. The mood was edgier. No music. Many of the innocents had felt the rod of their first battle, and it steeled them. Had some deserted the battlefield? Perhaps, but the numbers swelled with reinforcements.

When Dave returned to the hospital room, Wendy was not there. After a brief panic, he found her in the lounge. A fresh and smaller bandage covered the wound on her face. The patch over her eye was gone.

"How's your vision? Can you see ok?"

"Shit yes, but I can't see the protests because they're not showing them," she said. "Fucking Mayor Daley claims an electrical worker's strike prevents live broadcasts outside the arena, but I think it's a goddammed coverup."

Dave and Wendy settled in to watch the televised events inside the International Amphitheatre, ground zero for the convention.

America's grandfatherly anchorman, Walter Cronkite, set the stage:

"The Democratic convention is about to begin in a police state. There just doesn't seem to be any other way to say it."

The opening day featured floor fights over the seating of competing slates of delegates from a few southern states. A racially diverse delegation from Texas lost its attempt to be seated.

On Tuesday, more maimed and wounded protesters from another night of Lincoln Park violence swelled the hospital lounge.

During a lull in podium activity, CBS journalist Dan Rather worked the convention floor, wearing headphones and holding a microphone as he attempted to interview a delegate when security guards attempted to wrestle him away.

"Take your hands off me unless you plan to arrest me," Rather shouted.

"I think we've got a bunch of thugs here, Dan," Walter Cronkite remarked on air with the whole world listening.

On NBC, Edwin Newman reported from the floor as Chicago police dragged off antiwar delegates.

"It's easily the first time that policemen have entered the floor of a convention," said co-anchor Chet Huntley.

"In the United States," said David Brinkley.

The only permit issued for protest marches was scheduled for Wednesday the 28th. Everyone anticipated a major confrontation with the keepers of law and order.

"We've got to get out of here," Wendy said that morning in the hospital lounge.

Dave was aghast when he realized Wendy intended to leave the hospital to join the march. He thought, and hoped, she wanted to return to Minneapolis.

If there had been 2,000 gathered in Lincoln Park on the day Dave and Wendy arrived, the numbers swelled to 10,000, maybe 15,000, gathering in Grant Park near downtown. Protesters swarmed over a hillock and atop a statue of a Civil War general like bees on a hive. Helmeted National Guardsman carrying M1 rifles lined the periphery to prevent the planned march on the streets south to the Convention Headquarters. Instead, the protestors followed sidewalks west toward Michigan Avenue and the Conrad Hilton Hotel that served as the headquarters for the Democratic National Committee. They were met by a phalanx of National Guardsmen. Behind the front lines, machine guns mounted on jeeps trained their gunsights on the protestors.

"Sit down! Sit down!" Wendy screeched while gesturing with her arms for everyone to stage a sit-down protest.

Others joined in and soon the mass squatted on the sidewalk and a chant went up, "The whole world is watching! The whole world is watching!" That wasn't immediately true because live television feeds were not happening, but film crews quickly rushed their evidence to their production rooms back at their stations and on to the networks.

Dave sat in a trance, watching the Battle for Michigan Avenue play out in slow motion. Tear gas burned his breaths and stung his eyes. Blood pooled in the gutters. Sirens, shouts, and screams climbed the skyscraper canyons, reaching the 24th floor and the suite of candidate Humphrey.

It was not a fair fight. The police wore helmets and wielded clubs with holstered handguns at the ready backed by the armaments of the military against the protestors' mere placards, slogans, and peace signs. The protestors protested, retreated, and rallied to protest again without looting, which saved lives, since Mayor Daley reportedly had issued a "shoot-to-kill" order for looters. The street level plate-glass windows of the Hilton Bar came crashing down around protesters squeezed against the wall by waves of police. Aides of Senator McCarthy escorted the wounded to his suite for emergency medical care. Dave thought he spied Alex, but he couldn't tell for sure through eyes smarting from tear gas.

Press cameras were visible here and there, but that didn't discourage the police from attacking their fellow Americans with their boots and their billy clubs. Perhaps they felt immune from responsibility after they removed their name tags. The police assaulted members of the press despite visible press badges or maybe because of them. The enforcers of law and order didn't care that the press was witness to their mayhem, or maybe they did, and they wanted their brutality to be seen, proud of their viciousness, anxious to make a statement. They seemed entitled, even encouraged.

This was the climax of the hot times of summer in the city. The apocalyptic battle in a season of urban violence. Pent up frustration at a foreign war gone bad and a domestic war in the streets and the hearts of a conflicted nation. The police and half of America recognized the enemy, and it was kids in tie-dyed shirts and bell bottom pants. Long-haired liberals indoctrinated by leftist colleges. Draft-dodging cowards. Bra-burning feminists. Queer perverts. If the establishment couldn't defeat her foes in Vietnam, they sure as hell would do so on the home front.

For seventeen minutes that evening, the whole world watched the filmed evidence of the street violence as the TV networks cut away from the convention floor. When they returned, Connecticut Senator Abraham Ribicoff came to the podium to nominate peace candidate, Senator George McGovern of South Dakota. At one point, he glared at Chicago Mayor Daley in the front row and denounced the use of "Gestapo tactics on the streets of Chicago." Boos and hisses rained down on him as Mayor Daley jabbed his finger at the senator and screamed, "Fuck you, you Jew son of a bitch!"

In the wee hours of morning, Dave wandered in a daze, looking for Wendy. It seemed an afterthought, but the Convention voted down a peace platform and nominated Humphrey on the first ballot.

Wendy slept while Dave piloted her Volkswagen Beetle along the Wisconsin freeway back toward

Minnesota. Suddenly he veered onto the off ramp toward Madison.

"Where are we?" Wendy said, yawning.

"Gonna revisit the scene of my baptism. Maybe I'll affirm my baptismal vows."

"What are you talking about?"

"Let's visit the University of Wisconsin campus building where the cops beat the shit out of a bunch of us for protesting Dow Chemical and the use of napalm. That was the day I got true religion. I wanna see if I can find that again."

The last summer session at UW had ended and fall term hadn't begun. Campus was nearly deserted. The building was locked, and they peered in through windows.

"It's empty, and so am I," Dave said. "It was a nice try, but there's not much fight left in me. Let's grab a burger."

Wendy clutched his arm as they retraced their steps to her car.

Chapter Twenty-five

Beans called the rocky outcropping at the edge of the firebase perimeter the "pissing rock." He emptied his bladder after completing guard duty during the 4:00 am to 8:00 am shift. Beneath the rocky perch, concertina wire defined the firebase perimeter as the hill broke away sharply into the valley below. The sun burned off the mist hanging over the valley.

He ducked into the adjacent defensive bunker that served as the guard post to retrieve his gear before depositing it in the tent that passed as a barracks. From there, he headed toward the mess tent to catch breakfast before returning to the barracks for a morning nap. As he scarfed down scrambled eggs drowned in ketchup, he heard the familiar *wump-wump* of arriving helicopters. After an early departure from Camp Enari, a pair of choppers delivered a dozen LRRPs to the hilltop firebase. LRRPs were grunts like Beans, only crazier, traipsing around the jungle in small units with little firepower and depending upon stealth.

The triple canopy jungles of the Central Highlands provided cover for tributaries of the Ho Chi Minh Trail spilling into South Vietnam through Laos and Cambodia. Interdiction of NVA infiltrators at such entry points was the responsibility of the 4th Infantry Division. Small teams of scouts called LRRPs (Long Range Reconnaissance Patrols) prowled the jungles to locate enemy activity. When the LRRPs identified a target, the army hit hard with bombs, artillery, or helicopter gunships.

Beans drained the last of his coffee and departed the mess tent to check out the arrivals.

The lurps wore camouflage fatigues in mottled shades of green. Under bush hats or head bands, thick paint smeared eight faces, but the other four remained clean. The eight face-painted men carried bulging rucksacks and an assortment of weapons: several CAR-15s—short commando versions of M-16s; an M-16 with a silencer; an over-under with an M-16 barrel on top and an M-79 grenade launcher below; and a trio of AK-47s captured from the NVA. The four bare-faced troopers merely carried M-16s and bandoliers of full magazines slung over their shoulders and a couple of PRC-25 radios with extension antennas. They would remain at the camp to serve as radio relay for the eight who would be inserted into the jungle.

"What the fuck!" Beans recognized Sam Baker, a fellow trainee in Fort Polk a lifetime earlier.

"Sam, what the hell are you doing here?"

The painted-faced LRRP looked confused for a second, and then pointed a finger at Beans.

"Beans, right? I remember you. Long time ago, buddy," and they exchanged high fives.

"Just hangin' out," Beans said. "Been pulling guard duty here for a while."

Sam nodded toward the valley. "Listen, I don't have much time to gab. They're keeping the slicks warm to drop us in the jungle as soon as our radio team is up and running."

"How'd you end up in the LRRP's? Seems like a shitty way to earn yer combat pay."

"After Fort Polk, I went to Ranger school at Fort Benning."

"Yer a fuckin' Ranger? No shit. Figured you were smarter than that."

"It is what it is. Hey, let's figure out how to grab some beers after this mission."

It didn't take long for the four with clean faces to set up in the communications center, and after a commo check, the eight bound for the jungle reboarded the choppers. The choppers lifted off and headed down the ridge into the valley below and inserted the LRRPs into a small LZ a couple of miles away.

Beans' curiosity prompted him to hang out with the radio team, and he learned that the mission of the field team was to follow and map a broad trail that wound through the jungle below. An earlier LRRP team had discovered the well-used trail that supported major NVA traffic into the valley.

For the next two days, Beans followed the three-way transmissions between the team in the field (Romeo one eight), the radio relay team on the firebase (Romeo deuce deuce) and the LRRP headquarters back at Enari (Zero). The LRRPs on the ground discovered that the trail curled back toward the firebase. A couple of times they reported sighting NVA personnel on the trail, but the LRRPs avoided exposure. Stealth was the hallmark of the LRRPs. With small teams and limited firepower, they depended on subterfuge to keep their asses undetected and safe.

On the third day, Beans heard the transmission from the field team.

"Deuce deuce, this is Romeo one eight. Do you read?

"Roger, copy."

"Holy shit, there's hooches everywhere. We've stumbled upon a way station, and it's crawling with NVA. We're backing off."

A few seconds later came ominous words. "Contact! Contact! Romeo one eight in contact. We're retreating under fire. Deuce deuce, do you copy?"

Beans heard small arms fire crackling over the radio.

"We're moving toward higher ground seeking an LZ to get our asses outa here. We need gunship support. Over"

"Copy, one eight."

"Zero, this is Romeo deuce deuce. Romeo one eight reports contact. Gunships requested. Please advise. Over."

"Roger deuce deuce. Wait one."

"One eight. Gunships requested. Keep your heads down and wait for the gunships to hail you on your push."

"Romeo one eight. This is Kilo 4. Redleg standing by." The commander of the artillery battery on the firebase piped in.

"Kilo 4. Roger. We're moving but fire at will at pre-plotted coordinate one zero two. That may not be right on, but it might get the Charlies to hunker down. Do you copy?"

"Roger one eight. Kilo 4 firing at will on pre-plotted coordinate one zero two."

An ear-splitting barrage of artillery from the firebase exploded.

"Romeo deuce deuce, this is Zero. Gunships enroute. Over."

"Roger, Zero. Romeo one eight, this is deuce deuce. Zero reports gunships are coming your way."

Several minutes of dead silence followed before the gunships came on station.

"Romeo one-eight, this is Gambler two six on your push. Be at your location in 04 or 05. Please standby to pop smoke. Do you read?"

"Roger, Gambler two six. Standing by with smoke. Over."

Another minute.

"One eight, this is Gambler, please pop smoke."

"Roger. Smoke popped."

"One eight, this is Gambler. We see banana yellow. Please confirm, and we'll lay down minigun fire around you."

"Roger. Banana yellow. Light 'em up."

Beans climbed atop the commo bunker for a view of the action in the valley below. Others from the firebase watched from the edge of the perimeter and from the perch of the pissing rock. A pair of Cobra gunships circled over the jungle for at least ten minutes firing rockets and bursts of their miniguns capable of spewing hot metal at 6,000 rounds per minute. The breeze carried snatches of the chainsaw growl of the miniguns.

"One eight, this is Gambler. That should quiet the SOBs," a Cobra pilot said when the firing stopped.

"Roger that."

"Deuce deuce. This is Romeo one eight. We haven't taken any recent fire, but I regret to inform that we have a broken bow."

Beans looked at the radio team listening with him. One of them set his jaw and shook his head. "'Broken bow' is code word for KIA. We've got a man down. Dead."

Eight men down there, including Sam. Odds are in his favor. But ...

Another transmission from the team in the field.

"Kilo 4. Is Redleg ready to change targets? We can provide coordinates for that way station. Time to blow it to kingdom come with the Howitzers sitting on the firebase."

"One eight, this is Kilo 4. You bet yer ass. Waiting for the coordinates. Can you walk the fire in from your location? Over."

Romeo one eight provided the coordinates, and a 105 mm Howitzer fired a targeting round.

"Kilo 4. Adjust target 500 meters, azimuth 230 degrees WSW."

After a second targeting round, Romeo one eight said, "Adjust target 150 meters, azimuth 270 degrees West."

A third artillery shell exploded in the valley.

"You got it, Kilo 4. Fire for effect."

All six Howitzers fired repeatedly for five or ten minutes. Beans and the others held their hands over their ears at the ear-splitting artillery fire. After the shelling stopped, the scout team made a request.

"Long way back to the LZ and difficult with a broken bow and with unfriendlies crawling around. Can you arrange a rope ladder extraction?"

"Wait one. We'll check with base."

"Zero. This is deuce deuce. One eight request a ladder extraction. Do you copy?"

After a few minutes, base responded affirmatively.

The relay team reported, "One eight. Standby. An extraction bird with a rope ladder is enroute."

Atop the firebase, Beans and dozens of others watched the activities in the valley below as the rescue Huey arrived. The door gunners on the helicopter lowered a two-sided rope ladder with rungs into the jungle. The Cobras continued to circle with occasional bursts of their miniguns to keep any NVA from taking potshots at the hovering Huey.

"Fucking A, Man, that's a long way to climb a shaky ladder into a hovering helicopter," someone said.

First, one man slowly climbed hand over foot up the ladder. The helicopter rocked with the weight on the ladder, but the pilot did a decent job of holding her steady. Behind the first climber came a second, and then a third, but his foot slipped off a step, and he dangled for seconds holding on with his hands before he regained his footing. He hesitated for a moment as if mustering his resolve to continue climbing. Or praying. After he made it and the door gunner pulled him into the hovering bird, a fourth, fifth, and sixth made it ok. As the chopper added weight, the bird bucked more with each addition. The whole episode took an eternity as the slick hovered in place.

"How the hell are they going to get the body out?" Someone wondered aloud.

The men watching from the firebase grew silent, anticipating the rest. Slowly, the helicopter elevated, rising straight up. When the bottom of the ladder cleared the trees, they saw the dead body draped over the bottom rung and the eighth man hanging there holding the body in place. With the live man and dead man dangling at the bottom of the ladder, the pilot slowly pivoted toward the firebase, but then the voice of the chopper pilot crackled over the radio.

"Freakin' heavy load. Running low on petrol."

The chopper gradually climbed toward the firebase with the ladder dangling behind, swaying in the breeze. By now, every swinging dick on the firebase had joined the silent audience. When the breeze finally carried the whir of the rotors, the crowd began to murmur.

"For chrissake, that's Sam hanging on the ladder!" Beans muttered to himself.

Sam Baker was the hero at the end of the ladder holding his dead comrade in place. Beans' friend survived the day, another mother's son didn't.

"Higher, higher!" Many yelled with gestures to the pilot to climb higher as the bottom of the ladder was about to smash into the pissing rock. Sam and the body scraped over, and clutching arms grabbed them. The door gunners pulled the ladder up, and the rescue chopper landed safely.

"Got a butt?" Sam asked as Beans joined him. "I quit, but I need a smoke real bad. And a shot of whiskey. Got any whiskey?"

Beans gave him a Kool and a light. Sam's hand shook badly, and he used his second hand to steady the cigarette.

Beans departed to find a jug. He needed a stiff drink also. When he returned, Sam stood alone at the edge of the perimeter staring into the valley.

"This is a hell of a way to share a drink. What happened down there?"

"Dunno. We thought we had eluded them, and we sat in the bush on the side of the hill. A single shot rang out, and he slumped over. Hit in the head. Doesn't make sense."

Beans was ready to tie one on, but then Lieutenant Farnsworth put out the word to his men. "Get your shit together. Fresh birds are coming to pick us up, and 1st platoon has orders to sweep the area and make sure the artillery barrage wiped out that way station."

A proper drunk would have to wait.

"It's hairy down there," Sam stated the obvious. "Watch yer ass."

As Beans headed toward the barracks to grab his weapon and gear, Sam offered thin courage.

"Next round is on me."

Chapter Twenty-six

The provocateur peered through the brush as he spied on the unsuspecting soldier standing alone in the clearing. Clouds scudded across autumn's night sky. *Wait, wait, let the clouds cover the moon, and darkness will blanket your approach. Move quickly but quietly. Don't rouse the unliving!*

In an instant, the deed was done, and red paint dripped from Iron Mike, the statue of a soldier guarding the Armory on the University of Minnesota campus. The Armory was the home to the ROTC program. Dave lashed out due to frustration, disillusionment, or a sense of helplessness; maybe he tried to convince himself, or Wendy, that he still had fire in his belly, but he immediately regretted his impetuous act, and the vandalism provided no relief or satisfaction. He wasn't cut out for the guerilla theater of the court jesters Hoffman and Rubin or the active resistance of the Berrigan brothers. What seemed bold and critical before seemed juvenile and petty after, and he realized his puny effort at performative protest would hardly change the ROTC program at the U, much less the course of history.

And then it got worse, and history would change—his own.

"You ok?" Dave asked.

"I've been better," Frank Nelson the house painter said.

A soiled t-shirt drooped loosely over sagging shoulders. Bloodshot eyes separated chin stubble from white hair furrowed like snow drifts following a blizzard.

"Where's your coffee?" Dave asked as he opened the kitchen cabinet doors. He found what he was looking for and began to brew a pot.

"Do you have any eggs?"

Dave didn't wait for an answer and opened the refrigerator door.

"Why don't you ask the real question on your mind?" Frank said.

"What's that?"

"Why do I drink?"

Frank picked at the scrambled eggs Dave placed in front of him.

"I have an easy answer even if you're too timid to ask the question. I drink because I'm a drunk. It is what it is and it's who I am."

Dave tossed an empty whiskey bottle in the garbage.

"Now the hard question, for which I have no answer, is 'why am I a drunk?' It's not something I chose. In fact, I swore I would never be like my alcoholic father, but I guess it's in my blood. There are mornings when I'm drenched in remorse, and I stand in the shower attempting to wash away the guilt. I swear I'll never drink again, but I do."

His voice tailed off followed by tsking sounds made by his tongue against clenched teeth.

"Sorry you had to see me this way. It happens sometimes when I have nothing to do."

"Have you tried AA? I hear there's a hospital or clinic just outside the Cities called Hazel Nut or Hazel Nut Den or something like that."

Frank managed a smile. "Yep, Hazel Nut, that fits me."

He stared out the kitchen windows at the Norway Pines swaying in the evening breeze.

"Actually, it's called Hazelden, and I do know about it. Doubt they can teach new tricks to an old dog like me."

"Take a shower. Shave. Get some sleep, and I'll be back tomorrow," Dave said. "Got some things on my mind that I want to bounce off you."

Dave was unsettled, and he had returned to Kalmar to regain his bearings. After the visit to Frank Nelson, he returned home for supper with his mother. His father was out of town. He downed two helpings of Swedish meatballs slathered with brown gravy, then helped his mother with supper dishes.

Harv and Meg had differing expectations for their son. Harv expected accomplishment, and when Dave's path appeared to be sidetracked, Harv became cold and judgmental. For Harv, 1968 had been a string of disappointments in Dave, and he took Dave's actions personally as a reflection on himself. Although Meg was disappointed that Dave's college journey was stalled, she remained warm and gracious, and her concern was for Dave's wellbeing, seen through his eyes, not her own.

Leaning over the steaming hot sink caused a solitary strand of Meg's coiffed auburn hair to hang loose, but her solid face with high cheekbones and understated makeup remained classy. Even in an apron, she was elegant.

"Is your deferment gone?" she asked, knowing the answer but wanting a discussion.

"I'm sorry I screwed up and lost my deferment."

"I don't want you to go and fight in Vietnam. I lost my brother, Dickie, in the war in Italy, but that was for a righteous cause, not this hopeless quagmire."

"I'm looking at my options."

"How are you and Ang doing?"

"Ok, I guess, but I'm not spending as much time with her as I expected."

Meg bit her lip and hesitated before speaking.

"I'm sure you've figured out that your father and I married soon after we learned that I was pregnant with your sister. We weren't smart about it. Of course, it's turned out ok with us, but it put a strain on the start of our marriage. It was much worse then, but even now there are a few old ladies at church who cast a look of judgment in their eye."

Dave had a good idea where his mother was going with this.

"You don't need to tell me if you're sleeping with Angie, but if you are, you need to be smart. I'm sure Angie knows about the pill, and you know about condoms. You have options that weren't available when your father and I got serious with each other, and I trust you are using those options wisely."

Dave didn't look his mom in the eye as he dried dinner plates, but he listened intently. When they finished with the dishes, Dave headed to the living room and switched on the TV. Meg followed him, and her comments switched from mom mode to school nurse mode.

"The teachers gladly assigned the task of teaching a class on sex education to me. My heart breaks for some of the stories told to me in private by high school, even jr. high, girls. They don't know that they have choices. Saying no is the best option, but I realize that isn't always realistic, and they don't always know about birth control. I'd probably get fired on the spot if the school board knew I handed out condoms and informed girls about the pill. Of course, getting a prescription is impossible without parental consent. If a girl gets pregnant, her options are limited."

Dave thought of his classmate who missed their junior year. Everyone knew she was pregnant and ultimately gave the baby up for adoption before returning as a subdued senior. What he didn't know was the hush-hush story of a high school girl from the mid-fifties, but his mom shared her story.

"I was just starting out as school nurse, and Wanda never came to me with her pregnancy. We only learned after the fact when she died from an attempted self-abortion. There were whispers in school, but never open conversations, and I don't know what I would have counseled her if she *had* come to me. Of course, adoption is an option as it was with your classmate. Keeping the baby will have lifetime consequences for the baby, mother, and perhaps the father. Back-alley abortions are dangerous and illegal. What I'm saying is that teen pregnancies don't present good options."

It occurred to Dave that he took his mother's compassionate wisdom for granted. It was rare for her to open up as much as she was doing this evening, but she spoke calmly and with matter-of-fact assurance. Perhaps the absence of his father accounted for her talkativeness. She concluded, almost as an afterthought:

"I think legal abortions should be available; at least, they'd be safe for the young girls."

Sock it to me.

Dave barely noticed Goldy Hawn speak the words with a mischievous, dimpled smile on the TV screen.

He never thought much about abortion, but his mother obviously had wrestled with it as a nurse who counseled young women. Didn't he see a recent news article about a Minnesota Catholic group forming to take a stand *against* abortion? Not that he knew much about Catholic doctrine, but a church that didn't allow priests to marry and which forbade birth control didn't carry much credibility with him on issues of human sexuality.

Sock it to me

Candidate Richard Nixon's stilted appearance on *Rowan and Martin's Laugh-In* was laughable but not comedic. Dave wasn't impressed, but his mother smiled. The show provided rapid-fire escape comedy-- silly but not serious, but that's probably what the public yearned for. *You bet your sweet bippy.*

Dave preferred the edgy *Smothers Brothers Comedy Hour,* even if the CBS censors did not. Anti-war activism in prime time, veiled in satirical humor.

Dick Smothers: "Our government is asking us as citizens to refrain from traveling in foreign lands."

Tom Smothers: "OK, all you guys in Vietnam, come on home."

Dave heard that the censors cut the truly bad-ass stuff such as a segment featuring Harry Belafonte singing *Lord,*

Don't Stop the Carnival while scenes of police violence during the 1968 Democratic National Convention played in the background. When the show booked folk singer Pete Seeger for his first network appearance since being blacklisted during the Joe McCarthy era witch hunts, the censors deleted *Knee Deep in the Big Muddy*, but the public outcry and the popularity of the show convinced CBS to allow Seeger to sing his song later that year. Only the dim witted failed to understand that the song protested the Vietnam quagmire.

"Your dad will be happy to see you," Meg Karlstad said as Dave trudged up the stairs to his bedroom, but he knew that was bullshit. Harv Karlstad would return from an overnight business trip to St. Paul the next day.

Dave tossed and turned in twisted, sweaty sheets as discomforting thoughts pinballed around murky half-sleep. *Angie's new dorm crowd. Wendy's scarred face. College sucked. Fuck politics, but what are Humphrey's chances against Nixon?* When he wandered downstairs for a glass of water, he made a list of things to discuss with his painter mentor. Frank may be old, *never trust anyone over thirty,* and an alcoholic, but he had proven to be a valuable sounding board for Dave.

"Hope he's sober tomorrow," Dave mumbled as he headed back to bed.

"How's Miss American Pie," Frank asked.

He looked much better. Clean shaven. His thick mop of pure white hair was carefully combed. Shoulders squared not hunched.

"I thought we'd see more of each other being at the U together, but she's caught up in the whirlwind of her freshman year. She's been hanging with new dorm buddies."

Dave drummed his fingers on the kitchen tabletop in time with the burps of coffee percolating on the stove.

"She was also cool and a little distant when I returned from Chicago. 'I don't know what to think,' Angie said when I shared the turmoil of the Chicago convention. Like America itself, she was frightened by the violence and unsure whether to blame the protestors or the police."

Frank poured two cups of strong, dark coffee.

"Cream? Sugar?"

Frank took his black, but Dave added cream and two teaspoons of sugar.

"Then there's Wendy. She's the gal who keeps hauling me off to protests. She's not ambivalent like Wendy, and the scar across her face from a policeman's baton doesn't faze her a bit. I'm pretty hollowed out the way things are going, but her spirit never wavers."

"Are you screwing her?"

Frank's directness startled Dave, and he jerked his gaze at Frank before quickly looking away.

"Well, no, I mean not since Angie and I have been going together."

Frank moved to the stove and poured himself another cup. He gestured to Dave by lifting the pot toward him, but Dave shook his head.

"Have you thought about campaigning for Humphrey?"

Dave rolled his eyes.

"No, I'm serious. There's still time for the disillusioned to rally. Still time for the left and middle of the Democratic party, the young and the old, the pale white and the people of color, the established and the disenfranchised, to coalesce around Humphrey and against Nixon."

Frank clucked his tongue against the roof of his mouth before continuing.

"History can be cruelly ironic. Your generation never knew Humphrey the firebrand, the liberal mayor of Minneapolis, who had presaged the civil rights movement in a rabble-rousing speech at the 1948 Democratic Convention. Back then, segregationist Dixiecrats, led by Senator Strom Thurmond of South Carolina, stomped out as Mayor Hubert Humphrey spoke:"

The time has arrived in America for the Democratic Party to get out of the shadow of states' rights and to walk forthrightly into the bright sunshine of human rights.

Frank paused to look at Dave to see if this was sinking in, but Dave's face was non-committal.

"I know Humphrey has become the bogeyman representing the establishment. Despite his personal progressive record and the historic civil rights legislation of the current administration, Humphrey is now a pariah to your generation due to the administration's war policy, but according to the law-and-order Republicans, he is a frightening socialist beholden to the riotous mobs of the hot summer. He *is* the best bet to accomplish an end to the war."

"I'll think about it," Dave said, but his body language belied a lack of conviction.

"How about school? Are you getting back into the rhythm of college?"

Dave dropped his eyes.

"That's one of the things I want to talk to you about. I screwed up. Big time. Campus police arrested me for a stupid prank, and the University suspended me for the remainder of the term."

A teasing smile creased Frank's face, but then his expression turned serious.

"Won't the draft board come after you if you're not enrolled?"

"That's what I'm afraid of. I need to figure out my options. I'm thinking about the Peace Corps. What do you think?"

Doubt squeezed the wrinkles on Frank's face.

"What are the requirements? Are you qualified?"

Chapter Twenty-seven

Too friggin' quiet.

The rainforest was normally a cacophony of birdsongs, chirping rodents, or chattering monkeys, but the silence said the jungle knew intruders were present.

Beans, walking point, held up his hand for the others to halt. The platoon of twenty men raked their eyes back and forth, but they didn't spot anything lurking in the ferns and underbrush at the edge of the jungle. After momentarily hesitating, they slipped into and through the heavy foliage. As soon as they moved under the triple canopy, the vines, shrubs, and small trees disappeared, and they stood in a clearing. The heavy cover prevented sunlight penetration to the floor of the rainforest and thus no underbrush.

Beans squatted to reconnoiter. His nose wrinkled, and his nostrils flared at the acrid odor of exploded artillery gunpowder. He made an exaggerated sniffing gesture to alert the others. They followed the scent. With each step forward, they hesitated and scanned for signs of life. Creeping on the jungle floor without ground cover seemed like parading naked down Main Street, but when a hooch--a bamboo hut on stilts and covered by a thatched roof-- appeared in front of them, they found what they were looking for, and soon a whole array of hooches came into view. The artillery shelling had destroyed many of them.

A patchy-haired mutt trotted toward them with one ear flopped back. Suddenly surprised by coming face-to-face with the interlopers, the dog tensed and growled as if to say, *Who the fuck are you? You don't belong here!* With a single yip, he wheeled and loped back the way he had come.

"The fuckers *didi maued* their asses out'a here," Frankie said, and Beans exhaled a bit of tension standing amidst the hooches of the abandoned way station.

"Maybe," Lieutenant Farnsworth warned. "Watch out for tunnels."

They inspected the hooches from the outside without entering. Could be booby trapped. Many of the hooches had collapsed and smoldered from the artillery barrage.

"Light 'em up," came the order from Lieutenant Farnsworth. "Like this."

The platoon leader picked a dry palm frond from the ground, flipped open his Zippo cigarette lighter, and held the flame to a palm leaf. When the frond started to crackle, he tossed it onto a roof, and the dry thatch exploded into flames. The men followed suit, and soon the hooches were ablaze.

Frankie yelled. "Got a tunnel here." He pointed his M-16 at a hole covered with thatch.

"Frag it," Lieutenant Farnsworth said.

Frankie pulled the pin from a fragmentary grenade and chucked it into the tunnel. With a whoosh, dust billowed out but no signs of life.

"Sir, lend me yer .45, and I'll take a look."

The lieutenant hesitated. Climbing down a tunnel was extra-hazardous, and many tunnel rats didn't make it out.

"Come on, I can do this."

Lieutenant Farnsworth relented and handed his .45 sidearm and a flashlight to Frankie who cautiously entered the tunnel and disappeared. Long minutes passed, and suddenly Frankie's head popped up twenty meters away.

"Ain't shit in there," he said, "but it smelled of piss. I suspect that's where they hid while the shells rained down."

"Wait one," Beans said. "There's something tucked behind that thick stand of bamboo." He tried to go through the bamboo, but it was impenetrable. "There has to be a path somewhere," he mumbled.

He backed off and circled around, and eventually discovered a narrow footpath curving around and coming in from the backside. The path led him into a small clearing in front of a small hut tucked into lush, head-high ferns.

Beans picked up a palm frond, set it afire with his Zippo, and tossed it onto the thatch roof. He lit a Kool, sucked in a deep pull of the mentholated nicotine, and stepped back to watch as the flames spread.

Then it all went bad.

When a burning chunk fell to the floor of the hooch. A woman screamed, and a dog barked.

"What the fuck?"

Beans bounded up the steps as the flames engulfed the roof. A young woman with afterbirth between her legs sat in the corner, cradling her bloody newborn. The umbilical cord remained attached. The same patchy-haired mutt snarled at Beans and showed his teeth. As Beans stepped toward the woman, the dog lunged at him and clamped his jaws around Beans' wrist. Dog and man tumbled back down the steps, rolling in a heap.

"Get the fuck off me, you mangy sonofabitch," Beans yelled at the snarling, snapping, clawing canine.

Burning pieces of thatch dropped from the roof, and flames curled up the bamboo sides. Inside, the woman's screams grew more frantic, and her baby wailed. Beans struggled to reach for the Ka Bar knife strapped to his right leg just above the boot. He pulled it from its sheath with a bloody hand and plunged the seven-inch blade all the way to the hilt into the beast's belly, then again into the chest. With a last whimper, the dog fell limp, and Beans scrambled to his feet just as the burning roof collapsed into the hut.

One last scream and then silence except for the crackling flames.

"The doctor stitched the gash on your wrist, but the scratches on your face and hands just need a sterile cleaning. Let me take a look." the female nurse said. "You're lucky he didn't order rabies shots based on the circumstances."

The heavy-set female captain with straight dark hair draped over the silver bars on her fatigues collar was a lesser version of Mama Cass Elliot in olive-drab fatigues.

Beans barely remembered the medivac helicopter ride from the jungle to the 71st Evacuation Hospital at Camp Enari. He paid little attention as she cleaned, medicated, and gauzed his wounds.

"Where you from, soldier?"

"Far away from here."

She got the hint and continued her work in silence.

For more than a week, Beans remained confined to the hospital, even though he was healthy, but SOP required monitoring the wrist wound for infection. He felt the fool as he wandered around in hospital pajamas, never more so than the night there was a sapper alert in the base, and all the patients took shelter in a Quonset hut bunker, safeguarded by a short, squat, pimply-faced orderly wearing a steel pot and a flak jacket and gingerly handling an M-16. He seemed like an overweight little boy playing soldier. Beans figured the biggest danger was not sappers but the orderly who didn't know shit about the weapon in his hands. Later, toward the end of Beans' hospitalization, beads of sweat trickled down the face of the same orderly as he removed the stitches from Beans' wrist.

Just before his discharge from the hospital, members of his squad visited Beans, accompanied by Lieutenant Farnsworth.

"On your feet, soldier."

Beans did as he was told, and the lieutenant pinned a purple heart medal on his pajama shirt. Apparently, a dog bite qualified as wounded in action. Beans was embarrassed. Seems when shit went bad, the army awarded a medal. When the rest departed to enjoy their well-earned standdown in the base camp, Frankie remained.

"What the fuck was she doing there?" Beans asked without expecting an answer. "Those goddammed cowards busted ass out of there and left her behind."

Frankie piped in. "I spect those fuckers didn't see any other way. When the shells started falling on them, they scrambled, but there was no way to take a woman in the middle of childbirth."

"Yeah, but what the fuck was she doing there in the first place?"

"The NVA use women to haul materiel down from the north," Frankie said. "Or maybe she was the station chief minding the place."

"That bitching hound tried to protect her but prevented me from pulling her out of that burning hooch," Beans said, shaking his head.

"It's the shits," Frankie said, "but it don't mean nuthin'."

Along with the Filipino band mimicking Ike and Tina Turner and their pounding, driving *Proud Mary*, Beans rolled, and the Non-Commissioned Officers (NCO) club rocked. A cloud of blue smoke hung in the rafters. Warrant officers who piloted choppers by day, danced on tables by night. The standing room only crowd in the rear swayed with the rhythm. Everyone wore standard olive-drab fatigues except for the cocky LRRPs in tiger fatigues and Aussie bush hats. Whenever the pushing and shoving got a little rambunctious, MPs quickly restored order, and the band played on.

After Beans stepped outside and emptied his bladder down a piss tube--the canister of a 105 mm artillery shell implanted in the ground—he joined half a dozen of his comrades mingling nearby.

"Have a toke and pass it on."

Beans took a hit on the joint, handed it to his left, and soon another OJ, an opium-soaked marijuana cigarette, circled his way from his right. Drunk and stoned, Beans returned inside as the band broke into the favorite wrap to every nightly performance, and the whole place shouted and swayed to the refrain of the rock anthem of the Animals band: *We gotta get out of this place.*

Chapter Twenty-eight

The Great Emancipator peered over their shoulders as they gazed across the reflecting pond while seated on the marble steps of his memorial. A slight October breeze rippled the water and scattered yellow elm leaves across the lawn where a quarter of a million folks heard the impatient words of dear friend John Lewis and the hopeful words of Dr. King half a decade earlier. So much hope swallowed up by gut-wrenching disappointment.

What did Lincoln think then and what did he think now?

Wendy Cragun and Dave crammed into Wendy's Volkswagen Beetle for a cross country trip to the District of Columbia, but their mission failed. Dave had lost his student draft deferment and hoped Senator McCarthy's office could expedite the Peace Corps application process, but even the influence of a sitting Senator could not overcome Dave's lack of qualifications. No degree. No foreign language fluency. No particular skills, and house painting experience didn't help. Even in the anti-war Senator's office, a desire to avoid the draft wasn't sufficient justification for the Senator to pull strings.

"Ever been to New York City?"

Wendy suggested an extension of their trip east with a short jaunt up the Eastern seaboard to the Big Apple.

"I've got a cousin who lives in Manhattan, and we can crash in her apartment."

"Nah, I don't think so," Dave said, but once again he followed the audacious Irish woman on a path far, far from Kalmar.

Wendy's cousin, Anna, and Lorie, her roommate, lived in a 2nd story apartment over a bakery near the corner of 11th and Bleeker in the West Village. The roommates met as coeds at Barnard College on the Upper West Side, and now they pursued graduate degrees. Anna studied fashion at the nearby Parsons School of Art and Design and Lorie sought a master's degree in art history at New York University located adjacent to Washington Square. The tall and slender women both left their pale, plain faces untouched by makeup. Twisted into a bun over a high forehead, Anna's burnt auburn hair lay tight against her scalp, but Lorie's straight, dirty-blonde hair draped down her back nearly reaching her waistline.

Lorie was oddly indifferent toward Dave, ignoring him as if he wasn't there, but Anna watched him with a beguiling smile as if she knew a secret. After pizza and beer, Anna lit a reefer and passed it around. Lorie took one hit before she reached out and smoothed a wayward lock of hair dangling over Anna's face.

"I'm turning in," Lorie said. "Night all."

"I'll be in soon," Anna replied.

After Anna left, Dave said, more as a statement than a question, "They're not just roommates, are they."

"Ahh … no," Wendy replied.

Andy Warhol posters adorned the apartment walls, and the stale aroma of incense reeked from the plush sofa where Dave slept. Awake well before the others, he felt conspicuous as the blue-lidded eyes of Warhol's Marilyn

Monroe watched him pull on his pants. The bathroom
called, and he gingerly stepped across creaking dark wood
floors, fearing he would awaken Wendy who lay in a tangle
of blankets on an air mattress that had miraculously
remained inflated through the night. He exited via the
stairway to the sidewalk, and he sat alone at a tiny, wrought
iron table in the bakery sipping coffee and munching on a
Danish while poring over the New York Times. A steady
stream of sleepy-eyed denizens passed through.

"Figured I'd find you here," Wendy said. "Up for a
walk?"

In NYC, you travel on shoe leather. After hoofing
along tree-lined streets fronting low rise brownstones,
studios, theaters, jazz clubs, bistros, and graffiti art on brick
walls, they passed through the Washington Arch into
Washington Square Park, where they encountered a medley
of Village life: pigeons strutting on sidewalks, street
musicians, the aroma of weed wafting on a kindly breeze,
protest signs (*Fighting for peace is like balling for
chastity*), chess players, pretzel vendors and hot dog carts,
street hustlers, a gigantic wand spewing soap bubbles,
Nehru shirts and bell bottoms, kids squealing and dogs
barking in a circular wading pool, poetry reading (is that
Alan Ginsburg?), and wannabe artists seeking to capture
the essence of existence—or maybe your pencil portrait for
twenty bucks.

Back at the Bleeker Street apartment, three New York
University undergrads dropped in to greet the Minnesotans.
Mark and Alan were NYU seniors and Debbie a junior.
Mark would be tall but for a slumped over posture. His
unkempt hair extended below his shoulders. Alan's bushy

black hair matched his beard. He was average height but heavy-set. Oversized oval-framed eyeglasses dominated Debbie's appearance. The tinted eyeglasses filled her face under a thick mat of brunette hair that crowded into her face from all sides.

Dave and Wendy, front line warriors in battles from New Hampshire to Chicago to Los Angeles, were celebrities of sorts, and the New Yorkers invited them to another skirmish.

"George Wallace will speak tonight at the Garden," Mark said.

"Why is that southern segregationist in New York?" Wendy asked.

"He thinks his third-party candidacy will appeal to the grievances of white working-class voters in the north," Debbie said.

"So, we mean to heckle him from the audience," Alan said.

The seven-person entourage boarded the Broadway and Seventh Avenue local and rode the subway under the streets of Manhattan. After a few stops, they would exit at Penn Station bound for Madison Square Garden.

"Quebec, man," Alan said as the train rumbled north. "That's what I'm thinking if I can't get a draft deferment for grad school."

"Montreal is a great city, and they welcome American draft resisters with open arms," Mark added. "Something to think about."

Dave avoided Wendy's imploring eyes. He needed a plan B after his quest for the Peace Corps failed, and he didn't have much time. With the loss of his deferment, his draft board re-classified him as 1-A, and the army could come calling at any time.

Even though they arrived at Madison Square Garden well before Wallace's scheduled appearance, thousands of screaming, frenzied supporters already jammed the circular hall and joined with country musicians in renditions of "Dixie" and "I'm a Yankee Doodle Dandy." Confederate battle flags scattered in the audience offered a jarring juxtaposition to the Star-Spangled Banners hanging onstage.

The seven troublemakers from the Bleeker Street apartment joined dozens of others heckling the Alabama Governor. Along with hoisting signs saying "Nazi", the hecklers offered mock Nazi salutes. Competing chants rose to the rafters. "N … s get out!" "Go back to Africa!" and "White Power!" from one side and "Two-four-six-eight, we don't want a Fascist state" from the other.

Curious more than confrontational, Dave moved away from his compatriots for conversation with the true believers. He moved to the back of the arena where hawkers selling bumper stickers and other campaign goodies supported the campaign's coffers.

"The country is going to pot, and we're fed up," a middle-aged man in a crew cut said. "Ever'body is against 'merica: the n … s, the college kids, the newspapers. Love it or leave it, I say. Well, I'm a proud patriot and so is the governor. As president, he won't stand for these silly-assed protests, and he'll crack a few heads to restore law and order. My God, did you see those fuckin' n ... s disrespect our flag at the Olympics? Black power, my ass. They should've put those traitors in front of a firing squad right then and there."

At the recent Mexico City Olympics, American Tommy Smith set a world record while winning the 200-meter sprint, and his teammate John Carlos won the bronze medal. During the medal awards ceremony, the two black athletes bowed their heads and raised black-gloved clenched fists aloft while the American national anthem blared through the sound system and the American flag rose to the top of the flagpole. They were immediately dismissed from the American team and prevented from running the 400-meter relay. Dave knew at the time that their protest would rile up a large segment of America in a swirl of action, reaction, counteraction, overreaction, backlash. Black frustration and white angst.

"I'm ex-military," the next man said, wearing an American Legion garrison hat tilted on the side of a balding scalp and sporting a tattoo of a battleship on a bare arm. "That used to mean something. Now they spit on our boys in uniform." As he spoke, his face flushed with rage. "They stopped saying the Pledge of Allegiance in my grandkids' school. Instead, they sing the praises of that fuckin' communist, Martin Luther King."

The next man, a carpenter, said, "The country needs to wake up and really see what's goin' on. The people been taken advantage of long enuff. I shake my head ever' time I look at my paycheck. The politicians take their share from the man who breaks his back and give plenty to lazy bastards who don't give a rusty fuck about work."

Another said, "Well, let me tell you, Governor Wallace is fer us and against them. He don't look down on us like the college crowd and the elites do. He's for the common man, and he says what he thinks—what we all think."

Dave thought of Clarence Pfeffer and the Wallace bumper sticker on his rusty Ford pickup. If Clarence felt disrespected in his manure-stained bib overalls, he was probably right, Dave realized, and Dave shared the blame. Condescension may be the biggest sin of the left and motivator of the right.

Just then, a scuffle broke out on the balcony above. When a pair of women hoisted a bed sheet with the words "Seig Heil" painted in dripping red, Wallace partisans ripped the sheet away from the women and pushed, shoved, and harassed them until they retreated.

"Women's liberation my ass," a man wearing a baseball cap from Teamsters Local 814 cupped his hands and yelled at the women, and Dave moved closer to listen. "I call the loudmouths 'women's lip,'" the union man boasted. "They need to get back in the kitchen where they belong. Raise their kids to show some respect. Ugly bitches who need attention just like those hags on the Atlantic City boardwalk who protested the Miss America pageant weeks ago." As the women disappeared into an exit, he yelled again, "Go ahead, dump yer hair curlers and makeup. Burn yer bras and throw away yer girdles and let yer fat asses hang free."

The next man glanced around before flashing a policeman's badge. "I'm one of New York City's finest, but I can't wear my uniform here. You should be thankful for the police. If'n it wasn't for us; you couldn't even walk the streets. The Democrats blame us for the breakdown of law and order, but it's not us. It's a sick society led by a sick Supreme Court and sick politicians in Washington."

Finally, Wallace bounded up the steps to the platform. He fed off the energy of the standing, screaming, adoring crowd. He teased with red meat, and their unsated appetite begged for more. They especially loved it when he chewed on the hecklers.

He pointed a finger at a long hair and said, "Hey there, sweetie." With immaculate timing, he paused before adding, "Oh, excuse me. I thought you were a girl."

Tilting his head toward the dozens of hecklers, he said, "You better have your say now, I can tell you that. After November 5, you anarchists are through in this country." When supporters attacked protesters in the balcony, Wallace said, "Well you came for trouble, and you got it."

He turned to his adoring audience, "That's what's wrong with America. Our system is under attack … It's a few anarchists, a few activists, a few militants, a few revolutionaries, and a few Communists." He demonized a laundry list of enemies: pseudo-intellectuals, theoreticians, anarchists, hippies, protesters, liberals, left-wingers, professors, the media—all those he claimed looked down on the average man on the street.

He took on the establishment.

"There isn't a dime's worth of difference between Nixon and Humphrey, and they're both unfit to govern this country in the next four years."

He singled out the Supreme Court and the Justice Department for civil rights decisions and inaction against "left-wing intellectuals and Communist professors who advocate a victory for the Vietcong."

He condemned the New York Times and the television networks for encouraging "the rebellion in our streets," and dishonestly reporting on his campaign because "they just don't want the people to know what kind of support we have. Well, don't worry what the newspapers say about us … they call us extremists and want to say we're Fascists. These large newspapers think they know more than the average citizen on the streets of New York."

Raucous applause interrupted him multiple times, and when he finished, his running mate, Curtis E. LeMay, the retired Air Force general, joined him as they raised clasped hands in victory as balloons floated down on the rapturous crowd. Each time the candidates bowed at the front of the bunting-lined platform the frenzy increased. The true believers didn't care that Wallace's national polling was slipping or that LeMay was dragging down the ticket as a loose cannon advocating use of nuclear weapons.

"Have we just witnessed a Hitler youth rally?" Wendy asked as they stepped into the brisk autumn night.

It was worse outside. Hundreds, maybe more, engaged in cultural warfare that threatened physical violence. Two sides pushed and shoved and hurled insults. Outnumbered police dodged rocks and soda bottles flung from both sides. "Seig Heil" taunts from protesters were answered with "Commie faggots" from the Wallace crowd.

The Bleeker Street seven ducked around the corner.

"Give the man credit," Wendy continued. "He may be a demagogue, but he's good at it. He skillfully blends racism and anti-government hostility into a noxious brew. He screams complaints without offering solutions, only a list of grudges. He's got charisma even if it's malignant. He had them swooning on every word like Elmer Gantry at a tent revival. I'm surprised it didn't end with an altar call."

"Where does that energy in the crowd come from? What feeds the passion?" Anna asked. "It was palpable. You could cut it with a knife."

"Resentment," Debbie said. "Resentment toward blacks, browns, and the educated. And women. Did you notice how white men dominated the crowd? We've got the pill, and that gives us sexual freedom, and it pisses off the patriarchy. They don't like the bra burners."

"The system—they resent whatever they think it is that leaves them with the short stick in life," Alan said. "It's crazy ironic. They tout patriotism and then attack American institutions: the federal bureaucracy, courts and the justice system, higher education, and the press—especially the press." Alan, the history major, continued with a chilling bit of history. "Did you know that the pro-Hitler American Bund held a similar rally here at Madison Square Garden just a few decades ago? Twenty thousand showed up. The backdrop to the stage offered a huge picture of George Washington flanked by swastikas. Seems like history just goes in circles, and populist demagoguery never goes away and rears its ugly head in trying times."

"It's more than resentment," Mark said. "It's full-blown anger bordering on hate, and it's about race. They think civil rights legislation is at their expense."

"I think it's an inferiority complex, a sense of inadequacy and insecurity," Lorie said. "It starts in the south where rednecks are still embarrassed about losing the Civil War, but Wallace has struck a chord with disaffected northerners as well. Think there were any professors in that crowd? Doctors? Lawyers? College graduates? Shit, I bet many of them never graduated from high school. These people feel like they've been ignored and put down their whole life, and they've developed a chip on their shoulder as big as a log. Along comes Wallace who demonizes the elites, and they lap it up. Respect. That's what they feel they're missing."

"It's fear," Dave had the last word. "The world is spinning too fast for them, and they're afraid of being left behind. They're frustrated because they can't slow down or stop the change they don't understand. They're afraid of blacks, hippies, protesters, reporters, and you name it. They blame, they accuse, they strike out against everyone who is different from them. Against anything that threatens their comfort zone. Against everything that contradicts their world view. It's the brown paper bag syndrome. When the man who lived his whole life with a brown paper bag over his head had the bag removed, he was confronted with a reality that he didn't know, didn't believe, didn't understand, and it frightened him, so he pulled the comfortable bag over his head again, and he lashed out against anyone who tried to remove it."

They all nodded.

"Whatever the hell it was, I need to shower off after that," Debbie said.

"Catch ya later," she said, and the three NYU students hailed a cab heading south toward campus.

"How about a drink before we call it a night," Anna said as she locked arms with Lorie. "We know a place."

The foursome scampered down the steps of Penn Station where they boarded a subway train with connections to the Christopher Street station back in the West Village.

Dave and Wendy followed Anna and Lorie as they ducked into a nondescript Christopher Street bar known as the Stonewall Inn. Far, far from Kalmar. Drag queens flirted in the corners. While Dave and Wendy awkwardly perched at the bar sipping watered-down bourbon, Anna and Lorie slow danced to Frankie Valli and the Four Seasons on the juke box. The dance floor filled with men dancing with men and women with women.

Back at Dave's high school dances, the girls often danced with other girls, and everyone assumed that was because the boys were too self-conscious to step onto the floor. That was true enough, but Dave wondered if some of his female classmates were truly being themselves, even if they didn't fully understand. Or, maybe they understood but no one else did.

"Hey, girlfriend. Care to dance?" A well-dressed biracial woman with a butch haircut approached Wendy.

"Oh, that's sweet, but I'm with him," Wendy said, and she planted a wet kiss on Dave's lips, followed by a lingering look into his eyes.

"No harm in asking," the woman said with a wink. As she stepped away, she turned back and said over her shoulder, "Ain't love grand?"

Suddenly, the pairings on the dance floor separated as the lights flashed and uniformed police rushed in. In the chaos of the police raid, Dave and Wendy soon found themselves in the back of a paddy wagon seated next to the woman who had just approached Wendy. Somehow, Anna and Lorie slipped away into the night.

"It don't mean nuthin', honey," the woman said to Wendy. "They'll haul us to the precinct station, snap our picture to scare us, but then release us without charges. They do this all the time. Stonewall is our safe place to be ourselves, and they know that. It's just frickin' harassment. I think it's how the police get their rocks off. One day, they'll go too far, and …" her voice trailed off.

Dave sat next to a diminutive man dressed in a cheap business suit. He removed his coke bottle glasses and dabbed at his eyes with a handkerchief.

"You ok, mister?" Dave asked.

The man blew his nose and shook his head.

"No, I'm not ok. The Stonewall is my safe place, and the police want to take that away from me. They violated my sanctuary. I've been bullied all my life. At work, I try to speak with a deep voice and act macho, but I know they talk about me and laugh at me behind my back. When I discovered the Stonewall, I found a family to replace the family that abandoned me long ago. In a world that seems so mean and angry, Stonewall is the sanctuary where we can unwind and forget about the darkness out there. It is home where I'm accepted for who I am. I can be myself. No pretending. No hiding in a closet. But those assholes in uniforms want to take that away from us."

Dave didn't know how to react or what to say. This was all new to him. It seemed his own world looked like the inside of a brown paper bag. He regretted laughing at and sharing queer jokes, but that was an abstraction, and now he was face-to-face with the real flesh and blood consequences of ignorance. Face-to-face with the effects of trivializing or demonizing others who were different. Face-to-face with the results of fear-borne prejudice.

He wondered which of his friends was in the closet. Who had he offended, or worse, frightened. Who was afraid to honestly share their true selves with him. That was on him.

Dave reached out to shake the man's hand.

"My name is Dave. What's yours?"

"Benjamin," the man said with a surprised but thankful look as if he appreciated Dave's recognition of his humanity.

Chapter Twenty-nine

Beans and the others returned to guard duty on the remote firebase. After the gunships had sprayed the valley with thousands of rounds and the Howitzers on the firebase obliterated the way station, with the help of Beans' platoon to raze the remains, the men on the firebase figured the ass kicking had chased the NVA out of that valley.

The NVA had other ideas. It seems they were pissed off, and they returned with a vengeance.

The firebase wasn't the only high ground, and the assault began at nightfall with recoilless rifle fire (mobile mini cannons) and mortar fire from surrounding hilltops. The shelling was as persistent as the monsoon rain. The Howitzers returned fire toward the unseen enemy, but mini cannons and mortars were mobile, and the enemy moved whenever the Howitzers began to zero in.

When the shelling started, Beans and his rifle squad scrambled from their bunks to man positions in a defensive bunker on the perimeter. Defensive bunkers were reasonably well-fortified, even if they didn't keep the rain out. The roof consisted of three layers of sandbags atop corrugated steel sheets laid across steel girders with a good seven feet of standing room below. Shooting slits faced outward toward the perimeter, and all their M-16s rested there, along with stacks of full clips of ammo. A single M-60 machine gun rested on a V-shaped muzzle support with belts of thirty-caliber ammo folded alongside. Sam, the tall and lean black man from Dallas, was the designated machine gunner. One end of the bunker wasn't as deep and stayed relatively dry. That's where supplies and radios were stored.

Shifts of two or three men at a time stood at the shooting slits to keep an eye on the concertina wire about thirty meters down the hillside in front of the bunker. The others sat on overturned pails in the mire to snatch some shuteye or engage in nervous banter. Sam's pet monkey chittered on his shoulder; the monkey didn't like the shelling any more than the men did. Minutes seemed to take more than sixty seconds and hours more than sixty minutes. Nothing to do but listen to the shells exploding topside.

THUD.

BOOM.

When mortar rounds landed close, they first heard the thud and then the explosion. The sandbag roof shuddered, and sand filtered down on the men following the direct hit on their bunker. There would be a pock mark atop the bunker and the roof a little thinner in that spot, but it would take multiple direct hits by the mortar fire to breach the bunker.

Sometime after midnight, the incoming stopped. Fifteen minutes passed, then half an hour.

"You figure they're finished?" Frankie asked. "It'll be daylight soon, and mebbe they're moving out before we can call in helicopter gunships to light up their asses."

"Could be, or mebbe they're just movin' around. Mebbe our artillery has zeroed in on their positions," Beans answered.

"Let's stretch our legs and see how the others are doin'" Frankie said.

"I dunno. Let's give it another ten." Beans said.

Ten minutes later, they stepped outside, carrying their M-16s with a bandolier of extra magazines slung around their shoulders.

"Don't look too bad," Frankie said, but the mess tent was a smoldering ruin.

A few others milled about from other bunkers, and the red glow of cigarettes lit up the night.

"Everybody ok?" Someone yelled out.

"No biggie," Beans replied.

"Shit. Look at that," Frankie said, pointing to the flagpole that had been knocked over. "We gotta fix it."

Frankie wasn't one to wrap himself in the flag, but it just wasn't right that Old Glory wasn't flapping in the breeze atop the command bunker. Beans followed him atop the sandbag roof to prop the flagpole back into position, and the muddy flag again took its rightful pride of place overlooking the firebase.

Just then, the unmistakable high-pitched whistle of an artillery round screeched overhead.

PHWWWWWHHT.

BOOM.

"Holy shit!" Frankie said as an explosion knocked over trees just outside the perimeter on the far side of the firebase. "That was no mortar. That was a big gun. NVA artillery is zeroing in from miles away, probably across the border in Cambodia."

PHWWWWWHHT

There was something ironic about incoming artillery; it was lethal as hell, but the screaming hiss warned you to duck for cover, and they hauled ass toward the bunker with Beans in the lead.

THUD

BOOM

Beans lunged toward the bunker as the exploding artillery shell pushed a rush of air that lifted him and slammed him against the corrugated steel entrance to the bunker. He bounced down the steps as pieces of gravel shrapnel peppered the metal behind him with chinking noises.

"You ok, brother?" Lieutenant Farnsworth asked.

Beans sat up holding his misshapen left wrist. A jagged edge of bone protruded through the skin. The artillery explosions continued for a few minutes and then stopped.

Sam, the machine gunner, surprised everyone by firing a burst from his M-60 into the dark.

"What the hell, man?"

"I thought I heard something or saw something," Sam replied. "I think there's movement out there."

"Throw an illumination grenade to light up the concertina wire," Farnsworth said.

Jonesy tossed a white phosphorous grenade to the left and another to the right.

"Fuckin' sappers are in the wire!"

Their bodies camouflaged with charcoal dust and grease, the elite NVA special forces the troops called sappers had crept close to the concertina wire while the firebase defenders lay low under the barrage of artillery fire, and the sappers opened a hole with wire cutters to penetrate the outer defense and infiltrate the base.

The sappers' coordination with their artillery missed by seconds; if they had been quicker and breached the concertina wire before the artillery stopped, they would have caused mayhem from inside the base tossing satchel charges into bunkers and mowing down anyone who popped out. As it was, the first sappers through the wire stepped right into the flashing muzzles of multiple M-16s spitting out hundreds of rounds while Sam the M-60 gunner fired in short bursts. Beans wiped the mud off his M-16 with the cleanest spot on his shirt and made it to the wall where the others fired into the night. Unable to cradle the rifle with his left arm, Beans rested the barrel on the shoulder-level earth and fired single rounds. The sappers attempted to fight back by firing AK 47s and throwing satchel charges uphill, but they landed short of the bunker. The first few through the wire died within seconds, and the others quickly pulled back.

"Conserve yer ammo! Hold yer fire. Flick yer safeties to single fire when they come again," Farnsworth yelled.

Beans stopped firing and looked around the bunker.

"Where's Frankie?" he asked. No one answered, and he knew. Frankie was behind him when they scrambled back to the bunker as the NVA artillery shell exploded, and he didn't make it.

Beans dropped down and squatted on the clay floor of the bunker with his back against the mud wall. He gulped the air that reeked of gunpowder. Adrenaline had masked his pain, but now he clenched his teeth and his eyelids against the throbbing in his wrist. Shutting his eyes had been nightmarish ever since he set fire to the hooch with the young mother and child inside, but now he saw Frankie squatting on a rocky outcropping alongside a bubbling stream, whittling a hollow bamboo shoot into a whistle, bush hat characteristically canted toward the right over a crinkly mass of brown hair, shirtless with dog tags dangling over a hairy chest.

Beans' eye slits opened to an empty bunker entrance with moonbeams filtering through smoke and dust.

Frankie had been the rock, the permanent fixture in their impermanent soldierly existence, the Bronx Gibraltar. Although others would have their day and die, Beans didn't believe that law applied to Frankie. Frankie had a cheerful fatalism about him, a whistling-past-the-graveyard sense of humor that seemed to give him an aura of invincibility as if his joking warded off danger. "A week from now, I'll be seven days dead," he would say with a laugh, white teeth flashing through dark stubble. *La vida loca.* Despite death always stalking the men of Alpha Company, Beans oddly assumed that Frankie was indestructible, but the blinding flash of an exploding artillery round exposed the fragile reality.

In the dimly lit bunker, wide pupils followed a spider scrambling to a fly writhing against the sticky sinews of web. With a sting, the spider injected venom, and the fly's struggles were soon over.

"Sting me," Beans mumbled.

When the NVA sappers pulled back, the mortar fire and recoilless rifle fire from nearby hilltops picked up, punctuated by occasional artillery rounds. Twice more before dawn, NVA sappers attempted to penetrate the concertina, but both times M-60 and M-16 rifle fire from Beans' bunker repelled them. When the morning sun burned through the mist rising from the valley, half a dozen mother's sons from the north lay dead, strewn in and around the gap in the concertina wire.

With the dawn, Puff the Magic Dragon arrived. Some called her Spooky. She was an old, WWII vintage, lumbering, fixed-wing prop plane that slowly circled the perimeter, but Christ Almighty could she bring hellfire from the sky. With three mounted miniguns with Gatling style rotating barrels, Spooky could fire up to 18,000 M-60 rounds a minute. Not that she did. To conserve ammo, she would fire short bursts from one or the other guns as she circled the firebase in a counterclockwise direction, banking with her portside tilted toward the target because the guns were mounted on that side. Since every sixth round was a tracer and with thousands of rounds fired, the effect appeared as a stream of fire pouring from the sky. If Spooky didn't kill the enemy, she sure as hell scared the shit out of them.

Spooky quieted the mortar fire, the small arms fire, and the recoilless rifle fire in minutes, and a few brave souls ventured outside the bunker to repair the breach in the wire. Dead sappers in black pajamas were draped in the wire like scarecrows to ward off unwanted visitors. If Charlie came again, he would have to blast a new hole. Others filled sandbags and added layers to the bunker roofs.

All they could find of Frankie was a single bloody boot with his name and number stitched inside. Everyone had a number preceded by RA for men who enlisted or US for draftees. Frankie was an RA who signed up to fight and die for the country that barely recognized him as a citizen.

Spooky didn't carry enough ammo to remain on station long. Soon after she left, the mortars again started exploding into the base. About the time the mortars would let up, recoilless rifles picked up. It was obvious that the mobile mortars and recoilless rifles kept repositioning. When they were moving, the shelling stopped, and then it would pick up again from a new direction. The howitzers returned fire. The men in the bunkers remained hunkered down like moles in their holes. Then the monsoon kicked in, and rainclouds hung low over the hilltop spilling buckets that muddied the red clay and pooled in low spots in the bunker.

During the close combat, Beans' pain was secondary, but when the shooting died down, intense pain flared up; at least, that's when he noticed it. In mid-morning, a medic scrambled into the bunker and did his best to clean the open wound before splinting the wrist and wrapping it in gauze.

"This is your ticket home, soldier. We'll land a dust off when the rain and the shelling die down and get you out a here."

"*When* the shelling dies down?' Beans replied. He figured he would spend eternity here shooting, and sweating, and pissing his pants, and alternately praying and cursing God. Maybe that was the same thing.

"You in pain?"

The sweat beads on Beans' chalky, pale face answered for him.

"This'll help for a few hours."

The medic pulled the wire loop off the end of a morphine syrette and inserted the needle just under the skin on Beans' arm. With thumb and forefinger, he squeezed the tube, and the narcotic flowed into Beans' veins which allowed him to catch snatches of sleep sitting on a pail, leaning against a muddy clay wall, as water from a leaky roof dripped into the pool that soaked his boots.

Toward evening, the pain returned, and the guys in the bunker expected a ground assault at any minute, but the sappers never returned. Only the fucking, relentless shelling. And the rain. Beans almost wished the dinks would come rushing in again because then he could forget the pain.

The medic returned the next morning and changed the dressing. Beans was a shivering, pale hulk. The persistent monsoon rains saturated everything and kept helicopter support from approaching the remote firebase.

"This is the last one I have," he said, as he injected another morphine syrette.

When the medic returned the third morning, he didn't say much, but Beans could see for himself. Telltale red streaks on his arm spidered out from the wound. He figured he would lose the arm to infection, and he half wished the medic would chop it off then and there if it would stop the pain.

That's when the rain lifted, Spooky returned quelling the mortar fire, and dust-off medivac helicopters came in and carried Beans and other wounded men out of there.

In anesthesia-addled consciousness, Beans imagined Cass Elliot of the Mamas and Papas floating around him singing encouragement to dream, but only nightmares visited his sleep.

What was that? What was that sound? Frankie, did you hear it? I heard a whimper. Nah, it wasn't nothing. Hell yes, it was a whimper. I heard it. Did you hear it, Sam? There it is again. Tell me you hear it. It's a goddammed whimper. Poncho, can you hear it now? It's growing louder. It's more than a whimper, it's a moan. Course it is. It's a fucking moan. Dozer, can you hear it? You must hear it. It's a wail. Cover your ears. It's so damned loud. Cover your ears, you sonofabitches. Can you see it? I don't see it. Mebbe, I do see it. I see something. It's coming closer and wailing. Can you see it? Can you hear it? I can't stop the wailing! I can't stop it coming closer! I see it now. Do you see it? It's black as soot. And red. Red cracked skin. Stop the fuckin' wailing, you goddammed burnt piece of shit! Get back! Get back! Stop screaming! You're making my ears bleed. Stop bawling, please stop bawling, please, please, please.

Beans awoke gasping, cheeks wet with tears. The room spun around him.

"Easy soldier. Breathe. Lay back."

He sensed he had been here before, but he struggled to get his bearings. He feared shutting his eyes lest the dream of the burned baby return, but he shut them anyway to stop the room from spinning. He wriggled his toes and flexed his right hand into a fist. He tried to wriggle his fingers on his left hand, but he couldn't feel anything.

The heavy-set nurse who had treated him weeks earlier wiped his forehead with a damp cloth. Beans remembered her, the captain who looked like Mama Cass Elliot.

"You don't feel warm. I think the fever has broken."

"Where am I?"

"You're back at the 71st Evacuation Hospital at Camp Enari. You were here before for treatment of a dog bite on your left wrist. Now you broke the same arm, and a nasty infection set in. You won't be here long. You're about to go for a jet ride to Japan for rehab and further treatment."

He attempted to make a fist with his left hand, but he felt nothing. He couldn't look.

"Did they cut it off?"

"No, it's there, for now at least, surgically put back together and numbed with a local anesthetic and pumped full of antibiotics. They'll decide the best treatment when you get to Japan. For now, you need to rest. Sweet dreams, soldier," Mama Cass said.

Beans walked alone down a long hallway to the rehabilitation center. The cityscape of Yokohama, Japan, loomed beyond the red leaves of trees ablaze in the sun outside the hallway windows. A squat Japanese man dressed in the uniform of a janitor bowed slightly as Beans passed. Beans paused to admire the view.

"What kind of trees are those?" he asked, and the janitor again bowed slightly, but did not speak.

Beans jabbed emphatically toward the red trees with the forefinger of his right hand.

"Trees."

The janitor smiled broadly and nodded.

"*Kito*," he said and mimicked Beans' jabbing finger. "*Kito*."

The janitors, cooks, and other workers were Japanese, but the doctors, nurses, and administrators of the 106th General Hospital in Yokohama were Americans. Beans rehabbed his left arm following surgery to set the compound fracture. He was airlifted to Japan for continuing treatment of the infection and rehabilitation soon after he regained consciousness. Heavy doses of antibiotics and daily wound care had the infection under control, and now daily therapy was improving the stiffness and mobility of his left wrist as the broken bones mended.

A short female orderly assisted his rehab specialist.

"Is *Kito* the name of the trees outside the hallway window?" Beans asked the diminutive Japanese woman.

At first, she looked confused. "Akiko?"

"No, *Kito*, the red trees outside."

"Ah yes, *Kito*. Red trees. *Kito* means calm."

Beans detected a slight blush in her face.

"I thought you asked my name," she said. "My name is Akiko."

"What does Akiko mean?"

She twisted her face as if to say, "I don't know," and they both laughed.

After therapy, Beans paused for a long time at the hallway windows. Of all the emotions that flashed through him in alternating waves--anger, resentment, remorse, loneliness, and too many more to name—fear was no longer one of them, but neither was calm. He realized how frightened he had been in Vietnam. Every hour of every day, fear lived with him, even if he didn't consciously know it at the time. Now, he recognized it by its absence.

Kito. Calm. At peace. He sensed tranquility in the brilliant crimson leaves, jangled branches, and twisted trunks of the *Kito* trees. There was harmony in the whole. He aspired to calmness even as agitation in various forms flared up regularly. Peace had come to his external existence but not yet to his internal psyche.

He expected to stay in Japan for weeks, and as soon as the surgical wound healed and the bones knit together, he would likely be shipped back to Vietnam. In the meantime, he wandered through the grounds surrounding the hospital and the Kishine Barracks that housed the American personnel, but he always found his way to a bench under the sprawling *Kito* trees with the brilliant end-of-summer leaves. Must be related to the sugar maples on a hillock on the home place half a world away, he mused.

Akiko the orderly saw him there and poked her head out the window.

"Officer Beans!" she exclaimed. Akiko didn't understand American naming conventions or rank any more than he understood Japanese.

"Hello, *Kito*." He intentionally mixed up her name with the trees.

"No, my name is Akiko. The trees are *Kito*."

He knew that, and she knew he twisted the names intentionally. It was their running joke.

"Come outside and sit with me," Beans said.

"No, no. On duty now."

"When are you off duty?"

Beans gazed across a pond at a pagoda rising above the trees on the far side. The pagoda looked like a stack of pyramids piled one above the other—a three-tiered tower with multiple squared eaves. Fall had begun to spray the foliage in multi colors, highlighted by the crimson *Kito* leaves. A mat of pinkish/purplish flowers floated as an island on the calm pond waters.

Akiko invited him to the garden on her day off, and it was easy enough for him to simply walk through the guard gate manned by MPs. All it took was a friendly wave, and it would be just as easy when he returned. Walking off base like that would have been unthinkable in Vietnam.

Beans and Akiko followed a path that meandered through the Sankeien Gardens on the outskirts of Yokohama. Decades earlier, a silk trader built this garden, and the city restored everything after WWII bombs had wreaked their damage. Her brother followed along and lingered nearby--a basket-bearing chaperone.

Beans towered over Akiko by nearly a foot and a half. Her close-cropped straight black hair in a soup-bowl haircut draped over her ears. A traditional white kimono with an understated floral pattern sash replaced her hospital uniform.

Akiko turned her head, scanning the garden. "You like?"

Beans breathed in the mixed scents of many flowers hanging in the air. He slowly exhaled through his mouth. He surveyed the garden grounds and then fixed his eyes on her. He nodded.

"I like."

The garden grounds were lush, verdant, and beautiful, and the traditional buildings mindful of a time and place with a culture and customs unknown to Beans, but it was the spiritual tranquility of the place that most appealed to him.

"Thank you for bringing me," he said. "I like."

A slight breeze rippled the pond water and rustled leaves. Akiko gently traced her fingers across the pink flowers of a bush.

"When we touch a flower, we are reminded that we are part of nature," she said. "*Ikebana*. When you arrange flowers, you forget worries. *Ikebana* and brewing tea are the two things a young girl must learn to become a good housewife." She glanced at Beans and blushed.

Her brother unpacked his basket on a grassy knoll and lit coals in a small brazier. He stepped aside and Akiko performed the simple, methodical, and highly ritualized steps of preparing tea for her honored guest. She performed her tasks prayerfully, glancing often at Beans, wringing her slight hands as she nervously waited for the water to warm.

"*Ichi go ichi e,*" she said. "Each moment only occurs once."

Beans' head twitched slightly sideways, subconsciously saying, "No!" and a soft sadness washed over him as it dawned on him that this bliss would pass, and he opened his hands as if to catch and hold the fleeting serenity. He glanced nervously at the chaperone brother as he restrained himself from clutching Akiko and holding her tight.

"Officer Beans, I have something for you." Akiko rapidly approached him several days later, holding papers in extended hands. He quickly scanned the paperwork. He would be leaving sooner than expected, but he would not return to Vietnam. His Japanese rehabilitation was over, and he received orders for a convalescent leave home. The flight would leave the very next day.

"You must be so happy," she said with misty eyes.

His war was over, or so it seemed, but he wasn't sure what he felt. He unclasped the shell necklace he had purchased in Thailand and placed it around her neck.

"For you to remember your tall American friend. You have been so kind, and your brewed tea chases away my demons."

Akiko stood on her tiptoes and kissed him, blushed at her boldness, and then scurried away, sobbing.

Chapter Thirty

Dave munched on Old Dutch potato chips and sipped a
Pepsi as he sat on Frank Nelson's couch watching the black
and white TV images of news anchors reporting election
results. The latest polls and early returns were promising.
The presidential race was close, much closer than the
Democrats dared hope just a few weeks earlier. Frank
shrugged his shoulders and raised his eyebrows as if to say,
"maybe," as he switched back and forth between ABC,
NBC, and CBS network news, but hope was an elusive
sentiment that dared not be voiced aloud following an
election season of discontent.

"Just two months ago, Humphrey's moribund
campaign was on life support," Frank said. "Polls said he
was behind Nixon by double digits and barely ahead of
Wallace. Following the recent civil rights legislation
enacted by a Democratic administration, the solid south
was gone for the Democrats."

"A noble effort, Dave said, but at a high political
price."

"You're catching on," Frank said. "But it's more than
that. The Democratic Party was in disarray following
assassinations, urban violence, and street warfare on
display at the Chicago Convention. Meanwhile, the glib
Nixon campaign ran television ads depicting bloodied
protesters on the streets of Chicago, neighborhoods ablaze,
and graphic scenes of Americans under fire in Vietnam.
Nixon exuded calmness and normalcy contrasted with
Democratic chaos. Nixon artfully avoided policy

discussions beyond platitudes in front of fawning questioners at staged town halls. 'I believe in progress,' Nixon said with a broad smile, or 'It's better to look forward than to look back,' but did he actually have a plan to end the war?"

"Of course not," Dave said.

Frank continued his monologue.

"Barely a month before the election, Humphrey finally became his own man declaring support for a bombing halt to spur negotiations that would end the war sooner than later, and his campaign turned on a dime. Protesters stopped appearing at his rallies with 'Dump the Hump' signs and instead claimed 'If You Mean it, We're With You.' Hecklers transformed into cheerleaders. Polling showed a narrowing race. The contrast between the bumbling Spiro Agnew, the Republican candidate for Vice President who couldn't refrain from insulting one ethnic group after another, and the calm, reasoned Senator Muskie, the Democratic Veep candidate, may have helped narrow the gap as well."

But, in the end, it mattered for naught, and by the time Frank went to bed, the sad results appeared ominous.

"Damn it," Frank said late the next morning when the networks finally called it for Nixon.

It was close and Nixon won by less than a percentage point in the popular vote, but he won. Humphrey easily carried his home state of Minnesota, including at the local town hall precinct where Frank voted. Dave was still underage. Wallace carried five states in the south and received nearly 14% of the popular vote nationwide, but Humphrey's late surge reclaimed much of Wallace's support in the union halls of the north, and the segregationist didn't come close outside of Dixie even if he had revealed a mass of disaffected white, blue-collar voters persuadable by demagogic rants.

"Two weeks. If the election had two more weeks, Humphrey might have caught up."

Frank shook his head.

"If Humphrey had broken with Johnson's war policy earlier, he might have pulled off a miracle comeback. When LBJ stopped the bombing just a couple of days before the election, Humphrey's position was validated, but when our supposed allies, the South Vietnamese government, refused to participate in peace talks, I smelled a rat. Don't know how, but I suspect Nixon's cronies somehow got to the South Vietnamese leaders and threw a wrench in the gears of the proposed peace talks just to stem Humphrey's momentum."

Soon after the networks called the race, Dave and Frank departed in his pickup. They had an appointment at the Hazelden Clinic in a small city north of Minneapolis. Dave had convinced Frank to give alcoholism treatment a close look.

A grim-faced Frank drove his pickup to Hazelden. Dave would drive it home and pick him up later if the counselor persuaded Frank to stay for treatment. The drive was silent, unusual for the usually chatty professor turned painter. Frank answered the counselor's questions honestly if half-heartedly, and he didn't put up much of a squawk with the recommendation for in-patient treatment.

Dave returned alone to Kalmar. He moved into Frank's house, and he would do his best to handle minor painting jobs in Frank's absence. Living in his father's house had become unbearable.

Even the old neighborhood of Kalmar seemed mean and foreign. The bituminous streets where the gang spent hours biking were now riddled with potholes. For reasons unknown, the stately elms in the front yard of the Lutheran parsonage had disappeared. The friendly old lady that the kids called Auntie Alice had passed away, and her house was shuttered and empty. No one picked the apples from her Haralson tree, and rotting fruit lay in the uncut grass.

How could the town change so much in two short years?

Business was booming at the United States Navy enlistment office situated in a strip mall store front. Dave leaned against Frank's pickup while watching the comings and the goings, trying to appear nonchalant, like a thief casing the joint. He gauged the look on the faces of the men his age who arrived compared to their disposition upon leaving. When he finally mustered the courage to approach the glass storefront door, he spied someone on the other side about to leave, and Dave ducked away as if he would be caught committing some grievous deed, an act of nefarious mischief. He walked slowly down the block, kicking at grassy clumps that sprouted in the sidewalk cracks, casting furtive side glances at storefront windows. When he finally approached the door a second time, he just stood there looking in, but then he was swept inside as if by fate when someone behind him opened the door and said, "After you."

"Ensign Gregory will see you soon," the receptionist in civilian clothing said, handing him a pen and a clipboard with a form to be completed, and Dave took a seat in a waiting area with half a dozen other young men.

Bright-eyed and bushy-tailed, the ensign appeared in a starched uniform and escorted Dave to a small interview room. The ensign was himself a newbie, fresh off a college ROTC program, but he was an earnest promoter of the Navy way.

"What kind of training are you looking for," the ensign asked, looking up from the questionnaire Dave filled out.

"Well, after college I'm thinking about law school."

The ensign pursed his lips and narrowed his eye slits.

"Hmm, the Judge Advocacy General Corps is where our lawyers go, but they are law school graduates not college dropouts."

Dave shrugged. He assumed the ensign didn't mean to insult him, but it was what it was.

"We do have administrative support positions for JAG, but those would require a six-year commitment."

"What's the normal commitment for a less specialized position?" Dave asked even if he already knew that a Navy enlistment would double the two-year service requirement of an army draftee, but at least he wouldn't get shot at in a hot war zone.

"Four years, and that will qualify you for the GI bill that will help pay for college and law school later."

"Can I lock in geographical assignments?" Dave asked, preferring to stay away from Southeast Asia.

"No, afraid not. You can make requests, but …" his voice trailed off.

"Do you have brochures that I can take with me to consider? Other helpful information?"

"So, you're not ready to enlist today?" the disappointed ensign asked as he pulled paperwork out of a drawer.

"I need to think about it, to figure out the area of training," Dave said, gathering up the publications the ensign offered.

Enlisting in the National Guard had already been ruled out. Their quota was full due to heavy demand from others like Dave seeking to avoid the draft. The Air Force required a service commitment similar to the Navy. Dave didn't even bother to look over the brochures received from Ensign Gregory. Even as his options appeared to be drying up, he was paralyzed with inaction.

Dave settled into a monotonous routine living in Frank's house. Soap operas. Game shows. Occasional painting gigs. Dave looked forward to weekends and football. The University of Minnesota Golden Gophers lost a riveting game to the defending national champions from the University of Southern California and their running back, OJ Simpson. The Minnesota Vikings pursued their first championship of the Central Division of the NFL under young coach Bud Grant, a U grad, but NBC left Dave and millions of fans howling when the network pulled the plug on the broadcast of the most anticipated game of the year. The New York Jets quarterbacked by Joe Namath faced off against the Oakland Raiders, but NBC switched to a telecast of a made-for-tv version of *Heidi* with only two minutes remaining in the game. It didn't help the outcry when the public later learned of the twists and turns and thrilling conclusion to the game that occurred while Heidi tended goats in the Swiss Alps.

Dave knew of Elvis Presley, of course, but not the heart throb of the '50s when he ruled as the King of rock and roll while Dave was still in elementary school. He never understood the swooning affection Hannah, his older sister, expressed. After Elvis joined the army in 1960, the luster of his star faded, and he embarked on a movie career rather than spinning hit records. He retained a following, to be sure, but the movies were crap. Then came a December Comeback Concert on network TV, and Dave tuned in out of curiosity and boredom.

Holy shit! Dude could sing with charisma oozing from every sweaty pore. He reprised his greatest hits, and Dave rose to his feet and danced alone in Frank's living room. Then came the finale, which Dave heard as an ode to the MLK *I have a Dream* speech but with achiness because the dream was elusive.

TV distractions barely masked Dave's anguish over the reality of his 1-A draft status. He felt guilty for screwing up, alternating with resentment for a system that put him in this quandary. Self-pity and a fatalistic sense of impending martyrdom loomed over him.

He was confused, for sure, as he wrestled with bad options.

He quickly rejected the idea of service in the Navy or Air Force even if they offered a safe alternative. All branches of the armed services were no less part of the war machine than the frontline Army and Marine Corps. The four-year service obligation made that decision easy.

His privilege smacked him in the face when he lost his deferment. If fate decreed that his generation must suffer the burden of Vietnam, why should the onus be on others to risk life and limb? How could he justify sitting on the sidelines while thousands of others sacrificed? Self-doubt pricked at his conscience. Was smug war resistance on moral grounds nothing more than rationalizing selfishness?

Maybe he should just accept the draft, put in his two years, and be done with it. Not all draftees were sent to Vietnam. Even many Vietnam-bound draftees were assigned to less dangerous specialties than front line duty. Surely the army would put his intellect to good use. Did he feel lucky? Should he roll the dice?

On the other hand, didn't he have the obligation to resist an immoral war? What does that even mean?

Should he burn his draft card and face criminal charges for draft evasion? Would a conviction lead to jail time? A black mark on his future resume? Disqualification for law school or admission to the bar or other pathways to the good life? Must he go along to get along as the entry fee for participation in the American dream?

The idea of fleeing to Canada or Sweden grew on him, but where would he go and what would he do in once he got there? When could he return? He would be alone leaving friends and family behind. He certainly couldn't ask Angie to join him.

Could he?

Chapter Thirty-one

Beans laid his weapon's muzzle across his left forearm to steady his aim at his unsuspecting quarry. The soreness in his left wrist had dissipated, but it remained stiff, and he had difficulty holding onto a gun stock. Not to worry, nestling the rifle barrel in the folds of his sleeve worked well enough. An opening in the brushy patch presented a clear shot. Less than thirty meters. No way he could miss a clean kill at this distance. The front sight hovered over the chest where his bullet would rip heart or lungs. He flipped off the safety. A single shot would do. He sucked in a breath and held it as the trigger finger on his right hand touched the resistance in the curvature of the trigger.

Steady, steady, squeeze, do not jerk, squeeze.

Suddenly he stopped. He lifted his head, raised his right hand crisply to his forehead, and saluted his target. The magnificent whitetail buck with an impressive rack snorted and bounded away with his tail held high.

Beans blew warm breaths over his chilly hands and pulled on his mittens. Instead of green fatigues, he wore a bright red wool coat with a blaze orange hat with ear flaps.

He climbed down from his tree stand and trudged slowly through the fresh fallen snow on the floor of the Tamarac swamp on the north edge of the Pfeffer farm. He smiled inwardly as he remembered the familiar sound of boots crunching through powder snow. He knew this place deep in his bones. The afternoon sun warmed his soul if not his skin. The breaths that steamed in front of his face reminded him that he was safe and alive.

Noble white pines and sturdy burr oaks on a hillside replaced triple canopy jungle and spurred wonder that he had actually returned home. The sugar maples had shed their brilliant autumnal colors, and he wondered about the bright red *Kito* trees of Japan. And Akiko. He often thought of Akiko, the petite orderly who befriended him and served him tea in a garden.

As he approached the farmstead, the old house seemed small and shabby. He hadn't remembered the chipped paint, or the drooping rain gutters, but now the disrepair made the place look sad and tired. The roof of the chicken coop where the hens laid their eggs sagged, and it seemed like a heavy snowfall would collapse the whole damn thing.

His homecoming was strange and surreal, and his mood changed as fast as the Minnesota weather. Tranquility was transitory with despondency always close at hand spurred by guilt at the very fact that he was home and alive and well. His minds-eye had often visited these haunts as he slept under the Vietnam stars, but now that he was here, what had been familiar now seemed strange and cold and barren.

He spied his ma through the kitchen window, hard at work—as always—preparing supper. She promised pot roast with potatoes and carrots for supper. He would ladle the brown gravy on thick. Ma seemed softer than he remembered, and her round, puffy face with pouty lips broke into a smile when he was around.

Pa warned him to come home from hunting early because an early season blizzard was blowing in, and the dark clouds on the western horizon said it was so. After he helped Ma with the supper dishes, he climbed the stairs to his second-floor bedroom where gusts of wind buffeted his window. Heavy snowflakes nearly blotted out the solitary yard light outside his second-floor window. As he gazed into the storm, the swirling snow carried the pleading eyes of the NVA soldier in the instant his life ended; he heard the wail of a newborn in the howling wind; and a wind gust slammed Frankie's empty boot against the barn. Suddenly, his heart raced, he drew rapid breaths, and then he collapsed onto the floor, chest heaving with sobs.

His minor scrape with law enforcement ended well enough, thanks to a forgiving manager at a St. Cloud department store. When Beans discovered plastic M-16 facsimiles in the toy section, he smashed the imitation weapons of war on the tile floor, but the policeman called to the scene agreed not to press charges after Beans paid for the damage, satisfying the store manager.

Beans' convalescent leave began with a flight from Tokyo to SeaTac airport. The airliner passed directly over the hollowed out, concave peak of Mt. Fuji. It appeared barren but who knew what bubbled beneath, awaiting a sudden and violent eruption when the pressure would become too great.

When he reached Fort Lewis for processing, he placed a collect call from a payphone.

"Hey Ma, it's me. I'm back on US soil. Can Pa pick me up at the airport?"

He heard her gasping for breath, but she didn't speak.

"Ma, did you hear me? I'm coming home. Can Pa pick me up at the airport?"

Between sobs, Mary Ann Pfeffer stammered, "When? What time?"

His Ma's voice on the phone crackled in his ear. The morning sun haloed the snowy peak of Mount Ranier. Fallen leaves rustled in a chill autumn breeze, and his cheek felt the bite of it. The aroma of steaks sizzling on a grill wafted past, and his mouth watered. After the phone call, he would visit the twenty-four-hour steakhouse where he would receive a welcome-home steak with real American beef.

Vietnam had been surreal, but this was reality as he remembered it. Sense had replaced nonsense. Normalcy. He gave his Ma his flight details with moist eyes and a catch in his voice. He was home.

The Kalmar Trucking Company cattle truck never carried a more esteemed guest riding shotgun. And silent. Not that Clarence Pfeffer was much of a conversationalist, but the journey from the airport to Kalmar passed quietly except for the rumble of the diesel engine. As they neared the Pfeffer farmstead, Clarence finally spoke, but the words caught in his throat.

"I'm glad… I'm glad you're home safe, Son."

Clarence usually called Beans "Boy."

Willard Lofgren was Kalmar's local grocer and his parents before him. He was Willie as a boy working in his pa's store, and he was Willie now. When holding court behind the counter, Willie sported a red bowtie behind an oversized white cotton duck apron that barely covered his barrel chest. His flabby-jowled face suggested a man of mirth, but when it came down to business, his eyes revealed earnest sobriety.

Willie took great pride in the orderly shelves of canned goods, breads and cereals, health and hygiene, household necessities, and everything else the denizens of Kalmar required in their daily lives. Narrow aisleways separated the shelves with a cooler behind the counter holding eggs and dairy, but no meat, except hot dogs, salamis, and prepackaged bacon, and it saddened Willie that the meat lockers in the back of the store were now relegated to mere storage. Town folks purchased meat from butcher Emil Mokros, or they stored up half a beef in their freezer purchased directly from a local farmer, or worse, from a supermarket elsewhere.

Only strangers paid with cash or a check at the Lofgren Grocery. The locals charged their purchases, and each item was carefully scribed into that customer's ledger tucked beneath the counter with bills due at the end of the month. With living quarters upstairs over the main street storefront, Willie and Mae, his wife, and their two teenage daughters, Lorraine and Lily, took turns behind the single counter. Sometimes Willie's sister, a nearby farm wife, helped when the Lofgrens took a rare day off.

Willie swam against the tide of commerce flowing from small town grocers, haberdashers, and barbers to city shopping malls. Times were changing and the future of the ma and pa store uncertain. The days when Willie bought a new Chevy every year had already ended. Even lifelong customers often did their grocery shopping at a supermarket in a nearby town, and Willie and Mae felt betrayed.

When Willie heard that the Pfeffer boy was home from Vietnam, he invited Clarence and Jeffrey to a monthly meeting of the Kalmar Lions Club. Clarence begged off, but Beans attended, and he was embarrassed when Mr. Lofgren offered a glowing account of the local basketball hero who earned a bronze star and two purple hearts while protecting the country from the scourge of communism. The standing ovation from the dozens of Lions and their wives in attendance, including Harv and Meg Karlstad, seemed awkward but appreciated. Thank God, they didn't ask him to speak.

Harv surmised that his own son would receive a cool reception from the Kalmar Lions due to his anti-war activism, but Meg was just glad to see Beans home safe and sound even if he looked older and thinner, especially in the facial skin stretched tight over high cheekbones. And his eyes. Meg knew the boys on the basketball team back then well enough, and the players loved her spaghetti dinners. Beans ate voraciously and with wide-eyed gusto, but now his sunken eyes were dark and defensive, even dodgy.

Beans knew the faces and names of the village gentry, but he didn't know them well personally because the Pfeffers weren't woven into the Kalmar social fabric. Did the townsfolk see him as a hero or perhaps merely a novelty—or a celebrity--someone who had seen things and done things and experienced awe-full and awful things they couldn't even imagine? What they saw on the black and white TV screen he witnessed in blood-red color, and he was their vicarious connection to the greatest adventure, for good or ill, of the generation they had birthed.

He heard the expressions of "attaboy" and "welcome home, soldier" along with back slaps and dainty handshakes from the women. The smiles of the good folks of Kalmar betrayed a smidge of doubt, but they found comfort in his presence as if he validated what they wanted to believe, and they remained confident that all was well for the brave boys fighting for America in a far-off land. Again, it was good that he was not asked to speak because his words would surely disappoint.

The warm welcome from the Kalmar Lions contrasted sharply with the ugliness alongside the roadway outside the Fort Lewis exit. When the bus to the SeaTac Airport carrying Beans and other soldiers home from Vietnam departed through the Fort Lewis gate, half a dozen protesters taunted the returning veterans with mean-spirited chants and signs.

"Join the Army; learn to kill," said one sign.

"Stop the mass murder," said another.

If the bus bound for the airport had stopped right there rather than whizzing past, Beans and the others might have committed murder with their bare hands.

"Fuck those cocksuckers," yelled someone from the back of the bus.

"Stop the bus, and we'll kick some ass," another threatened.

Beans fumed all the way to SeaTac. Why the hell did the self-righteous little pricks target the troops? Protest the war all you want, but for chrissake, it's not the soldier's fault. They're victims, too. The roadside protest was hostile and nasty, to be sure, but mostly it was sheer idiocy. Nothing like pissing off the folks you want to convert, and scenes such as this on America's TV screens greatly damaged the cause of peace. *Support the troops* became a rallying cry against the protesters and a convenient euphemism for supporting the war policy.

Then there was the strange situation with a beautiful woman on the flight from Seattle to Minneapolis. Beans traveled in his dress uniform that allowed him to fly standby for a deeply discounted fare, and the Northwest Airlines flight was nearly empty. When the young, attractive woman came down the aisle looking for a seat, she spied Beans and asked,

"Are you just back from Vietnam?"

"Yes."

"Can I sit with you and buy you a drink?"

"Sure. Why not?"

After finishing the drink, Beans soon fell asleep. After Clarence picked him up and they traveled in silence to Kalmar, he wondered what the woman had in mind. Her interest seemed odd. As the flight neared the Twin Cities International Airport, she asked if he was meeting someone at the airport, and there was the hint of an invitation if not. When he answered yes, his Pa would pick him up, the conversation ended, but he later wondered if she was genuinely interested in a liaison or whether she had larceny in mind. She may have suspected he carried a large sum of cash after he collected all his back pay, a normal situation for the soldiers who had little chance to spend money in Vietnam, and perhaps she planned to disappear from a hotel room in the middle of the night with his money. Her booty for his. Or maybe he had merely become a mistrustful, suspicious person, and the woman had nothing in mind except to honor his service by visiting with him and buying him a drink.

Beans never knew his Pa had a political bone in his body, but on election day, Clarence said he and the wife were headed to the town hall to vote and Beans should come along. Beans turned twenty-one overseas, so he was eligible to vote for the first time. He supposed he should vote because that was what he was fighting for, wasn't it? Mary Ann sat between her husband and son in the rusted out red pickup on the election day trip to the town hall.

"Gonna vote for Wallace, and you should too," Clarence said. "We're tired of this mess. The feds put the n … s ahead of hard-working Americans."

Beans thought of Nate Harris who quit high school to support his mama and sisters, and then he got drafted, and then he got killed.

"I heard Wallace was a cab driver," Clarence continued. "His cab driver logic makes sense. He's for folks like us. Truck drivers. Meat packers. Policemen," he nodded emphatically. "For sure, he'd put more police on the streets to bash heads of the long-haired hippies and n … s who burn down their own neighborhoods."

Beans didn't even know who Wallace was, but he sounded like an idiot. Beans voted for Humphrey, only because he was a Minnesotan and the only name he recognized. He didn't tell his Pa.

When he received a phone call from the Perfesser inviting him to a three-way meeting with him and Angie, Beans almost said, "Don't bother. Ain't interested," but a get together was arranged at Margie's Café. Later, the location was changed to the Olson cabin. Better to meet in private.

While Angie spruced up the cabin, Dave attacked the snow drift across the driveway with a scoop shovel. The wind had piled the snow deep, and he hoped the exertion would calm him, but a sticky verse from *Rocky Racoon,* a silly Beatles ditty, kept him anxious as it rattled around his thoughts. The honky-tonk tune and Paul McCartney's voice warned him that Rocky came to shoot up the one who stole his sweetheart. As John Lennon riffed on the harmonica, Dave fantasized about joining a blues band—not that he could play a lick or sing a note, but joining a band made as much sense as any other plan for his future.

Dave finished with the driveway and retreated inside the cabin half an hour before Beans arrived. Beans paused before approaching the cabin. He surveyed the snow-filled yard and the mist rising from the lake. The lake hadn't frozen over yet, and the water was warmer than the air. *Someone better pull that dock out of the water before it freezes in.* He had been at Ben and Joyce's cabin a few times before. He fished for sunfish from the dock, but he had never carried on in the bedroom like Dave and Angie, which he didn't know about, but it wouldn't surprise him.

Before he knocked on the door, Angie opened it, and he awkwardly stepped across the threshold into the kitchen. After briefly hesitating, she hugged him, but he didn't hug back.

"Hey, Beans," Dave waved at him while seated on the counter, but he didn't step forward to shake hands.

Beans glanced at him but quickly looked back at Angie.

"Sorry about yer dad. I heard."

Angie nodded.

"Oh Beans, it's so good to see you. How's the arm?"

He raised it and looked it over like he noticed the surgical scar for the first time.

"It's ok. A little stiff."

"Are you home for good? Did they discharge you?" Dave asked.

"Nope. I'm done with the Nam, but I'm just home for a convalescent leave. I still gotta put in my two years. I'll report back soon, and I've put in my request for a duty station overseas. Got one in mind. Course, I don't expect the army to do right by me."

"I heard about your medals," Dave said. "Was it rough over there?"

Beans shrugged.

"Yeah, I guess," he said, but he quickly changed the subject.

"How you guys doin'?"

Angie glanced at Dave.

"We're good. We're both studying at the U; well, I am and Dave's taking a break."

Dave saw more in the glance and heard more in her tentative answer. She hadn't openly questioned his anti-war, anti-draft escapades, but he knew she had her doubts. And her dorm crowd. She hung with them more and more and with Dave less and less. They hadn't had sex in a while. Even as Angie assured Beans, Dave was less assured.

"If you ain't enrolled in college, won't you get drafted?" Beans asked, looking straight at Dave for the first time. Beans shook his head and pursed his lips. "No man, you don't want to do that."

"I'll think of something," Dave said.

Angie scowled at him before turning her attention back to Beans.

"You know how sorry we are that we ended up together while you were over there and all," Angie said. "Hurting you was the last thing we wanted to do."

Beans shrugged.

"It don't mean nuthin'."

Chapter Thirty-two

"Sobriety looks good on you."

Frank Nelson's face glowed, and his eyes sparkled. Instead of a handshake, he clutched Dave in his arms and squeezed him like a grizzly, but he was not grizzled. Under a well-combed mop of white hair and revealed by a clean-shaven face, even his wrinkles seemed to smile.

"You don't know the half of it," Frank replied. "From the day I arrived, I knew I belonged here. Hazelden has been what I've needed for a long time, my whole life, really. I've learned more damn trite sayings, but for chrissake, I'll keep repeating them. 'One day at a time.' 'Easy does it.' 'Let go and let God.' 'Keep the main thing the main thing.' 'Keep it simple, stupid.' 'First things first.'"

"You wanna drive?" Dave asked as they strolled through the parking lot. He had driven Frank's pickup to retrieve Frank after weeks of inpatient treatment for alcoholism at the Hazelden Treatment Center in a small city north of the Twin Cities.

"Nah, I wanna enjoy the scenery and Christmas lights."

And talk.

"I've been out of touch, but dang it, Humphrey almost pulled it out. When he finally broke from the LBJ war policy with serious conversation about a negotiated peace and withdrawal, he changed the momentum, but now we're stuck with Tricky Dick for four years, maybe eight. Overall, the election of 1968 may portend the end of the party of FDR. The solid south is gone. White, blue-collar workers are drifting away. It's hard to imagine how much has changed since the Democratic landslide of 1964. Not sure yet what the party may become, but I fear 1968 will haunt the Democrats for a long time."

If Frank was pessimistic, Dave sounded cynical.

"I'm burned out. We all are. It's like we can't have nice things. America, I mean. Just when her promise was within reach, this goddammed war that no one wanted and served no purpose screwed it all up. Imagine if there was no war. The great accomplishments in civil rights and anti-poverty wouldn't have been pushed aside, overshadowed by protests and counterprotests, violence and counterviolence. We could have seen a generation of progress in the lives of all Americans like that following FDR's New Deal. Instead, we lost sight of who we are together and started hating on each other."

White knuckles clenched the steering wheel in the ten and two clock positions.

"I doubt that American leaders will do the right thing," Dave continued. "I've lost confidence that protest effectively leads to change. My cynicism has swallowed up my idealism. Knocking on doors in New Hampshire led to the kitchen of the Ambassador Hotel in Los Angeles and then to the battle for Michigan Avenue in Chicago. The nation needed Bobby Kennedy, and probably wanted him, but fate decreed Richard Milhous Nixon."

"Slow down, you're racing," Frank said, looking at the speedometer.

Dave took his foot off the gas, and his voice became a mere whisper. "If Bobby Kennedy had lived, that might have changed things. That was the day the music died for me. Some say God is on America's side, but that's pure bullshit. If that was true, why does he keep kicking us in the ass."

Snow flurries swirled from ashen skies. Darkness fell early during the wintertime solstice, and Frank's pickup lumbered along in the twilight. The occupants remained silent for many miles.

Finally, Frank spoke. "Tell me about your plans and switch on the headlights while you're at it."

"I've really wrestled with a shitload of bad options. For the first time in my life, the path forward isn't clear. Maybe patriotism is just doing the government's will, without question. That's what some say. 'My country right or wrong.'"

"You don't really believe that, do you?"

Dave imperceptibly shook his head, but he thought a moment before speaking.

"I strongly considered joining another branch of the military to avoid combat. That would take a couple extra years, but I wouldn't get my ass shot up, and I'd still be eligible for the good life. I mean, I'd still be in America's good graces. I want to be a lawyer one day, and that path could take me there. As a recruiter told me, I'd have the GI bill to pay for law school."

Frank's giddiness at his own change in fortune melted away as the windshield wipers flicked away the wet snowflakes.

Dave strummed his fingers on the steering wheel, staring straight ahead. He started to speak, but he choked on his words. He cleared his throat and started again.

"I'm leaning toward Canada," Dave said.

"No shit," Frank whispered.

"Wendy, my activist friend from the U, turned me on to a manual with many copies floating around campus. It's put together by someone who's already fled to Canada with input from many sources. It answered a lot of questions. Turns out you can simply cross the border into Canada without any questions and then apply for student status or landed immigrant status once you're there. The manual claims that there are no worries about extradition back to the states and that the Canadian government and populace are basically welcoming. I'm thinking Montreal and maybe McGill University. Local peace groups will help me get settled and dot all the i's on any paperwork."

Frank turned his face away from Dave and looked down the road. A few minutes passed before Frank spoke again.

"My young friend, I hope you understand the difficulty with that path. There will be icy patches on the road ahead."

"Do you think I'm a coward?"

"No, but others will."

"How about selfish? I mean, guys like Beans didn't have a choice. Why should I be different?"

"Again, I don't think you're selfish, but that's how others will see it. How 'bout you? Do you feel selfish?"

"Nah, I don't think so," Dave replied. "Hell, the four years of military service might be peanuts compared to relocating to Canada. Who knows when, or if, I will ever return from across the border?"

Frank clucked his tongue against the roof of his mouth. "It's a big sacrifice. You see that, don't you? You mentioned being in America's good graces. That's what you will give up."

"Yes," Dave said, voice rising. "I've protested. Worked for peace candidates. Gotten mauled by riot police. And, nothing changed. But, my friend Angie says we can't give up. We can't stop doing the right thing and speaking up just because we don't immediately see the results we want. I may be just a lonely voice crying in the desert, but I won't be silent. Most will see a move to Canada as selfish cowardice, but I see it as a sacrifice based on principle. A political statement. I hope some of my friends and family will see it that way, too."

"A noble gesture, indeed," Frank said while emphatically nodding his head. "I believe you've found your way forward, my young friend."

"Are you ok with it? I mean, I guess I'm looking for someone's blessing."

"Of course. What do your folks say? And Angie?"

"Haven't told them yet. You're the first."

"You're a selfish bastard." Angie said. Her tone was more matter of fact than Dave expected. "Why couldn't you just stay in school like a reasonable, responsible person?"

She was right, and Dave had no defense.

"I guess I expected it," Angie said. "That girl snaps her fingers, and you run off to change the world. God, how self-righteous and self-important you are. And naïve."

She mimicked Wendy's voice in sing-song fashion.

"Let's go to New Hampshire. Let's go to Chicago. Let's go to New York. Let's go to Canada."

"Wendy doesn't even know," Dave replied. "I haven't told her. I came to tell you first and bring you home for Christmas break," Dave said.

"No thanks. I'll find my own way home. Maybe I'll ask Brian to drive me to Kalmar."

"Who's Brian?

"He's just a guy from the dorm. He says that protesters are just whiney cowards."

"Has he surrendered his student deferment?"

"Course not. Why should he?"

Brian. Just a guy from the dorm. Angie said she wasn't surprised. It dawned on Dave that he wasn't surprised, either. It seemed that Angie had been moving on for some time. So, it was over, not in a thunderclap but with a whimper.

Dave plopped down on the floor outside Wendy Cragun's dorm room awaiting her return. Someone said she was taking her last fall term final. He waited for more than an hour. Down the hall, a reel-to-reel tape player blared favorite anthems of the counterculture. Dave enjoyed pot, to be sure, but he had never tripped on LSD. Nevertheless, he enjoyed the psychedelic music: *Eight Miles High; White Rabbit; Sunshine Superman.* Jimi Hendrix; Janis Joplin; the Grateful Dead. Jim Morrison and the Doors and their haunting *The End* seemed just right for Dave's mood.

"Hey, Davey, what's up?" Wendy said when she returned and as she inserted her key into the door lock. She was the only person who called him "Davey."

"I've decided to go to Canada. Montreal, actually."

Dave sat on the chair by her desk, and Wendy fiddled with her backpack that she threw onto her bed. A huge poster of Che Guevarra, the romanticized martyr of revolution, adorned the wall over her bed. She spoke with her back toward Dave.

"When do you leave?"

"Right after the holidays."

"Miss America going with you?"

"Nah, she dumped me. Can't blame her with the chaotic year it's been. I've changed. The world has changed." Dave paused for a second. "She's changed--I think she's seeing someone else."

"How are you getting to Canada?"

"Still working on that. Although I've made up my mind, I still need to sort out the details."

Wendy finished emptying her backpack and sat down on the edge of the bed. Dave knew her to be a naturally bubbly person, but now serious wrinkles lined her forehead, and she chewed on her lower lip. For a moment, her gaze shifted from Dave to the window overlooking the yard separating dormitories. Heavy snowflakes sifted through the branches of a barren oak tree.

"Let me go with you," she said, choking on the words as she turned to face him. Her misty eyes pleaded with him as a tear trickled over the pale scar that marred her ruddy cheek.

"I can't let you drive all that way and then drive home alone," Dave said.

"I won't drive home alone. I'll stay with you. You're an innocent, and you need me."

Dave's eyes narrowed. "What are you saying?"

She stood up and mussed his hair.

"Davey, Davey, Davey. For a smart guy, you can be dense as hell. Who loves you, Davey boy?"

Dave struggled to breathe. His mouth opened, but no words dribbled out. But then, an epiphany washed over him. The Red Sea parted. Clarity rushed in, and it was all good. For a year, he had waffled. He had clung to Angie as an idealized memory of the past, of a happy childhood, of high school days that were innocent but naïve, of a world that no longer existed. Looking back. Meanwhile, Wendy encouraged him, inspired him, motivated him. Looking forward. And, apparently, she loved him. He would gleefully return that love.

Dave rose to his feet and cupped Wendy's face in his hands. Their eyes locked and then their lips.

Chapter Thirty-three

While Dave hung the tinsel, his sister, Hannah, and his mom strung blinking lights on the spruce Christmas tree and then the delicate bulbs adorned with wintery scenes. Ever since he could remember, the stringy, silvery, fake icicles had been Dave's favorite part of the tree, even if Hannah always criticized his method.

"Hey, not in clumps!"

She was the delicate artist who dangled single threads just so. Meg's Siamese cat, Ramar, pawed at the low-hanging shreds.

"Dave, please climb the ladder and place the star," Meg said.

With the star taking its place of honor, Dave folded up the step ladder and crawled under the tree to pour water in the tree stand. Prickly needles on the low branches scraped against his exposed skin. He remembered the year that Harv said they should cut their own tree, which they did, but all the needles turned brown and fell to the floor by the time Christmas rolled around. Harv picked up the current specimen from the local feed store/farmer's co-op.

The doorbell rang, and Dave jumped up. Meg and Hannah stopped what they were doing and watched with anxious curiosity. When Dave opened the door and greeted Wendy with a kiss, mom and daughter exchanged glances. They expected Wendy, but still …

Christmas Eve began with the Karlstad foursome plus Wendy sipping rum-spiked eggnog. That helped to break the ice, a little.

"Thank you so much for allowing me to be part of your family Christmas," Wendy said. "I don't have much of a family. No siblings, and my parents are divorced and dysfunctional. You're so lucky!"

Meg's traditional dinner consisted of a bone-in ham, scalloped potatoes, candied carrots, and lefsa slathered in butter and sprinkled with brown sugar. They finished with sweet rice covered with tangy cranberry sauce served with coffee. With each course, the tension dissipated a bit more. Wendy was disarming. Chatty. Warm.

Harv and Dave retired to the living room and TV while the three women cleaned the dishes, but Hannah soon left to join friends.

"You two should talk," she said as she dried her hands and departed the kitchen.

"Mrs. Karlstad, please put your mind at ease. Dave and I know what we're doing, and we go into this with our eyes wide open. There will be bumps, and the biggest thing will be missing you. This may be the last family Christmas for a while."

Wendy's eyes moistened.

"Your son is a good person with a kind heart, and I've been in love with him since we campaigned in New Hampshire. We'll take care of each other."

With tears streaming down her cheeks, Meg hugged Wendy and held her close.

"Yes, yes, please take care of my boy."

Meanwhile, Harv and Dave talked in the living room.

"I heard Frank Nelson got sober," Harv said.

"Yeah, he went to treatment, and he's pumped about sobriety."

"You help with that?"

"A little."

"You know, Son, we can't all save the world, but helping Frank counts for something, too. A lot, in fact. Good for you."

Suddenly, Harv called to the women in the kitchen. "Come in here. You've got to see this."

Meg and Wendy joined them, and they watched scenes captured from a spaceship, Apollo 8, as it orbited the moon with three astronauts on board—a first. NASA claimed they would put men *on* the moon in the coming year.

A breathtaking image appeared above the barren lunar landscape. Earth rose over the horizon in the lunar morning, displayed in vivid blue colors. She seemed so small and fragile in her small corner amidst the vastness of space. Oceans and continents appeared shrouded in massive weather systems, but cities and national boundaries remained invisible. No separation of mother earth's people according to class, ethnicity, culture, or politics. No hot war in Southeast Asia or cold war elsewhere. No riots in the streets. No evidence of man's inhumanity to man.

The astronauts offered a Christmas message to the world.

In the beginning God created the heaven and the earth. And the earth was without form, and void; and darkness was upon the face of the deep. And the Spirit of God moved upon the face of the waters.

"Bet there's folks all around the globe watching this with admiration for American know how," Harv said. "You know, son, America is still the city on the hill and many still see American democracy as the gold standard as to how a people should manage their common affairs."

"Absolutely. Right on," Dave said. "Imagine how much better America could be if she only lived up to her own ideals."

Harv's face looked like he wanted to say something, but he merely nodded slightly. He looked at Meg and said, "I'm headed up."

"Wendy, you can sleep in Dave's room; let me show you where it is. Dave will sleep here on the couch."

"Thank you, Mrs. Karlstad," Wendy said as she followed up the stairs.

"Please, call me Meg."

Everyone knew that Dave and Wendy slept together and would live together in Canada, but sometimes following convention is the most comfortable path.

After a few minutes, Wendy and Meg returned with bedding and a pillow for Dave.

Meg handed Dave an envelope.

"Merry Christmas," she said. "This will help in Canada. Don't mention it to your father."

The envelope contained twenty, crisp one-hundred-dollar bills.

"Mom! Dad already gave me a thousand and said I shouldn't tell you."

On Christmas Day, Uncle Ken would host an expanded Karlstad family get-together. Dave passed.

"Uncle Ken won't understand why we're going to Canada. We don't want to make a scene."

Meg protested, but Harv said, "Maybe it's best."

Dave realized that he had only thought of himself without realizing the dilemma he imposed upon his parents. Even if they wouldn't be ashamed of him, they would be embarrassed—at family gatherings, Lions Club meetings, Sundays at church, or delivering fuel oil to Harv's customers. Friends would offer wan smiles and quickly move on. Local tongues would wag. His decision reflected not only on him, but them.

On the other hand, they didn't want him to die or become maimed in Vietnam, either. His quandary was theirs. The right answer was also the wrong answer, but it would equally be so if he chose differently and accepted being drafted into service. It wasn't win-win, it was lose-lose. What was the brave thing to do? What was the honorable thing to do? What was the moral thing to do? He regretted that he would be seen as a coward or draft dodger or deserter, and that would all redound to his family. His sacrifice was also theirs.

Icicles draped along the edge of the sheet metal roof over the Kalmar High School gym. New Year's Eve morn dawned sunny and bitter cold with sun dogs haloing the pale-yellow orb as it peaked over the horizon. Dave's breath clouded in front of him, and his boots crunched through several inches of fresh snow on the sidewalk. The maintenance crew enjoyed the New Year's holiday like the rest of the staff and shoveling the sidewalks would wait. The school building thermostats had been set low, and the gym remained chilly.

Dave slowly put up shots until he zeroed in, and then he moved to the free throw line. He once made thirty in a row following varsity practice, but then he had someone to shag the ball, and he never left the line to break his rhythm. Dribble twice, inhale a deep breath, bend the knees, flip the wrist, extend the fingers, hold the follow through. Muscle memory.

Swish.

The sound of another basketball thumping behind him broke his concentration. Beans appeared at the other end of the gym. At first, the former teammates ignored each other, but when Dave's ball bounced across the ten-second line, and he went to retrieve it, Beans challenged him.

Dave picked up his ball and attempted a jump shot, but Beans, at least half a foot taller, blocked it. Dave faked a second shot, and when Beans left his feet to block it, Dave went around him and scored a layup. Dave tossed the ball to Beans and went into a defensive crouch as if to say, "your turn." Beans dribbled twice attacking the basket, but Dave held his ground taking a charge. The men tumbled into a heap. Spirited competition continued for the next hour, but neither man spoke. Beans had the size and strength advantage, but Dave could hit long range jump shots, and he was quicker. Both men worked up a sweat in the cold gym.

Breathing heavily, Dave finally formed a "T" with his hands.

"Time. Call it even?"

"Right on," Beans replied with his hands on his knees.

They walked together to a drinking fountain in the corner of the gym.

"Froze my ass driving here this morning," Beans said. "The heater in Pa's old beater pickup don't work. After months in the Vietnamese heat and humidity, I still can't get used to the Minnesota cold, but I'll be leaving soon."

"Heard you got orders for Japan," Dave said.

"Yep. The army surprised me and honored my request. Goin' back to Yokohama where I received treatment for my arm. I'll be part of the support team for the Kishine Barracks and the 106th General Hospital. Yokohama boasts beautiful gardens, and I spent many hours relaxing in the shade of red-leafed trees. They call them *Kito,* which means calm."

Beans drew a deep breath through his nose and breathed out through his mouth.

"I'm looking for some peace, and I hope I might find it there. I also found Akiko. She's a sweet Japanese girl. She brews tea and arranges flowers," Beans said, remembering. "We been exchanging letters, and I think we may have a future. Least, I hope so."

"Sounds like a plan," Dave said.

After they pulled on their winter coats, stocking caps, boots, and gloves, they exited the building and entered the parking lot. They paused and turned to look at the old brick building where they spent their school days. The sun glinted off the sheet metal roof of the gym.

"Maybe you heard. I'm headed to Montreal," Dave said. "Hope that sits ok with you."

"No skin off my ass," Beans replied.

"You won't think I'm a coward?"

Beans looked him up and down and then shielded his eyes as he looked skyward. "Shit, for all the crap you'll take, it'll be the bravest thing you ever do, and damn sure the smartest."

Dave canted his head toward Beans letting the unexpected comment sink in.

"That girl goin' with you?" Beans asked, still gazing upward.

"Wendy?" Dave gave Beans a look that said, *You know about her?*

"Yeah, she'll be coming along. I think we've got a future, too."

"Been a helluva a year," Dave said, pulling off his glove and extending his hand for a handshake. Beans did likewise.

"Hell, yeah," Beans replied. "It's been somethin'."

Beans climbed behind the steering wheel of the red Ford pickup. Just before he pulled the door shut, he said, "Guess it didn't work out for either of us with her."

Dave assumed Beans referred to Angie, but maybe he meant America.

www.ingramcontent.com/pod-product-compliance
Lightning Source LLC
Chambersburg PA
CBHW072045150726
47996CB00015B/1602